Published by Under the Moon, LLC
Pelican Rapids, MN

Dedication:

To my Sam, lover, friend, supporter and most of all, my husband. I love you, now and always.

Part One: Slave

Chapter One

"You have no idea just how fortunate you are to be chosen for this honor," her mother muttered to the sharp rhythm of the brush being tugged through Alayna's unruly hair, each snarl torn free with a painful yank of bristles. "You're still young enough to be a part of the presentation, and all you can do is complain about that fact you'll have to take a few days out of your life in order to take part. Don't you know what an honor this is?"

There seemed little point in going over the subject for what would have been the twentieth time in the past two days alone. There was no more point in arguing, no more than she saw any point in the entire presentation service in the first place. She'd stand there along with a dozen other men and women of her age group, only to be sent home at the end of the service. It made no sense. No one had been picked from one of the ceremonies in over fifty years. Why would that change now? The idea of spending three days at the temple, maybe longer if she were unfortunate enough to catch the eyes of one of the Devoted, made her stomach turn.

"This is a waste of time, the Gods don't even exist."

"Hush!" The back of the hairbrush slapped against Alayna's arm.

"Ow! What did you do that for?" She rubbed the now sore, reddening spot. "I thought you would have grown used to my comments by now." What had gotten into her mother? Even when they had been getting ready for service, she'd never resorted to striking her before now. Sure, there had been the threat of one of the Devoteds finding out, but never this.

"Now of all times you have to let that irreverent mouth of yours loose. You'll bring misfortune on us all with your stupidity, and the Gods know that I raised you with better respect than that." The brush clattered to the surface of the dressing table, only to slide from the wood and onto the smoothly tiled floor. "I waited at the temple when I was your age, but unlike you, I hoped to be chosen. The Gods never answered my prayer. Now it's your turn, and the least you can do is remember that this is an honor. Not all are chosen to be presented, and out of those presented, only ten will be picked if the Gods decide this is the time for a re-blessing of our lands."

Alayna almost bit into her lip in order to keep silent as her mother spoke. Gods, indeed. No one could remember seeing one, and even the numbers of the Devoted had dwindled in the past fifteen years. Fewer men and women sought out the 'honor' of serving in the temple with each passing season. Even with the power they held over the town, it hadn't been enough to call more than a small handful into service each year. Who would want to spend all their lives in the temple worshipping nonexistent Gods when there was an entire world beyond the town walls waiting to be explored?

"You will not disgrace me today...is that very clear?" Her mother's sharp fingers dug into Alayna's shoulders. "I will not permit you to turn me into the laughingstock of the town."

"Yes, Mother." She tried not to wince, but through the polished surface of the mirror she could see the cold anger within her mother's gaze--a depth she had never seen before--and it was enough to silence even her tongue. Without the protection of her mother, there would be no one to prevent her being dragged up to the temple steps and thrown into the tender mercies of the Devoteds. Regardless of what she thought of their religion, they still held the power of life and death.

"If I so much as think you are going to open your mouth at the wrong time, I will ask to offer you up to feed the lands myself." The grip on her shoulders increased. "Don't think this is a joke. If you allow your irreverence to gain life during the ceremony, I'll beg permission to hold the dagger and draw it across your throat in the middle of the fields." If she had held any doubt prior to this of her mother's dedication to the old ways, it vanished with those words. The sheer ice of her voice, the look within her eyes, the way those fingers almost pierced her skin; they all combined to convince Alayna of just how serious the older woman truly was. "Is that clear, my daughter?"

"Perfectly." She struggled to keep from adding anything else, even when the painful grip finally eased.

"Do you really think I believe you, Alayna?" Her mother snarled, her hands clenching as she spoke. "I will not take this risk with you. Jeramiah!"

She blinked and then stared at her mother in open shock. Never before had her mother called for the hired guard that worked within their home to enter her daughter's chamber. Neither the guards or the servants had any reason to enter her chambers, let alone when she was in the process of preparing for the temple.

With near silent steps the dark-eyed guard strode into the room, a look of confusion clear in his gaze. "You called for me, my Lady?"

"Yes, my daughter requires a lesson in silence before she is called to attend the ceremony in the temple." Her mother snapped as she picked up the hairbrush from the floor and handed it to him. "I want you to teach her to guard her tongue."

"My Lady?" he stammered, taking the brush as he looked between mother and daughter. "Are you sure about this? I mean, she is to be presented to the temple this day. Do you truly wish me to send her there with her backside tanned?"

"If that is what it takes to teach her to keep silent, then yes." Her mother crossed her arms, stepping back enough that Jeramiah would have the room to move.

He shot a quick look back and forth between the two women, blinking. His brow furrowed slightly, the corners of his lips twitching upwards. His gaze narrowed on Alayna, tracing openly over her form. "Are you sure this is something you want me to do, my Lady?"

"Get on with it, man, before I start to think that I need to have you replaced in my service. I am sure there are a dozen men or more who would willingly take your place. Perhaps someone that has been at the end of my daughter's less than pleasant mouth before now would delight in administering a little well-placed correction."

He needed no further encouragement in order to move towards Alayna. His gaze turned flint-like as he gripped the hairbrush tightly enough to turn his knuckles near white. "We can do this the hard way or the easy way, Lady Alayna."

"Mother! You can't be serious about this." She finally voiced a protest.

The silence she was offered chilled her soul, leaving her flinching even as Jeramiah grasped her shoulder and pulled her up from the chair. Her bottom lip caught between her teeth under the tight grip on her form. Without a word, Jeramiah took position on the very chair she had been sitting on and pulled her over his lap with a firm grasp that she knew she would not be able to fight her way free from.

The soft cotton robe that had kept her body covered he now raised to her waist. He grasped it with one hand, holding her and her clothing in place over his knees.

With the way her mother was behaving, she doubted that escape would be an option. Alayna could only begin to imagine what orders her mother would give should she find her way free of the guard. How many others would the older woman call into the chamber if she did fight?

No, better that she accepted this, got it over and done with.

Color flamed across her cheeks at the way her ass was now exposed to both her mother and the guardsman. With the preparations for the temple rights, she had been dressed in only the robe with not even a slip of cloth to guard her loins, a fact that was now foremost in her thoughts as the air caressed her flesh. The first strike of the back of the hairbrush against her bared ass sapped the breath from her lungs. Pain and heat flushed through her body, the second crack against her skin. Her lips parted in a gasped cry. Her legs kicked against the stone floor even as she struggled to hold position across the man's lap.

A loud snap echoed within the chamber, her cry now more of a gasp for breath as heat mixed with the burning pain. It flooded between her thighs as she clenched them tightly together. Shame added to the fear; the wicked heat, both sets of cheeks turning a deep red with the cracking blows that landed on her upturned ass.

Crack!

The sound was louder than ever. Pain greater than before throbbed through her ass, a burning following its growth, a slick heat gaining life between her pressing thighs.

Five more blows colored her cheeks, five more cries of pain masked the unholy pleasure brought to aching life within her wicked flesh. She barely even knew when his grip released on her robe, a shiver claiming her form with the touch of the soft fabric being pushed back down over her ass. Only when Jeramiah pulled her from across his lap did she become fully aware of what the spanking had caused. Not just for herself, but for the man who had administered it. Whilst her thighs now felt slick, she could also see the tenting of his pants before he finally stood.

Wicked. Deep inside she had become a wicked woman, not the untouched purity she strived to be. Her hands moved to touch her heated ass through the cloth, her gaze lowering shyly as she felt the path of Jeramiah's gaze across her form. The smile that shone within his eyes offered a dark hunger that she craved to learn more about.

"Good, now finish your preparations. We will be leaving for the temple before the noon hour. You're beautiful, I can only hope those of the temple agree and grant you the honor I was denied."

Her mother waved Jeramiah out of the room, seemingly unaware of the results the task had brought to pass. Now instead of the cold determination of earlier moments, warmth seeped into her mother's eyes, if only for a moment before the older woman left the room, the door closing with a soft click.

Her hands moved to touch the throbbing, punished skin of her ass. How could her mother have demanded such a thing from her?

The same way she now expected Alayna to prepare for the temple.

She glanced toward the mirror and shook her head.

A few days and this would all be over. If she were lucky it would end before that; perhaps she wouldn't even pass the initial inspection. No, not with the care that her mother had taken with preparations. She was guaranteed at least three days of waiting before being able to return home. At least then she could leave home. She'd be an adult; even without a mate she'd have the freedom to pack, leave the home. She'd have the freedom to find out just what lay beyond the boundaries of the town.

A waste of time all, because of her mother insisting she follow some outdated tradition. An honor. In no way did she see going to the temple as any form of honor. As for beauty, well, maybe others did find her attractive, but it's not as though she had ever acted on the offers that had been made to her. At first her mother had assumed it was part of her daughter's belief in the old ways, so she could be presented to the temple as a pure soul. At least she had, until Alayna's doubts had gained voice in the past year. The truth of the matter was far simpler; not one of the men that had approached Alayna had interested her. The punishment from the Devoted if she had been caught with a man prior to her presentation might have played a larger part in her decision than she had previously admitted. Breaking the laws of copulation carried stiff penalties. Men had been castrated before being sold to mercenary forces, women racked in public, then handed to the highest bidder, sentenced to life as a prostitute, denied family, home, the right to travel--and those were said to be the lucky ones.

Only five days before, she had stood in the central square and watched a woman reduced into life as a prostitute. Before hundreds, the woman who had been close to Alayna's age had been stripped to her skin, her clothes burned into ash before she had been hauled to a stone pillar. Leather had bound her wrists, pulling her hands high above her head, and even now Alayna could hear the sound of the whip snapping through the air, a sound that had left her squirming, her thighs slick with a need she did not understand. No, not a need. It had to be something else that she'd missed. A fear, perhaps? Sweat built at what could be her own fate if someone other than her mother heard her words against the ancient beliefs.

Fear. Those of the temple ruled the lands through terror; stories of retribution from the Gods; threats of blood being spilled to appease those dark protectors. She'd seen the way people reacted when asked about the temple or the events that would occur within the dark stone walls, all in the name of imaginary Gods.

"Three days," she promised to her reflection. "I can hold on just three more days."

With forty-nine other young men and women she waited in silence within the antechamber, each one dressed in an identical white linen robe as they kept their focus on the main temple doors. Their faces were schooled into calm repose, hands clasped before them. All traces of her arguments had been forced from her face as she waited with the others. Her mother and all the other hopeful relatives were behind them, escorted from the temple grounds for the duration of the wait.

Nothing had been said to the gathered men and women, not since the wooden doors had been barred behind them, nor had they been given any hint of how long they would have to wait until someone came to escort them to the chambers set aside for this time of year. Several of the faces she had recognized, most she hadn't, but that had been no surprise. Some families even traveled in from beyond the town for this, others might have journeyed further. She would have the chance to find out more about them when they were finally led from the chamber.

If that ever happened.

She wasn't sure what was more irritating; the waiting, or having to do so under the stern watch of the marble statue at the front of the room. It had to be a good twelve feet tall, and towered above their heads. What nightmare had sparked the artists' creation of such a thing she didn't know, but the look on the face of the male God left her feeling sick. High cheekbones, an arrogant gaze that she was sure had followed her through the room as she had taken her place with the others, his lips turned upwards in a mockery of a smile. He might have been handsome under other circumstances--she might even have had a real interest in a man who looked like that--but there was no mistaking the cruelty in his features.

Her toes curled against the tiled floor. How long had they been waiting now? At least the heat of the spanking had dissipated, leaving her body unmarked beneath the fresh robe. No one here could or would know of the humiliation she had faced only a few hours beforehand.

Without appearing to move, she tried to find something that would help keep her occupied, her gaze drawing to the bolts on the doors, silently counting them. Sixty-five bolts that she could count, though the three people in front of her prevented a true accounting.

Someone stifled a yawn behind her. At least she wasn't the only one bored. Eventually the habit of the presentation would die out and no more younglings would have to wait barefooted in the cold chamber. It didn't matter that the setting was ornate, with heavy carvings decorating the walls, small braziers, torches and even a rare woven hanging on one wall depicting a woman kneeling naked at the foot of a statue where she stared upwards, her hands raised to the silent God. Alayna couldn't be sure if the woman was praying or pleading, but all she cared about right now was finding a way to keep her mind from slipping into a numb boredom.

No clocks, no way to measure time beyond the mental count she kept. It had to be nearly half an hour now, maybe a little longer than that, and her feet had grown cold within the first few minutes.

Foolish.

One bolt, two, how many times would she count them before her temper finally got the better of her? Fifteen bolts, sixteen, if there was a better way of wasting time, she didn't know what it might be.

"Welcome, my sons and daughters, welcome." The new voice snapped her from the mindnumbing routine of the count. At the head of the room now stood a middle-aged man with pale blue eyes. Shoulder-length brown hair curled against his red-robed shoulders; one of the Devoted. "Come, come, let's get you out of here into a warmer room so we can finish the preparations."

More to do, well, as long as that new work meant they would be out of the chamber. One by one they followed the red-robed man out through the iron-wrapped door. By the muted sounds of relief, she hadn't been the only one who had grown cold during the wait. A few soft chuckles mixed with the sounds of bare feet against the stone, the light rustle of the linen robes, the tension of the wait under the stern face of the statue lost by the time they entered a smaller room.

Torches burned along the walls; a fire added extra warmth at one side from a large fireplace that took up a good quarter of the wall space. No statues watched them here, large cushions offered places for them to rest, a table lay spread with food and drink, and even blankets had been folded to one side of the table, should they need them.

"It will be a long wait, so make yourselves comfortable, have something to eat and drink, and someone will be here soon to explain matters to you," the gentle-eyed man explained as he waved his hand around the room. Strange, anytime she had spoken to her mother about the ceremony, Alayna had had the distinct impression that those within the temple were to be feared. How could anyone fear the man that played host to them now? He didn't even match what she had witnessed in the temple grounds and town square.

"Devoted?" A blond young man with delicate features spoke. "I don't understand. I thought we were to be inspected?"

"Inspected, yes, of course you are, but when the Father has time. Until then, rest, relax and try to enjoy the gifts of the temple. This is a time of celebration for you, for us, enjoy it." The older man smiled, gesturing towards the room. "Someone will come for you soon--one at a time, of course--so you can make your offering to the Gods alone. We wouldn't want others to intrude on your prayers when your time comes around, now would we?"

The warmth of the room, food, blankets and the scattered places to sit were all too good to pass up to the shivering men and women. Under the watch of the red-robed Devoted, the group moved through the room, taking what they needed before seeking out places to rest. Alayna and a handful of others avoided the food, taking only a blanket before sitting down.

Something didn't sit right. Maybe it was foolishness on her behalf, but she couldn't match the stories she had heard, the things she had witnessed, with the kindness now being offered to them. Maybe refusing the food would have her sent home faster, more likely it showed her to be foolish, either way, her choice made more sense than the expanse of food that had been laid out for them.

"One of my brothers or sisters will return soon to choose the first of you for your prayers," the Devoted informed them as he moved back towards the door, his gaze appearing to settle on Alayna for a moment as he continued to speak. "You are all very welcome to the temple. You've no idea how excited we all are. Today marks a turning point in your young lives."

Even with the gentle smile the Devoted offered, Alayna could still hear the sound of the leather whip against the back of the woman in the square, the scene all too willing to replay itself in her mind...

Chapter Two

"Child?" Something shook her shoulder as the unfamiliar voice urged her to wake, the two combining to pull her from the odd dreams that had plagued her light sleep. Images of blood and fire had combined behind her sleep-claimed mind, dark figures without faces had walked through the smoke, statues with soulless eyes had come to life in the middle of banquets so they could feast on those gathered. Cold, depraved dreams that had left her coated in a cold sweat before the woman had laid a finger on her. "Are you awake?"

Alayna slowly opened her eyes, focusing on a dark-haired woman in the robes of the temple. "Yes, I am. Sorry, I must have drifted off."

"With the length of the day that you've had, I suppose you think it acceptable that you could fall asleep. That is not a view I share." The woman's voice lacked any sense of real warmth and her gaze left Alayna's skin crawling. After the Devoted that had brought them to the room, the woman's lack of hospitality came as something of a shock. "I tried telling him that laying out blankets was a mistake. The time for sleeping is over; on your feet, child. I don't have time to wait on your laziness. Up now, or I will have you dragged from the room by your hair if I have to."

Child, the very term irritated her, but Alayna managed to school her expression into what she hoped was one of calm acceptance. Only a small handful remained in the room, mainly those who had chosen not to partake in the offerings from the table, and they were avoiding looking at either Alayna or the Devoted with her. Had they been deliberately kept waiting because of their refusal? Well, she paid for it now; her stomach growled even as she rose, leaving the blanket to pool on the floor.

"Yes, Devoted. May I ask where we are going?"

"Perhaps your memory is in need of a little extra training?" The woman's eyes narrowed her voice dropping into a low whisper. "Or have you already forgotten what you were told earlier in the day?"

"I'm sorry, I was still--" She began to protest, sleep still half-clouding her vision.

"Excuses will not be tolerated, best you remember that." The woman cut her off with a sharp wave of her hand. "You will follow me and there will be no more questions from you, child, not until you are given leave to ask them." The deep red robes whispered over the floor as the Devoted turned, leading the way through the now open door.

No questions, that was like asking the sun not to rise. She had grown used to questioning everything, from why it rained to what was the point in learning the language of the Gods when very few people still used it, no one that she knew outside of the temple. However, openly disobeying one of the Devoted was not something she planned on risking, so no matter how loudly the questions spoke in the back of her mind, she kept them trapped behind her lips as she followed the woman down the hallway.

Where had everyone else gone?

The hallway appeared empty except for the Devoted and herself. No other robes, white or red, traveled through the stone-lined corridor, and no voices reached her from behind the closed doors they passed. The silence unnerved her, adding to the growing tension that built across her shoulders. With the amount of people she knew to be in the Temple there had to be some sign of them, a hint of noise, something.

The Devoted stopped, pushing open a door into a small dimly-lit room. "This is a prayer chamber. It's one of several within the temple that we keep for this time of year. Here you will wait here and offer your prayers." The woman turned, fixing her with a calm look. "I suggest you focus fully on your offerings; through those you will be inspected by the Gods and no doubt found to be lacking. I cannot imagine someone like you ever being picked to serve the Gods."

"Yes, Devoted." She tried to sound pious, but it didn't appear to fool the other woman. The quicker this was over, the better.

"Foolish girl, do you really think I haven't escorted ones like you before to this room? I'm well aware of what you really think. It oozes from you, that flippant nature, a refusal to accept your proper place in this life. Pray hard whilst you have the time or you will find yourself being a part of another type of prayer to the Gods." The red-robed woman pushed Alayna into the room, closing the door behind her before any protests could be offered.

A door that then locked behind her.

Where did they think she was going to go running off to?

Her nails dug into her palms. So this was it, this was the great turning point in her life. Time spent alone in a small, dark and bare room to offer prayers to Gods she didn't believe in, for what? So she could satisfy a dying religion, her mother and a group of mindless zealots?

Her gaze moved over the walls of the small room as she realized she'd been wrong; it wasn't completely bare. Runes had been etched into the stone walls, a single oil lamp hung from the ceiling, coating the chamber with a soft orange light. Like the first chamber, this room also held a statue of the same male God she had seen earlier in the day. Where did they find people to make these things?

Sick. Anyone who could create a work of art like this had to be sick. Just that look in the statue's eyes had been enough to turn her stomach, now she was locked in a room with it until they decided she had done enough time on her knees.

With a slow breath let out through clenched teeth, Alayna eased to her knees, taking position at the booted feet of the statue. At least this way if someone looked in on her or there were peepholes within the room, she'd appear to be fulfilling her duties. Her fingers intertwined, head lowered, completing the image of a woman praying before her God. At least one thing remained in her favor; these types of offerings were normally done in silence, so no one would expect to hear mumbling words of praise spilling from her lips.

Cold seeped through her body; the linen offered little in the way of protection. Not that she had expected them to really care, the antechamber, now here. The warmth and kindness of the other room had felt out of place. Maybe that had been why she had refused to touch anything other than a blanket?

Her brow furrowed.

No, there had to be something, a small grain of reason behind her choice not to touch what they had offered her.

"Or maybe you knew we were watching you?" A man's voice pulled her from the mix of thoughts, catching her off-guard. No one else should have been in the room, she'd not heard any doors open, or the sound of footsteps.

"Who?" She turned, still on her knees, searching for the source of the voice.

"We were right; you're stubborn, headstrong, arrogant and yes, attractive. Very nice indeed." His words sent a chill down her spine. Where were they coming from?

"I'm right in front of you, Alayna." The mocking words taunted her.

That didn't make sense, the only thing in front of her were walls and the...

"Ah, I see, you're unwilling to accept the obvious answer?" Wherever he was, his voice was smooth, silk-like, holding a cold, deadly quality that turned her stomach even as she searched for the source.

The statue moved, dust falling away from the boots, white stone turning into black leather. That wasn't possible. Statues didn't come to life.

"That is, unless they aren't statues at all but your Gods,

child." Fingers twined into her hair, grasping it tightly, arching her backwards until her gaze rose to meet the now living face. His eyes burned into hers, violet pupils, lips turned upwards into a sneer. "Yes, I'm real and yes, I can hear your thoughts. What else did you expect? But of course, the Gods don't really exist, do we. We're nothing more than an outdated concept, a product of the fears of weak-minded fools, a belief encouraged by zealots."

"This isn't happening." She tried to hide the fear that fueled her words.

"Oh, but it is." His free hand slapped against her face; the only thing that saved her head from snapping to one side being the very grip he had in her hair. Pain lanced through her face; the inside of her lips carried the taste of her own blood as it seeped out from the corner of her mouth. Only twice before in her life had she been struck, and both those times had been that very morning. Now her face throbbed from a slap that had dazed her vision and left her trembling under the gaze of a man she feared to be left with. "Such a delicious-looking offering you make, Alayna, and I plan on tasting you to your fullest over the coming weeks."

His smile offered no comfort to her; if anything it made matters worse, only serving to remind her of a predator. With the stone covering now lacking, she could see every elegant line of his face, smell the odd musk-like smell that seemed to emanate from him. Under other circumstances she might have called him handsome--dark and cruel, but not someone that most women could have ignored.

His grip tightened on her hair and pulled her up from her knees, twisting in her hair as he kept her back painfully arched even as his lips lowered to hers. She tensed, expecting a kiss to claim her or a hand to move over her body, perhaps tear the linen from her form. Her breath caught in the back of her throat and something more sparked into life, an unwanted desire that gained life even with the fear that rose. She could feel it, that odd clenching sensation between her thighs as he closed the gap between them.

A shudder ran through her body at the touch of his tongue against her chin, following the thin trickle of blood as it seeped from her lips. Something gained life within her, a need to press more tightly to him, to seek out his touch even though her mind screamed no. Only now did his hand move across her body, touching through the linen, caressing from her thigh upwards.

"Yes, you'll do nicely." His words brushed against her cheek. "A tender new pet at my feet, so ripe for the training I can mold you with. All the delights I will be able to teach you as you enter my service more deeply with each passing day."

"I don't understand. Why me, why not someone who wants to serve you?" Her protest gained life as he moved his lips from her cheek. This wasn't real, it couldn't be happening, she didn't want to believe that this man who held her could be anything more than a trick of the Temple.

The Gods didn't exist.

"We do exist." He all but laughed in her face as his hand closed on her breast, tracing slow circles over the tight, firm mound until his fingers closed on her nipple. Nails dug in, twisting sharply, tearing a cry from her lips as she arched in his grasp. Pain burned through her taut nipple, rippling down into her breast, through her stomach to tighten between her thighs in a way she had never expected. "Such a delicious sound, the first of many you will give to me. Why you? So strange how they all say that, when the answer is really quite simple. When I want a light snack, I'll choose a mind that comes to me willingly, sweet Alayna, but I find the unwilling to be far more satisfying in the long run."

His painful grip released from her nipple only to find a fresh hold on her robe, the linen torn from her form in a single yank only to be tossed against the wall, his gaze moving openly along her now exposed form. Heat claimed her cheeks, shame and fear mixing with a desire to approach him that made little sense even to her. Her face throbbed from the slap, she could still taste the lingering blood on her gum, her nipples had grown hard either from the cold or the pain. Every part of her felt exposed to him, yet the idea of trying to run never entered her mind.

Images ran through her mind; chains, bonds that would hold her, restraining her body against stone, against wood. A terrible haunting image of her body marked with her own blood, whimpering in need, in desire, wanting to cling to the dark-eyed cruel man who now held her. Every fiber of her being wanted, in that moment, to be flung to the stones beneath his body, to feel his flesh pressing within her own, claiming her, taking her, spearing her sex until all she could was scream, whimper, cry out to him for more.

"You can see it, can't you? Taste it within your mind, all the pleasures to come under my touch, the service you will endure." He turned her tightly within his grip, looking into her eyes without sign or hint of mercy. "My Chosen."

"No." A whimpered plea of a word that gained no sympathy from him, offered no sign of kindness or change in his stance.

"Open the door, my Devoted ones." His cold smile never faltered, even when he threw her against the stone floor. "I have chosen!"

Uncaring hands grasped at her arms, pulling her out of the room before the door had barely opened. Red robes, white ones, yellow tunics marking those who worked as servants in the temple, a hallway that had been empty only a short while before now thrived with life.

"Bathe her, prepare her and then you will bring her to my chamber. Make the announcement that one of the Gods has returned and chosen. This woman, this one of the offered will become of the Blessed...if she survives the training."

Clarity returned with the distance between them as two red-robed women hurried her away from his side, followed by a tunic-wearing servant. She had to have been in shock, that was the only thing that made sense. An elaborate trick, powdered rock coated over his clothing that had cracked when he had moved?

What about his ability to hear her thoughts?

Perhaps he had just been reading the emotions on her face, or she had mumbled something without realizing it?

"Where are you taking me?" She regained control of her voice long enough to ask as they half carried, half pushed her through the throng of people.

"You've been chosen and should count yourself fortunate amongst women," the same dark-eyed woman who had locked her within the small room earlier informed her.

"That's not what I asked." She tried pulling free of their grasp. Escape…there had to be a way she could break free of the temple.

"You're being taken to bathe and prepare, just as he decreed. Stupid girl, don't you realize the honor that is being bestowed upon you? Not only have you been welcomed into the temple, but you've been chosen as his new consort." A coal-dark gaze fixed on her. "I would have slain my own mother for such a chance as you have been given."

Right now she'd had seriously thought about killing her mother if it had meant being given the chance to escape. "You could take my place, then."

The Devoted stopped without warning, her hand tightening on Alayna's arm, turning her sharply to face the narrow-faced woman. For the second time in less than an hour she experienced the mix of pain and shock that accompanied the loud slap across her cheek. "How dare you try to tempt me that way! Everything I have ever prayed for has just been granted to you, and you try and toss it away? If I didn't believe His Holiness would have me killed for it, I'd see you whipped to within an inch of your life! Be assured when he grants me permission to aid in your teaching, I will take delight in correcting your errors then."

Until that moment Alayna had never seen such a look of

jealousy and hatred as she now saw within the older woman's eyes. "I'm sorry, Devoted. Forgive me. The stress of the moment, the shock of meeting one of the Gods..." The excuses hurried from her lips.

"I'm not fooled by you, Chosen. I don't know what his Lordship sees in you, but I know what you are. Sooner or later he'll see it and when he does, I pray I am the one that wields the dagger and sends you on your way." Thin lips hissed the cold words into her face.

"Devoted Isabella, if it pleases you, we are supposed to be overseeing her preparations," one of the other red-robed women spoke quietly.

"Yes, of course. I have permitted myself to be distracted by her foolishness. No longer. Come, the bathhouse awaits."

In stunned silence, Alayna allowed herself to be led down the hallway past the mixture of bemused and awed onlookers. Did most of them truly believe that being chosen was some form of honor? Even her few brief moments with that creature had left her shaken. What his plans were for her she didn't know, and wasn't sure she ever wanted to find out. There had to be a way of escaping the situation.

Doors opened before the small group, the large hallway replaced by a narrower, more ornate one and finally terminating at a set of heavily carved wooden doors. Steam curled upwards from the open baths, delicate scents mingled, low voices carried into the bathhouse even as the doors closed behind them.

"Clean her, prepare her fully, the Immortal Traven demands it." Isabella demanded, scattering the attendants through the room even as she pushed Alayna towards the largest of the steaming baths. At least she had two names to work with now. Isabella, that name was familiar. There had been a woman presented to the temple when Alayna had been a child, one her mother spoke of in near awe, speaking of rumors that had told of the woman being destined to be the highest of the Devoted before her cycles dried.

Enslaved By Blood

Could it be the same one? She couldn't imagine two of that name, with that level of harsh loyalty existing within the same Temple.

Traven, that name she knew, one of the highest of the Gods, revered for his intelligence and cruelty. Entire families had been given to the fields and forests in his name, some walking willingly under the knife, and she had been chosen by him. She tried remembering the images she had seen of him in the scrolls. Dark violet eyes, midnight hair, a whip curled into his belt, that full but cold smile. The man she had met within the prayer room matched the stories appearance-wise at least.

The water lapped along her legs, caressing her chilled skin, though it did nothing to ease her fears as she let the women of the bathhouse do their work. Her thoughts kept drifting from Isabella and Traven, then back again. A Chosen. One who belonged to the God that picked them out completely; body, mind and soul, flesh and blood for their taking, their pain, their pleasure, their very sustenance if the God so wished. That part of the stories had to be false. Isabella would not so crave to be in her place if there was a chance that she would be slain for the amusement of the Gods.

When the soft fingers of the attendants parted her thighs, she finally responded to their presence. "Don't touch me like that, what do you think you are doing?" She tried pulling away from them, heat rising in twin spots on her cheeks.

"We're doing what is needed and preparing you for our God, Chosen. Such traditions have been set down in stone since before the temple was built." The nearest attendant smiled, her voice softer than those others she had heard, a hint of a kindness that felt out of place within the temple. "The Gods are strict in such matters."

"I can wash myself, especially there. I don't need any help like that." Alayna turned away from them within the warm water. "Leave me."

"No, we have our orders, Chosen, and until you are used

to what is expected of you, these rituals will be enforced," the woman explained even as she turned Alayna back to face her and the others in the bath. Despite the task, the young attendant kept a smile on her face, her voice gentle. "Chosen, please do not make us restrain you for this."

One look towards the gloating Isabella made it all too clear that that was exactly what they would have to do if she did not comply. With both cheeks burning in shame, Alayna let them part her thighs, tensing as the women pressed their fingers between her lower lips, cleaning between them. Firm hands turned her fully to rest her face against the edge of the bath, parting her ass cheeks with a gentle care as that same intimate cleansing continued, even including slipping a soapy finger within the tight rim of her ass.

How much was she supposed to endure in silence?

"Lift her out." Isabella commanded.

She tried not to fight as they manipulated her from the bath, water pearling across her skin, falling to the floor in light droplets. Towels far softer than any she had seen before now smoothed across her skin, drying her in light pats until they pressed her to lie on her back across a bench. Oil-slick hands moved over her skin, rubbing in soothing strokes until some of her tension finally eased. Having the hands of a strange woman knead into her breasts felt strange, bringing a warmth of more intimate nature to life within her body. Her nipples were teased, pulled firmly into small points before those insistent hands continued down over her belly, circling her taut skin in firm touches. This part of the preparations she could accept, even enjoy, at least so she thought until those slick fingers moved her thighs until her feet sat on each side of the bench.

Alayna closed her eyes against the touches now, wanting to shut out their path over her sex. Her thighs tightened at the gentle touch that eased between her heated lower lips, a small jolt pushing through her hips as one light finger circled her clit. How could she even begin to enjoy such a series of touches?

Wicked, a part of her had to be wicked to find anything but humiliation in the handling she was being put through. Then, as she began to doubt her ability to shut the touches out any more they were gone, and the word was given to roll onto her belly. Firm strokes moved the oil over her back from shoulder to ass and worked her thighs, calves, even the soles of her feet, but any doubt she might have had on just what the attendant planned on doing vanished with the touch of the oil to her dark star.

"Don't!" She half rose from the bench, her escape prevented by two hands pressing firmly against her shoulders, forcing her with a gentle pressure back against the stone.

"It is part of the ritual, Chosen. All of you must be readied in case he wishes use of you in any fashion." One fingertip slipped within her ass, despite the clenching of her cheeks and thighs. "Relax, you are only making this worse."

Her grip tightened on the bench, teeth grinding under the intimate ministrations. A fingertip became two, working the oil in, stretching her ass just a little, never going deeper than the first knuckle, though even that was enough to bring tears of pain.

"You will grow used to this in time, Chosen." Isabella smirked. "Just as you will come to relish whatever delights our God wishes you to experience. You can, of course, fight against his desires, but you will not escape him. Or those with him."

Somehow she doubted that she would ever come to enjoy such ministrations as the ones she now endured. Those terrible touches soon ended, leaving her trembling, naked and oiled on the stone bench, her flame-colored cheeks hidden beneath the veil of her own hair. Would this be a daily ritual?

"Stand up." Isabella snapped the order at her. "I've no time for your laziness, and you will not keep his Holiness waiting."

She could still feel the lingering ghosts of those touches over her skin, especially between her thighs and ass cheeks, as she moved slowly to her feet.

"I said stand up!" Isabella grasped her hair, pulling Alayna upwards with a tight tug. "Next time I tell you to do something you will do it, Chosen or not."

"Devoted!" One of the Attendants protested, the same woman that had tried to offer some kindness during the bath. "She is the Lord Traven's property, he might…"

"I seriously doubt our God will find fault with me speeding his Chosen to his presence. Do not think to correct me again, Lily, or I will take great delight in having your screams replace more mundane prayers in the temple." Isabella turned her anger on the trembling young woman.

"Devoted, Mercy, please, I beg your forgiveness for speaking out of turn." Lily dropped to her belly on the tiled floor, visibly shaking under the cold gaze of the red-robed woman. "I forgot my place and beg your correction."

If the way Lily had moved to the floor had startled Alayna, the sharp kick Isabella inflicted on the prone woman only served to sicken her further. A sharp cry of pain followed the kick, one that became a whimper when Isabella grabbed the sobbing girl's hair, yanking her face from the tiles to hiss at her, "Crawl, slut, crawl now to the main temple and beg each Devoted you pass to strike you to help remind you of your place here."

"Yes, Devoted, thank you for your Mercy." Lily pressed her lips to the floor before Isabella's feet. In silence and under the watchful gaze of the Devoted, Lily crawled slowly out of the room, the choked sobs following the trembling woman from sight.

She wanted to scream at Isabella for her cruelty, to find a way to encourage Lily to stand up for herself, but what good would it have done? She'd spent less than one day within the walls of the temple, but now she had been taught that at least some of the stories were true. The knots in her stomach had become snakes that squirmed with each new breath. What of the other tales, those that spoke of screams, of blood offerings, lives taken for no other reason but to ease the passage of the night into day?

"Now we will finish your preparations without any further interruptions." Isabella turned her cool gaze back towards Alayna, assessing her openly as she spoke. "If I hear one more protest from you over this ritual, then you will beg to crawl to Lord Traven's feet before I am through with you. Is that very clear, Chosen?"

Chapter Three

A short, almost nonexistent robe of silver-grey clung to her form, outlining the swell of her breasts. It barely covered the curves of her ass when she stood, despite how much she tried to tug it down. How much more it would reveal should she have reason to sit was blatantly clear to Alayna. Why even bother to dress her at all, if this was what she was going to have to wear?

"Well now, I cannot see Lord Traven having any issues with how you have cleaned up." Isabella walked slowly around her, tracing her short, tapered nails across Alayna's shoulders. "Such a delicate little offering you turned out to be. All it took was a little cooperation on your behalf. Pity you couldn't see fit to comply earlier, then perhaps that slut Lily would not have stepped out of line."

Her cold smile only added to the discomfort Isabella took obvious delight in inflicting on her. "You've a sweet body, Chosen." Cruel fingers closed on Alayna's breast, her nails digging slowly into covered skin. "Perhaps in time he will permit me to take a little sport with you. If I am lucky that time will be soon, as a way of teaching you your place. I'll even bring Lily in to watch. You'd like that, wouldn't you, Chosen? A good lesson in what is expected of you here?"

Her jaw clenched at the words. So that was the plan; blame the punishment of the attendant on her, perhaps explain it that way to Traven, and then sit back to watch the fallout. Letting her see the momentary fear wouldn't help matters, and she doubted there was anything Isabella could do to her. Better to wait it out, play the game of being subdued and find a way free of the Temple when the moment arose. "Devoted, this is all a shock to me, everything happening at once, but I am sure Lord Traven will see fit to correct those responsible for Lily's behavior."

The momentary look of hesitation in Isabella's eyes confirmed that that had been the right thing to say as the older woman's hand drew back. It didn't matter how proud or bold the Devoted tried to appear, she still feared the potential anger of the false God, Traven. She still didn't know how Traven had managed to know what she was thinking, but that was something she would figure out in time. A trick, or perhaps he was one of the gifted ones. Even in this day and age, one like that might appear to be a God.

"He's waited long enough for your appearance, Chosen." Isabella closed her grasp on Alayna's arm, pulling her towards the door. Despite the concern in the woman's voice, Alayna had no hesitation on doubting her sincerity. "I expect he is quite anxious to take a look at how you turned out. I believe taking you there on your hands and knees leashed like a beast would have been far more fitting, however, I am not one to correct a God. No matter how tempting the thought might be."

Keeping silent as she was pulled from the room and down the stone corridor took every ounce of control she could lay claim to. Leashed, yes, she was sure Isabella would have enjoyed that. How would she had displayed her to the others along the way, perhaps had her kiss the feet of those passing by, a whimper only permitted as a form of greeting, or something far worse? The woman was cruelty incarnate, a willing devotee to a God of darkness. Before entering the temple, Alayna had believed that every human being had some small redeeming quality. Now she knew that to be a false assumption.

Calm, she had to stay calm or it would only urge on Isabella and any other of the Devoted that might be present into some form of corrective action. The spanking she had been forced to endure before entering the temple would be mild compared to the actions Isabella might inflict on her. Worse, it might give them just cause to report her behavior to the man she was being delivered to. She had to maintain at least some appearance of acceptance of the situation.

Robed men and women watched in a near-stunned awe as the Devoted led her through the corridors, finally halting before a large set of double doors. Their gazes left her skin crawling, an itching she couldn't ignore as the hairs on the back of her neck rose. Runes far older than she had the ability to decipher had been carved into the heavy wood the iron that bound the doors themselves had turned almost ebony with age and two red-robed members of the Devoted stood on either side of the closed entrance.

"I bring his Chosen." Isabella announced. Nothing more was needed to be said, it seemed, as the doors opened before them with little more than a low creaking of hinges.

There had to be easily twenty people waiting within the large, well-lit room. Torches burned along the walls, small braziers sat in each of the four corners and a fire burned at one end, offering further light and warmth. No one spoke, and of Traven there was no sign. That shouldn't have surprised her. Why would someone who wanted others to believe he was a God, wait on the arrival of a mere mortal?

Isabella pressed her hand on Alayna's shoulder, forcing her without words to her knees. Just as she had feared, the short robe rose, the only thing keeping her sex covered being her own thighs as they pressed tightly together. That same hand pushed on the back of her head, making sure she kept her head bowed, and her eyes lowered to the stone floor. Another set of stones to count, another lesson in keeping herself quiet.

Perhaps in a few days the constant watch from the members of the temple would ease up, and then she would be able to find a way free of this place. The edges of the stone tiles under her knees adding ridges to her skin, she tugged at the robe, trying to find a way to keep her body a little more covered. Now as she knelt she could feel the oil on her skin--more than that, she still felt the ghostly memories of fingers pressing into her ass, over her clit, between her slick lips.

Shame added to a growing heat across her cheeks at the memory. What was it about this man that left her fighting a need to squirm?

"You have done well in preparing her, my Devoted one."

She struggled not to raise her gaze at the sound of his voice. He hadn't been in the room, she had been sure of that, and no door had opened, nor had she heard any footfalls to announce his arrival.

"You honor me with your words, my Lord." The honeyed tones fell from Isabella's lips. "Though I regret to inform you that your Chosen incited one of the temple Attendants to step out of line to a point where she dared to correct your Devoted servant in her actions."

"Look at me, my Chosen."

Alayna's gaze rose from the stones, meeting his. Violet, they were still violet, unlike any other sets of eyes she had seen before entering the temple. That had to be a trick of the light or an accident of birth; no human being had violet eyes.

"Is this true?" His voice soothed and frightened her at the same time, lulling her to answer even as the hair rose on the back of her neck. He hadn't lost any of his strange beauty, nor the danger he carried within his gaze. That smile reminded her clearly of a hunter and she knelt close to his feet as the offering. Her thighs pressed more tightly together, a heated uneasiness rising between them. Nerves, that had to be the answer. She couldn't imagine any other reason for the growing dampness that now seeped against the tender skin of her inner thighs.

"I do not know what prompted the attendant to speak the way she did, my Lord." She took a cue from how Isabella addressed him, hoping it would be the right way that it might ease any anger he would otherwise direct towards her. What punishment would he impose on her if he believed her to be the cause of

Lily's actions? He'd put her through something far greater than a spanking, of that she had no doubt. "I only know that the Devoted, Isabella, punished the girl and sent her on her way."

The thought of being pulled across his lap, her ass well bared as his hand cracked against her taut skin left a shiver running across her already chilled flesh. Then what would happen? Her mind was unwilling to form any suggestions.

"Ah, so a punishment has already been meted out." One dark eyebrow lifted as he addressed Isabella. "Why was that part of the incident left unspoken until my Chosen informed me?"

Cloth rustled behind her, as though someone had quickly knelt. Isabella, no doubt, there was no other within the chamber that Alayna could imagine finding a reason to kneel without an order snapped in their direction. "Forgive me, my Lord, I did not think you would want every small detail."

A laugh preceded his reply, a sound that knotted her stomach, as the mirth was a cold, chilling presence. "It is for me to decide what information I require and you would do best to remember that in future. Take this as a warning, Devoted Isabella. The next time it is you that will find yourself on your hands and knees, crawling for my punishment. A punishment I will let the girl, Lily, oversee."

He'd already known? Some member of the temple had informed him, no doubt. It didn't surprise her that there would be some politics and power shuffling that took place here. In fact, it made perfect sense that each Devoted would seek a way to be rid of their possible rivals.

"Yes, my Lord...I beg your forgiveness." She couldn't be sure, but it almost sounded as though the woman had lowered to her belly. A small glimmer of triumph threatened to turn her lips into a smile; that Isabella had been found lacking by the very God she wished to serve was in more than one way amusing.

"That you will earn at a later time, now leave us. You no longer have my blessing to remain for the first part of the claiming." Had there ever been any warmth in his voice, it now vanished. "Leave us!"

Swift steps carried Isabella from the room, the doors closing behind her. Even though she knew Traven might glance her way, Alayna still struggled to keep a smile from her face.

"Crawl to me now, my Chosen," he ordered as he stepped back and took a seat on what might have easily been mistaken for a throne. Well, what else did she think a 'God' would sit on? Crawl indeed, just a few days of this and she'd...

"Now!" The single word growled across the short distance at her.

She bit into her lip as she lowered to the floor, her hands curling a little against the stone. The robe rose, baring her ass fully to anyone stood behind her. Could they also see the glisten of her sweat against her inner thighs, or would they assume that was from the oiling? Her breasts pressed against the soft material of the brief robe, swaying with each hesitant crawl towards his booted feet. Dark leather lay within her line of sight, black cloth wrapped about his legs of a finer weave than she had seen before, her nails tapping on the stone as she edged forward until his boots were nearly under her lips.

"Kiss them."

A stone formed in the pit of her stomach. Kiss his boots? What other choice did she have if she wanted to keep up the image of a faithful Chosen? She lowered her lips to the smooth leather, brushing them across the surface in a light touch.

"No, kiss them fully. Lick, kiss, caress, offer me your worship with your tongue, my Chosen. Show all those here how well you wish to serve me, to learn from me." His words were little more than a low growl, a coldness touching them that only added to the discomfort and odd dampness between her thighs. "Remember the path into the darkness that I offer you now, prove to me that you are worth my attentions, or I shall be forced to turn you over to my Devoted ones as their plaything."

She swallowed hard before trying again. Being handed over to the likes of Isabella offered nightmarish images that she wanted no part of.

Dirt. She could taste the dirt on his boots as her tongue slid over the smooth leather. The leather carried a taste of its own, a deep smell, a power within it that she had never imagined. Her back arched, lips parting over the leather in her attempt to placate him, to offer what he wanted. She shivered, her thighs opening under the attention she paid to his boots, tasting the leather, dirt, the stitches under her lips. A low groan filled her ears and it took a moment for her to realize that the sound had come from her.

No, this wasn't possible; the noise had to have gained life elsewhere. Such a groan would suggest she enjoyed what he had commanded her to do when every part of her being denied him.

"Better." A tight grip found her hair, tangling into the long strands, using the hold to pull her up to her knees, his free hand brushing against her cheeks when he spoke. "That groan pleased me, though you have a long way to go, my Chosen. Sooner or later you will accept that I am exactly what I claim to be, a God. Your God, and you will come to live to serve me in whatever manner I so desire."

There was no escaping the intense look within his violet eyes. The protests that would have otherwise gained life so easily now stilled under that gaze. She could still taste the leather on her lips, still feel the oil between her thighs, within her ass, her nipples pressed against the thin cloth that molded to her body. Reactions that gained life despite that soft warning voice at the back of her mind. Dangerous, he offered death, pain, humiliation, she could see it all shining within his eyes...

She wanted to pull away, deny him, leave, but she couldn't. That desire had been caged, locked within her by the key that existed in his gaze.

"I offer you what no mortal ever could, Chosen. A life such as few dream of. All you have to do is give yourself to me freely." His hands moved from her body, the grip gone from her hair, the light touch missing from her cheek. Now he simply spoke and waited with his hands on his thighs, a dagger with a blade of red metal resting in his left hand across his leg.

She didn't want to take that step, but how else could she make them believe? No, it was more than that; a part of her wanted to, more than a part. His eyes, she couldn't pull away from his eyes, nor deny the heat that throbbed between her thighs. No man had ever touched her there, no one save herself until the preparations within the bathhouse, yet she knew what she wanted, needed. Just a touch, his touch, his lips across her skin, his hand within her hair once more, would that be so wrong to want?

"You want it, don't you." He smiled. "You can feel it, the offers of my touch, how it might be to curl at my feet?"

No, this was wrong. He had had her drugged, or there was something she was missing. It didn't matter how good his words felt, how they teased her with images that left her pressing her thighs together, almost squirming on her knees, she couldn't do it.

"Remember how it felt just a moment ago, how your tight little cunt clenched as you obeyed me and worshiped at my boots? That feeling is only the beginning. I can teach you so much more, bring you to the lowest in your life before I raise you to heights you have yet to even dream of."

"How?" Hadn't she screamed a denial? So why had it sounded more like a question, a way of seeking a path into the very service he offered?

"Bare your throat for me," came the soft whispering growl of a reply.

It didn't matter anymore why his words pulled at her core, or that a dozen others were watching her. Without hesitation she moved, tipping her head back, lifting her chin. She didn't even flinch when the blade touched her skin, slicing a small nick into her flesh. Before she could cry out, his hand returned to her hair, holding her in place so tightly that even if she had been able to try and move, that option was now taken from her.

Fear erupted into life, a cry torn from his lips at the touch of his teeth against her throat. Sharp, she had never expected teeth to feel so sharp and so compelling at the same time. Her back arched within his grasp, she fought to keep her hands from reaching for him, from clawing into him with a hunger she wanted to deny.

"Your blood, your life and your very being belong to me. With the offering of your neck you make yourself mine for the training of your own free will." His words vibrated into her neck in the moments before she felt his lips close about the small cut, a warmth flooding through her even as her mind screamed that he was drinking from the wound.

A low moan escaped her lips as he suckled openly on the small wound in her neck, drinking from her as he might a fine wine. Fear, disgust, the small amount of pain, they gave way to something else, a desire given full life that she wasn't ready to face. Her thighs parted as she pressed towards him, gripping at his hands, though his touch offered no kindness as it nearly tore strands of hair from her.

"You are claimed. As per the laws laid down by my kind from before the dawn of time I name this woman, this female beast, this living offering as my own." He lifted his lips from her skin. "Let no one else touch her without my consent; she is under my training, my teaching and belongs to me. She has no name, is nothing more than a Chosen, until she earns it."

She could barely blink at his words. Her mouth dried out as her heart raced, skipping beats only to race once more. A cold sweat coated her flesh even as her stomach knotted, rolled and threatened to empty. Only sheer willpower kept her from disgracing herself in front of those gathered in the room.

How could he do this to her?

Turn her into a creature without a name, what did he think she was?

Enslaved By Blood

The feel of the metal about her throat, the harsh click of a lock as the collar closed in place filled in the blanks.

Chosen, he called her, but the collar marked her as nothing more than a slave...

Chapter Four

A slave, she'd given herself to him as a slave. How could she have committed such an act of her own free will?

Had there been something in the bath or the oil that had left her so easy to be manipulated?

"My Lord, what do you wish sent out as orders in regards to your property? What word should be sent to those others in the temple?" A new voice inquired, one she had not heard before, nor did she think to turn and seek out the owner. Her mind was still reeling with the knowledge of what she had done and the weight of the locked metal about her throat. All grips Traven had had on her body were gone, leaving her with just the collar on her throat and the sting of the small cut above where the band of metal now lay.

"In time I might send her amongst my Devoted in order to experience other delights, but for this night I will complete my claiming in private. Leave us." He didn't even look down at her now. His focus was on the others in the room even as they began to file out, leaving her half curled on the floor, shivering with the events that had left her locked within steel.

Silence followed the closing of the double doors, the sounds of the Devoteds, their robes, their presence, it all faded, shut behind the heavy wood. She didn't even think of moving from where he had left her; a part of her couldn't move, not even to touch the collar to see if it were real.

"Of course it is real." The mocking tone of his words would have been hard to miss. "You still cling to that odd belief, don't you, that slender hope that this is all some trick of the mind, perhaps lack of food, maybe it is the water you must be craving by now. How many answers has your frightened little mind offered you?”

"It...this cannot be real," she mumbled. "Gods, the Gods don't even exist. I shouldn't be here. I'm going to wake up soon, home in my bed, where it's safe."

"Oh, I know that is what you believe. I've heard your arguments with your Mother as you've grown into womanhood. I've sat and watched you over the years, waiting for the time when you would be presented to me. I even watched today as you went through that delightful spanking under the hands of the guard your mother employed. Did you enjoy it pet? Your cunt clenched with his strikes, didn't it, your body wanted something else from him, no matter how you would deny it.

"Oh, they were brief moments to someone like me, they've really been quite amusing, some of the excuses you have offered others, better yet have been the ones you have told yourself. So now what will you do, my little toy? Will you accept without argument what I am?" He leaned back in the throne. "No, of course you will not. That would be too easy, and I would not enjoy our time together quite as much if you suddenly gave in like that."

Her lips felt dry, but under the mocking gaze he had fixed her with, she felt unable to move. What else did he know about her, how did he know it, the more life the questions gained, the more obvious the answer became. It didn't matter that she was loath to believe it, he had either paid off her mother over the years or he was exactly what he claimed to be.

"Very good, my pet, very good indeed. So now your mind begins to grasp the concept, but will you accept the answer it gives you?" He smirked, swinging one leg over the arm of the throne, leaving it to dangle there as he watched her. The light played off the leather of his boots, refreshing her memory of how it felt to have that same leather under her lips. How smooth it had been, the taste, the tickle of her own hair as it had fallen over her face.

She shifted on her knees, her thighs pressing closed. How

could this all be affecting her in such a way?

"It will become far more intense," he promised coldly. "Stand up."

Alayna looked up quickly, seeing the way his gaze had narrowed. The last thing he looked willing to deal was an argument. With a shudder she rose, tugging the tunic back down over her thighs, seeking somewhere to fix her gaze, anywhere but meeting his. The power within his eyes, the way her skin crawled yet ached to be touched at the same time, the need to step closer to him and seek out what ever he wanted of her all mingled within her shivering form.

He moved with a silent grace she had not expected from a man of his build, clearing the distance between them. Without a word his fingers curled into her hair. She'd expected that, though, it seemed to be a habit with him, a way to use an inbuilt leash her body offered him.

The grip tightened, pulling her up onto her toes, arching her back as he marched her towards a smaller door behind the throne. One he opened without word of explanation to her, forcing her through it with a pleased growl. What lay in the other room caused her heart to sink whilst her pussy tightened.

Small torches offered a low light that played over the dark stone walls. Whips hung from the walls, some with a single tail, others with multiple ones, flat tails, braided ones, ones with heavy knots in. Crops, leather straps, cuffs, canes, knives, each one laid out in neat order on a smooth wooden table. Chains hung from the ceiling, from wooden beams against the wall and from a wooden x frame that stood in the middle of the room.

"Strip." His fingers slipped from her hair.

For a moment she stood there, watching as he walked away towards the frame. No matter how brief the tunic was, it at least offered some protection; the idea of stripping it off didn't appeal to her, especially in a room like this. If he had to give the order again, she had no doubt that he would punish her for not obeying.

Reluctantly she grasped the edge of the cloth, tugging it over her head until she then held it clutched to her body, holding on to the limited protection it still offered.

"Drop it and walk to the frame." He barely even looked at her, yet expected her to just walk to that damned frame?

Her fingers unlocked from the deathlike grip she had on the tunic, letting it fall to the floor. How could he expect her to just walk to the frame that way? Because he did, because she would, and because she already had done exactly what he had wanted. As her mind had played over the arguments, somehow her body had let the tunic fall and brought her to stand before the frame.

One strong hand pressed her against the frame, the wood smooth under her body. She didn't protest when he grasped her wrists, locking them into the manacles on the frame. His breath caressed a path down her bare back, his hands smoothing along her hips, down her thighs before he parted them harshly, locking her ankles against the frame.

"You have a lot to learn from me." He spoke softly. "Pain, pleasure, denial, your screams will sate one hunger I have, your tears another, perhaps you will bleed for me tonight, or I may just leave you hanging here when I have done with you." She couldn't see what he was doing, but the sound of his footfalls marked a passage across the room.

Leather cracked through the air, the violent noise pressing her tighter against the frame. "Please."

"Please what, my Chosen?" She could hear the smile in his voice.

"Don't do this to me." Alayna tugged at the bonds that held her against the wooden frame. Leather straps firmly buckled into place, there was no way she could slip free of this, no matter how she tried. He'd taken care to fasten them close, leaving just enough room so the blood could flow freely to her fingers, but nowhere near enough that she could release herself.

"Ah, but I want to do this. Nothing you could say would offer me even a moment of the delight I will gain from this first night with you under my touch." Leather sliced through the air, biting against her back in a long strike.

A scream tore free from her lips, her body arching upwards onto her toes, pressed tight against the frame. It burned, a deep, searing pain scoring into her flesh. Pain had been almost alien to her prior to coming to the temple, and even the brief amounts she had experienced held no comparison to the touch of the single tail whip.

"Now, some like to work their way up, warming the body with a flogger first, but I prefer the virgin-pure screams that using this whip creates. Perhaps another time I'll build you up for a longer night of play." He spoke calmly, curling the whip back away from her form. Her breath came in low sobs. Just one strike had brought a cry and had left her shuddering against the wood. "So we will play this game and see how much you can take."

More? He wanted to use that thing on her again?

The hiss offered a brief warning, enough that she could tense before it lashed against her back, wrapping from left hip to right shoulder, a new line of fire-fueled pain raising a welted path across her back. One scream melded into the next with the third crack of leather through the air, laying a new welt across both ass cheeks only to tear back through the air and add a second, then third line, one under the other in tight precision. He was tearing her open, her mind screamed that she felt blood. Surely no human being could be struck in such a manner without bleeding.

"This is just a beginning," he murmured against the back of her neck, his hands moving over the heated and raised welts, cupping her ass before he traced the single welt across both of her cheeks. "A simple beginning, but you already feel as though you could take no more, you want to plead for mercy, yet you have no idea just how much the human body can take. You move so nicely against the frame, little beast, like a dancer following through the play of the music I prefer. A dance that could fire the blood of even the oldest of my kind."

Soft, wet and warm, his tongue traced the first welt over her back, almost welcoming against the pain that still seared a path through her body. A slick, wicked but soothing touch that had her squirming against the leather straps. "Such a wonderful taste, but it will become better. We just need to change pace a little, baste the beast in steel."

A loud smack echoed in the room, his hand cracking against her ass cheek, a second one striking her other cheek, both mounds reddening under the blows. After the powerful pain of the single tail the spanks created more heat than pain, but still held her pressed to the frame.

"You'll come to enjoy our times within this room." Twice more his hand lashed against her ass as he spoke. "You'll even eventually ask to be brought in here. I've seen it before; you'll become addicted to what I can offer you." His hands moved down over her thighs, only to scrape a path back to her taut mounds, striking her ass four times in sharp beats. "Pain, pleasure, they combine under the right touch and with the right woman. You, my dear little beast, are such a woman."

"No." She whimpered a protest, biting back tears, arching to the wood as his hand slipped between her thighs to cup at her exposed mound. "Please, I'm not like that. I just want to go home."

"Oh, are you so sure, little beast?" One finger moved between the lips of her cunt, wriggling a deeper path into her willing body. How could she feel this way, how could she be so willing to accept his touch? "This seems so warm, inviting, just a small amount of pain and you're already slick here. You're so ready for more than just a finger within your tight pussy, aren't you?"

She tried biting back a groan, her body clenched about his finger, hips pressed backwards towards his body. This didn't make sense, how could she want his touch after the pain of the lash? After the way he had locked a collar on her throat, taken her name, called her nothing more than a beast?

Drugs. There had to be some form of drug involved. The bath, the oil, maybe something in the candles, inhaled with the smoke?

With a mocking chuckle, he pulled his finger from between her lips. "Soon, beast, we've only begun to build to that moment." That laugh followed him across the room, the whip tossed down on the table, something else collected instead. Her body wanted that wicked touch between her thighs to return, maybe more than one finger, something she could move against, rock back to, build to something she had only the basic understanding of. Was it wrong to want his touch like that? Her mind screamed yes, whilst her body whimpered no.

"There are so many interesting toys here you won't get the chance to experience them all tonight, but I can at least introduce you to a few of them. By the time we've finished tonight, you'll believe pain never ends, but it will be nothing more than a simple beginning." He walked back towards her, snapping something against the palm of his hand, the same something that then slapped between her thighs to sting at her swollen lips. She jerked at the touch, a cry more like a moan following the sound.

Why wasn't she screaming for him to stop?

"Be honest with yourself, beast, it's because you don't want this to stop," he answered her silent question. "Not yet, at least."

The small square of leather slapped rapidly between her thighs, striking from side to side, whipping the tender skin of her inner thighs. She couldn't help but cry out, her body arching up onto her toes, trying to draw away from the quick slaps of leather against flesh. Pain, heat and the breeze the tool created all brushed against the lips of her sex, vibrating through to her clit until her cries became soft gasps A crop, something translated the leather into being a crop in his hand.

"Yes, beast, a crop, quite fitting for use on an animal, don't you think?"

The strike that followed his word formed a line across the top

of her thighs under the tight swell of her ass, a blow that tore
a full-fledged scream from lips that had parted only moments
before in low moans.

"You're nothing more than a little beast under the control of
her Master."

Alayna's mind reeled between his words and the pain. A beast,
a thing, a toy under his fingers, is that what she was to become?
How could any living being be so cruel to another? Even what she
had witnessed of the Temple's punishment had offered nothing
that prepared her for this.

"It's really very easy to understand. Pain is addictive, it
sweetens the blood, drives the mind into places it might otherwise
be unwilling to explore. Some humans can learn to appreciate the
delights it offers, others shun it, some rare few, though, can use
it to take a step from this life into another existence." His words
whispered against her back, the crop still grasped in his hands as
he ran his fingers over her flanks, following the dip of her waist
before reaching about to cup her breasts. Sharp teeth laid a path
of nips along her shoulder, his fingers closing on her nipples,
pulling them out, tugging, twisting until she could not help but
whimper.

The welts on her ass radiated pain through her body, meeting
the fresh throbbing of her nipples, mingling down into her clit,
then deeper within her trapped body. In open betrayal her hips
rocked forward against the frame, matching the deep clenching of
her heated cunt.

"Pain mingles with pleasure, doesn't it? No matter how hard
you try to fight it, you can't stop what it does to you." Mocking
words caressed her neck and urged another rock from her hips.
"It offers something greater, a doorway you're afraid to walk
through. Well, don't worry about it, beast, you will have no
choice but to crawl through that door when the time is right." His
fingers tightened on her nipples, nails digging into either side of
the tight buds, twisting, pulling at them until she thought they

would be torn from her body. The release of his grip brought but a moment's relief, then fresh pain as the blood returned to her nipples, throbbing sharp pain through the tortured buds.

Tears spilled down her pale cheeks, the salt leaving a tacky trail that encouraged her dark hair to stick to her face.

His nails racked a path down from her breasts, her belly, then around her hips, nail scores to add to the pattern he was building on her pale skin.

One hand cupped between her thighs, his thumb playing over her clit, teasing a soft circular pattern over the tight, slick nub. He rubbed the hood between his fingers only to pull away, leaving her body wanting more of his touch.

"Time for a little more work," he growled against the back of her neck before stepping back, the crop connecting with her thighs in sharp cracks. Each strike landed on her taut skin, lines covering from the back of her knees up to the curve of her ass, a breath or two only between each strike. Little enough time to cry out before the next would land, welts, bruises, aching muscles, she'd be barely able to move by the time he had finished with her.

Sweat beaded across her body, falling with tears to mingle on her parted lips. Pain and heat ruled her now, thought fleeing a little further with each new strike. It didn't matter what she wanted, he'd continue with his game, wasting energy on pleading would have no affect on him even if she had any spare energy to waste. All she could do now was hang in the leather straps against the wood as her hips rocked in time to the strikes.

"Closer, each touch of the crop brings you closer to where I wish you to be this time." The square of leather tickled between her ass cheeks, trailing down over her reddened inner thighs only to smack up against her mound three times in quick succession. Even to her ears the sound was a damp, squishing noise. "Your body wants something else now, an answer to the craving."

"Yes." A single word, but fueled by the drive he had forced to life.

"Do you ask for it?" The leather tapped in quick, light slaps against her pussy lips. "Do you plead for it?"

"Yes," she whispered before her mind could scream no.

"Are you sure...you don't seem to be quite sincere enough for me." A rapid beat played over her lower lips, tapping against her clit, sliding between slick flesh. "You seem to be missing a word. I'm sure you know what word I mean, little beast."

Word? What word?

"Think of what you are now," he urged.

Slave, the collar made her a slave, his slave even if such a thing was barely known of beyond the walls of the temple. She didn't want to be that, not a beast, a piece of property, but the collar was locked about her throat, her body already marked at his whim as it burned with a need to feel something between her thighs. Her entrance into the temple had turned her into nothing better than an indentured whore.

"Say it." The rod of the crop pressed between her slick lips.

"Please...Master." The words gained a life of their own, slipping from her lips before she could think enough to prevent them. "Please, I need something."

"What do you need? Tell me." She could feel the crop turning in his hands, slipping between her lips, pressing against her clit.

"Need to feel..." Feel what, she'd never known this before. Her inner walls rippled, a heat claimed her core, demanding attention. Pressure cupped her sex, brushing against her lower lips as they tried to part.

Ache didn't even begin to describe it.

"Do you need to feel me between your thighs, to have my cock buried in that sweet, innocent cunt of yours?" He leaned closer, murmuring the words against her shoulder.

"Yes, Master." Flame danced over her cheeks at the shame of her words.

"Then beg me to fuck you." She could feel him smiling as he spoke, the shape of his lips changing against her skin. "Plead for what your body craves."

She couldn't. No matter how much this new craving burned within her body, how deeply her hips rocked towards the frame, then back against him or how the crop teased at her wicked flesh, she could not shame herself to that level. Her bottom lip caught between her teeth, trying to hold the plea within her body; a body that needed more, that rocked, pressed back towards him, her welted ass touching a swollen outline against his pants.

Something to press into her body, to fill her and find a way to end the sensual pain that flooded through her helpless body. Yes. Gods, yes, she needed that.

"Please, fuck me, Master." Tears coursed down her cheeks, spilling onto her lips. "Please, my Master."

His fingers tightened on her hips, pulling her ass back away from the frame as far as the leather straps on her wrists and ankles would allow. Smooth, hard flesh touched her welted skin, his cock pressing between her thighs, seeking the entrance to her cunt.

"No, please, not like this, Master," she pleaded. Not this, not bound this way, taken in bonds without care.

"Yes, exactly like this. You're my slave, and will be used as such." The head of his cock drove between her lips, into the tight, clenching confines of her vulva. Pain soared within her body as his cock parted her unused sex without a moment to prepare, nudging at the barrier within her body. She cried out, pressing towards the cross, but his grip on her hips denied her leave to move, driving into her body hard and fast, piercing the simple barrier in a single painful thrust.

It wasn't supposed to be this way. How often had she been taught that the first time needed to be gentle, with your life partner, taken with care so the woman might turn again to her mate?

He didn't move but remained buried within her body, his cock twitching at the inner walls of her pussy. Giving her a moment or two to catch her breath, he began, a deep, full rock that drew him from her only to drive back into her tight confines. Her body rose, trying to move away from him, only to find she had already started to rock back, to seek his cock, to welcome it within her sex.

Only now did his hands move from her hips, cupping her breasts, seeking out her nipples. With each harsh thrust into her cunt he pinched at her nipples, each rock of her hips he matched with the feel of his nails into the tight nubs. Her cries of pain turned into need as the slick sounds of his cock within her pussy echoed in the small chamber. A beast for his use, his pleasure, the play of pain across her body, she knew that, even accepted it for now, the drive he had given life to would allow her no other choice. A desire growing that claimed her, robbing her of sense.

She couldn't permit this and dare not let it rule her this way. Pain, pleasure, she no longer knew where one ended and the next began. Fear grew enough to grant her speech. "No, please. I don't want this."

"You can't stop it." His teeth closed on her shoulder, biting into her skin, his hips pressing deeper into her body. "It's there, building in you, wanting release. Give it life, my beast."

The walls of her cunt rippled along his throbbing cock. No matter what she said, her body wanted it, needed it, craved the release of the pleasure that had risen within her treacherous body. He twisted at her nipples, tugging them hard away from her breasts, his thrusts into her body adding to the pain from the welts. Each rock, each thrust, each painful twist of throbbing nipple only added to the depths of need that now ruled her bound form. "Gods!"

"Yes." The single word mocked her more deeply than any other.

"Need to...need something." She couldn't stop the rocking of her hips.

"You need to cum." He pulled from her body fully, only to thrust deeply back into her heated depths. "Such a tight, needful little cunt. It knows what you need. It needs to be the beast, the creature on its hands and knees, helpless and willing to serve my desires. Leashed, chained, owned, pleasure and pain can all be yours. I'll teach you the depths of the darkness I enjoy, lead you into the night with me. You'll dance under the lash, scream within my chains, crawl willingly to the feet of those I wish you to serve for my amusement; all this and far more will you come to enjoy."

No, she wanted to scream out no, but all she could do was accept her body rocking back against his, seeking to drive further onto his cock. His taunting words sparked images she wasn't ready to face, faceless men and woman staring down at her as she writhed under the body of another, bound against the stone floor. Mocking laughter that drove her onwards, pain, bonds, shame, need. Gods, the need. She couldn't control it any longer, didn't want to even try and control it. All she knew was she had to give in fully.

"Cum for me, beast," he growled against her body, driving harder than before within her walls. "Cum now!"

A scream tore from her lips, her body arching to the wood, a reaction freed from the last of the chains of restraint within her being. Her cunt tightened, released, only to tighten again, her thighs locking in place as she felt her body shake. Slick heat claimed the tight walls of her gripping sex, slipping over his cock to mingle with the sweat on her thighs.

"Mine!" he growled, his teeth sinking fully into her shoulder in two sharp points, piercing her skin, blood and pain mixing with the delight of her body's first release. Even with the deep shudders that rocked through her limp and helpless form, she knew what he was doing. With a low moan her mind slipped into a welcome darkness, fleeing from the knowledge that he was drinking from her body.

Her mind drifted away from the pain; she knew it was there, it called to her, but for now she was free of it. Her body wasn't her own, it lay within the bonds against the wood in a soft, limp heap, yet somehow she could see it. Not just her body, but the marks that were livid over her skin and the one that had placed them in such painful precision.

Traven's lips were still pressed to her shoulder; small trickles of blood dripped to the floor. Even like this, she could hear the suckling sounds of him drinking. What sort of demon did she belong to?

Uncertain, afraid, her mind refused to return to her body, yet somehow she could still see what he was doing. Only when he finally lifted his lips from her shoulder, only when she saw the torchlight reflecting from his blood-marked lips, when she could no longer ignore the two sharp teeth that now rested against her top lip did her mind finally return to her body with the knowledge she was owned by no demon, but by something far worse.

"My slave." His voice, she could still hear his voice. "You're my pet, my beast, and one day you could become so much more if you but have the courage to see what I can offer you."

Lord Traven, the dark God that had claimed her, her owner, her Master, was a drinker of blood. A Vampyre Lord, just as the darkest of the tales had hinted at...

Chapter Five

Pain, every breath brought a reminder of the suffering he had put her through. She no longer felt the wood against her body, but something softer; cushions, smooth fabric, soothing damp cloths that pressed to the welts marking her back. Still, that failed to chase away the pain completely. She wanted to shut out what he had done to her, and at the same time her mind embraced it, sought out the memory of the blows, his touch and the feel of his cock deep within her cunt as she had squirmed with his thrusts.

"So you survived his embrace." Her harsh voice pulled Alayna from her thoughts. "Such pretty marks, though, the first of many, no doubt. He is a master of such marks, and you came out lightly, though I have little doubt you think that way right now."

Lightly? Her body was burning from the touches of the whip. How could that be seen as light? Someone must have carried her from the chamber to this new room, though her mind refused to let her know who had been behind that.

"Leave us, leave us now, I would speak with the God's new pet," Isabella snapped at the servants, sending those tending the marks fleeing from the room. She'd not even seen their faces as they had worked on her body; her eyes had been closed and remained so until the door shut Somehow, by keeping them closed she had almost made herself believe she was alone, that no one else knew of the marks, of the play of blood that had been between her thighs when she had been carried into the chamber.

"Ahh, I see, he took your maidenhead and tasted you all in the same day." Tapered fingernails traced over the two puncture marks. "Quite the blessed one, aren't you? Did you writhe well for him, slut? Did you scream for him to fuck you, or did you deny yourself that pleasure?" Those same fingers curled into her hair, grasping tight until Alayna cried out in pain.

"I obeyed him, Devoted." She swallowed hard even as she spoke. "Just as was expected of me. What other choice was there for me? He is a God, an Immortal one, and I nothing more than his beast."

"A nameless beast at that. The entire temple knows that order." The hold in her hair released. "What a strange situation we find ourselves in. You would do almost anything to be free of this honor, and here I sit, someone who would willingly take your place."

Offering to swap places again would have done nothing more than anger Isabella, and that was the last thing she needed to risk doing. The woman had a core of ice; even her brief encounters with her so far had shown that. "I will try not to displease him, Devoted."

"See to it you don't displease him, not unless you truly do wish to experience his anger." Did Isabella still blame her for being sent from the chamber? "Now he has left specific instructions on how you are to be prepared for your rest. Move yourself, beast, get off that bed and onto your hands and knees. Creatures such as you do not yet have the privilege of using furniture."

Alayna bit back a complaint. Snapping out at the Devoted would do no good, and she knew enough of the temple already to be well aware that such as she would not speak of instructions from Traven unless those instructions did indeed exist. In silence she moved from the bench, looking up at Isabella as she did so, her body barely containing the trembling that moved so obviously over her limbs. The stone was cold beneath her hands, the edges of the tiles scraped against her knees as her hair slipped down over her back, caressing the sides of her breasts, nipples tightening into firm points.

"Much better, don't you agree, beast?" The taunting voice followed her to the floor. "Ah, yes, there was one other instruction you need to be aware of right now. Until the God decrees otherwise, you are to remain a beast in all things, with neither speech nor the ability to move on your feet. You will be a pet for his training."

No, she wanted to scream no, to run, lash out at the woman who took such great delight in putting her into this position, but there was nothing she could do. Unless Traven permitted otherwise, she had to obey. The welts on her body, the way being in this position pulled at them and the burning memory of his teeth in her flesh all served to keep her silent.

"Such a low little beast you now appear to be, naked and collared on her hands and knees at my feet. I must remember to thank Lord Traven for this favor, for allowing me to prepare you in the manner he has dictated. It would seem that my fall from grace lasted but a short few moments." Alayna struggled to hold position under the touch of Isabella's fingers through her hair, those sharp nails that trailed down across her back, catching the welts, adding new small shards of pain to her already brutalized body. "I will enjoy parading you through the temple to the quarters our God has ordered readied for you."

Alayna's nails threatened to crack under the pressure, catching on the edges of the stone as she shifted her weight a little. Beast, a thing, a pet, how many other indignities must she suffer before becoming free of this place and the creature that had locked steel about her throat?

"Well now, first we must finish your tending. Though your wounds are well earned, he wishes them cared for, no doubt that he may add fresh marks to your body." Isabella turned, calling two women back into the room. She heard the sound of water sloshing in a bowl, a cloth being wrung out. Before she had the time to adjust to what was to happen, a warm, damp cloth was being moved over her skin, washing her free from oil, sweat and blood alike. She'd seen horses cared for in a similar manner, but to undergo this herself only added to her growing frustration.

Gentle touches followed the path of the cloth, checking the

welts, pulling the skin on either side of them, looking for signs of the skin splitting. She hissed between clenched teeth at the small, sharp pains, but at least there appeared to be no further sign of the skin tearing, no feel of blood that trickled down her skin. That was one blessing, at least. Despite her anger, she still managed to remain on her hands and knees, even when a soft cloth was pressed between her thighs, cleansing the traces of Traven's brutal use.

Her thighs clenched, a deep shiver running through her body at the soft touch, her pussy still throbbing even now. How could the touch of a woman have that affect on her? That was just as confusing as how she had reacted to the events in the small chamber. Brutal touches, soft ones, pain, pleasure, her body still remembered how she had reacted, how such had affected her.

Twisted, somehow they had worked to twist her already to his whim.

"Salve the wounds." The order came from close by. Isabella had moved away enough that the women could see to the work, but had stayed within the room. The touches changed again, pushing her hair away from her body fully, smoothing a cooling salve across each welt. The pain, what there remained of it, eased with its application.

"Good, that should reduce any chances of infection and speed the healing time. Such a gift the God has granted you. I have seen many left to suffer for his amusement." The path of her steps across the stone made it clear just where Isabella was and that the Devoted watched her for any signs of disobedience. "Oil her, fully."

Oiling, they had already put her through that once, perhaps this time it would be easier to undergo. So why did she tense at the words?

Slick fingers moved across her skin, coated with oil, adding to her humiliation just as they had before taking her to Traven the first time. All she had to do was remain still, accept it, not fight the touches. It wasn't so hard to undergo. Or so she thought until those seeking fingers parted the soft petals of her cunt, slipping through her heated flesh, gently applying the oil that would make it far easier for someone to take her body in the same manner that Traven had, or worse.

Endure. Silent endurance, obedience and the time taken during whatever Isabella put her through to then plot revenge upon those who forced her to go through this. For a moment an image arose: Isabella on her hands and knees, her body marked with welts Alayna had placed there, screams she had heard from the touch of the whip. Isabella forced to become little more than a collared animal.

No, she wasn't like them. She would never do that to another living soul no matter how badly provoked she might be. So why was the image so tempting?

Slender fingers parted her cheeks, oiled, slick as they moved between them, seeking out the tight, dark rim of her ass. Humiliation grew into a raging heat as the first finger slipped into her ass, slippery, wicked touches that caused her thighs to clench, her hips to rock towards the floor. Shame colored her face, her thighs parting wider under the ministrations, that cold chuckle reaching her ears.

"That's it, little beast, enjoy the touch. Sooner or later he will take that ass, and what we do today will help prepare you for that use. Beasts need tails, wouldn't you agree?" Mocking words, hateful glances, was Isabella capable of anything more? No, she doubted that the Devoted had a gentle or caring bone in her body.

Tail, she was human, a person, despite Traven's orders otherwise, how could she suddenly have a tail? A low cry tore from her lips, one finger becoming two within her ass, both buried to the second knuckle, worked with a steady pressure past her ring of muscle, stretching, pulling at her ass.

"Enough, she is ready." The women moved away at the words. Ready for what?

Something firm pressed against her buttocks, smooth, heavy, a form of stone? Whatever it was, it had been left slick from oil, the edge pressing tightly to her curves, surely that wasn't to...

She cried out, pain and fear claiming her, the stone, wood or something else, whatever it was, pressed past the ring of her ass, working within her body. Slow thrusts buried it deeper with each rock, filling her, pushing the walls of her ass wider, beyond anything it was meant to endure, or so the pain told her. Worse than the pain, far worse than the humiliation was the sudden rise of wicked pleasure that rose within her. Her body clenched, hands tightening on the stone, her thighs parting wide as she rocked back against the intrusion into her ass.

"Good beast, embrace it, enjoy it, ready yourself for when he wishes to claim your ass," Isabella hissed in cold delight.

No, Gods no, this was wrong. She couldn't let herself react this way, she wasn't like this, no matter what Isabella or others wanted of her. Not a beast, not a slave, a woman with her own mind.

A low groan echoed through the chamber, her hips rocked to meet the thrust, a throbbing from her clit brought waves of shame and need with the slow rape of her ass.

"There." Soft strands of hair brushed at her inner thighs, the plug buried fully within her body, a tail now hanging free just as any animal would wear. The oiled hand of the Devoted slapped against her ass, sending the tail swinging between her thighs. "Such a pretty tail, beast, matches your hair, and I am sure you will become quite used to showing it off."

The plug burned within her ass, pulling it, stretching. Every breath reminded her of its presence and of the way her hips had reacted, the need that had burned into life within her cunt. How could one time within the dark chamber had resulted in her turning into a slut, hungry for the sexual touch of any that offered it to her?

The price of his claiming, the bite, the collar and all boiled down to this humiliation. He had forced her into this.

No, not true, in many ways she had entered the temple of her own free will. Even if she tried to tell herself otherwise, there had been a choice. She could have refused the presentation, claimed illness, claimed unclean thoughts, something, anything that would have kept her from the temple. Even with the threat of her mother, there had always been a way out. Her pride had told her there would be nothing to fear in entering, that the Gods didn't exist and because of that it would be a worthless exercise. One that would, at the end of the day, prove her right.

Now she found herself a collared beast, and proven so very wrong.

How many others would find themselves beaten, marked and owned because she had somehow aroused Traven's interest?

A clip snapped onto the collar, tugging her head upwards so she had no choice but to look fully into the eyes of the coldhearted Devoted. "Now we go to your quarters, little beast. Such a fine sleeping arrangement he has planned for you as well. You should be honored."

Her heart sank into the pit of her stomach.

The door opened with a soft creak, the leash tugging on her collar, pulling her towards the corridor. With shame claiming her face in a vivid blush, Alayna crawled after the smirking Devoted. Her breasts rocked with each step, the plug moved within her walls, the soft strands of hair brushing against her tender inner thighs. Each step, each rock only tugged at the plug, bringing her body back to an unwanted life, a need that had reluctantly crept into hiding for a brief moment. Now it soared, surging into the hardened tips of her nipples.

Where was she being led, and why like this? To drum home her new status in life?

A dozen sets of robe-covered forms were crawled past in the corridors, silence, mocking gazes, perhaps envy from a few. Those who, like Isabella, craved to be the one wearing the collar of a God. Well, they were welcome to it. Calm, she focused on being calm, on her breathing, on the feel of the stone beneath her hands, anything other than the presence of those around her during the trip through the corridors. Doors opened, new voices, new gazes to follow her path through the temple.

Where she was being taken she couldn't be entirely sure, but the path felt familiar in many ways, as if she was being taken to the main temple room. Her heart turned to lead as the double doors opened up into the very room where she had waited earlier in the day. It had been that day, hadn't it?

"There you are, beast. Such a pretty set of quarters, fitting for a low beast such as yourself. What a great honor, though, in the placement of your sleeping quarters, wouldn't you agree?"

Her breath caught. There within the large, cold room lay a low-set cage, empty save for a rug and a bowl, built in such a manner that it would be impossible for her to stand within it. A cage for a beast in the middle of the main temple room, where any who entered to offer their prayers to the gods would be able to view her.

Her hands curled into claws and she grasped the edges of the stone, her back arching in protest against the image that lay before her, the fate of being left overnight or longer within such a cage. How many would see her like this? How many of her peers, perhaps her family, her mother? No, she couldn't allow it, she couldn't permit such a thing to wrap about her like this.

"You will sleep within the cage, eat and you will use the larger bowl to relieve yourself. Twice a day you will be taken from the cage, re-oiled, your bowels allowed to move over the bowl. No privacy, no speech, no protests. Open to the viewing of all."

Isabella's grasp changed to claim her collar fully, tugging her towards the open door of the cage. She couldn't prevent what was happening, no matter how deeply her nails tried to dig into the stone, to find a way to keep from drawing closer to the cage she had no way to fight. If she tried, if she put too much effort into resisting, it would only make matters worse; others would be called for to aid Isabella. Her fight folded, slipping from her body, tears stinging her heated cheeks, shame taking its place.

With that mocking laughter ringing in her ears, Alayna heard the cage door lock behind her, sealing her within the low bars, naked, collared, a tail brushing against her legs. A beast on display without even the ability to protest, and stripped of every dignity she could imagine.

"Sleep well, little beast." Isabella tapped against the bars, smiling coldly before she swept from the room.

A cage, a rug, a small bowl of water and one to relieve herself in. What else did an animal expect?

Chapter Six

Four days. For four long, humiliating days she had remained in the cage, open and on display to anyone who entered the temple. As promised, she had been removed from the cage only long enough each day to have the plug removed, her body worked with oiled fingers, herbs added until she had had no choice but to relieve herself over the large bowl. Soft, warm, damp cloths had then been used to cleanse her body before fresh oil had been applied, the plug replaced and the cage once again locked shut.

Alayna peered out between the bars into the large room.

She'd lost track of just how many men and women had seen her within the steel bars. The first night within the cage had been an exhausted sleep, undisturbed beyond the soft memories of pain that marked her body, the plug pressing deep into her ass, dreams of his touch, his cock buried deep within her cunt, a need she had tried to deny over the hours of restless sleep.

Dawn had brought the first visitors to the temple, the first whispers that she had fought to shut out. A few soft voices had become many, some mocking, many in awe, how many hours had her cheeks remained the color of flame?

Worse though, far worse than she had imagined, remained the lack of knowledge as to when she would finally be removed from the cage.

Isabella had taken delight in visiting the great hall, though she had said nothing directly to her. The comments to others had teased at her, mocking her as she had remained curled in the cage. Of Traven there had been no sign, no calling for her to appear at his feet. Nothing that summoned her from the shameful hell she had been forced to endure.

He had claimed her, wanted her, so why hadn't he appeared to save her from this?

Because he wanted her to endure it? So she would know that there were worse things than being beaten, fates that she would do almost anything to avoid?

Perhaps it just amused him to have her go through this.

Tears, pain, the weight of the collar, she couldn't ignore them any more than she could ignore the voices of those who visited the temple. Even small tasks such as eating and drinking had taken on a new level of humility. Her hair had become coated, slick from trying to eat from bowls, from drinking on her hands and knees. She'd fought to learn how to lap from the bowls, though her first day had resulted in more food being spilt than consumed.

Anything would have been better than one more day within the cage as a beast on display, even if that meant abasing herself before Isabella and a hundred others like her. Just as long as she didn't have to spend one more night in the cage.

"Is the pretty little pet ready to leave her quarters?" Isabella smirked, her steps carrying her across the chamber. "He has some new orders for you today, little beast. Some plans for you that require you leaving the cage."

She looked back around the confines of her temporary home. Strange, only a few moments ago she had been willing to do anything to leave the cage and now—-now she wanted to remain within the safety of the bars.

Her stomach tightened into a knot. Isabella offered nothing but further steps into pain, of that Alayna was only too sure. Still, she did not dare protest when the cage opened and that slender hand grasped a tight hold on her collar. Whatever had been planned appeared to be due to take place elsewhere. Instead of the plug being removed and the bowl brought so she could shed her body of the waste that had built up overnight, the leash was snapped back onto her collar.

Relief instead of shame flushed her body as she was tugged through the corridors; this time she barely even noticed the robes she had passed by, the gazes of the men and women of the temple. All she cared about was being free of the cage. Her nails had grown ragged during the time in the cage, her eyes red-rimmed with tears she had shed, then learned to keep locked within her being. Now she focused on being free from the bars, free of the watchers within the large chamber. Time to recover, perhaps?

No, recovering would not have involved Isabella's presence. Someone kinder would have been sent for her, one who might have spent some time with her, offered her something in the way of comfort.

Did such a person exist within the temple?

No, if they did, they would not be wearing the robes of a Devoted, of that she was very sure. For a moment she recalled the girl, Lily. There had been a kindness within her, she'd seen it, but she was a rarity.

What had happened to the young woman? Had she survived her punishment?

One last set of doors opened before them, closing smoothly once she had been led within the new room. A private chamber, warmth, soft rugs decorating the floor, a woman's room, from what Alayna could make out right now. It didn't make a lot of sense. Why would she be taken to someone else's chamber and not Traven's?

Isabella's room, it had to be. Where else would she be taken except Traven's room, a bathing room or Isabella's? Had the woman found a way of regaining favor fully with the God? That had to be what had happened, or she would not have dared to bring Alayna into the private room.

The leash unhooked from her collar, Isabella's steps carried her back across the room where she hung it from a hook on the wall. When she turned, when she looked at Alayna, that single look chilled her to the core. "Well now, slut, are you ready to obey me and by doing so, learn to serve him in a new manner?"

She nearly spoke and then remembered in time that she had been denied even human speech until Traven decreed otherwise. Instead she offered a low whimper, nodding softly as she did so. Whatever this woman wanted of her, she had to look at it as but one step towards regaining her ability to speak, walk and act like a human being again instead of a beast on her hands and knees.

"Good, that will make this so much easier." Isabella smirked, her lips curling upwards in a tight, cruel line. The woman took a set of steel cuffs from a small table, the chain between them delicate and deceptively thin, but still strong enough to hold her wrists in place. Then she turned her attention back to Alayna. "Get down on your belly, little beast."

Without any protest, she moved from her hands and knees to lying flat on the soft rug. Her gaze followed the path Isabella took across the room, the robe making little more than a whispering sound as the woman moved.

"Your hands...I want you to place them behind your back."

Biting back a whimper, Alayna obeyed, crossing her hands in the small of her back, blinking through her hair as it slipped across her eyes to block her view. There seemed little point and the quicker she obeyed, the sooner she could return to normal.

Stupid idea, normal didn't exist anymore, the time in the cage should have taught her that much. Instead she still found her mind seeking an answer, looking for hope that didn't exist anymore. She was collared, naked, a tail and plug in her ass, nothing more than a nameless beast. Foolish to think she could ever be anything more; the only option was to find a way to endure.

The metal locked into place on her wrists, securing them behind her back. Even if she had thought there would be a way to break free of them, Alayna was only too well aware that she had no other choice but to obey the woman. At least with obedience she had a chance that the tail would be removed at last.

"You learned to use that tongue in order to feed and sate your thirst, now we will put it to another use." Isabella grasped her hair, forcing her up onto her knees. With that firm grip she half dragged Alayna towards the edge of the bed, releasing her only when the Devoted sat down. "I have no doubt that I will have to find a way to encourage you with your new task, but have no fear, little beast, I will not let our God down in this matter." She lifted what looked like a long, thin rod. Attached to the end was a single cord of leather. It looked braided, but Alayna couldn't be sure, she did, however, see the knot that had been tied at the end very clearly.

With a crack it snapped through the air, the knot biting into Alayna's ass, forcing a cry from her lips. The small welt rose almost instantly on her skin, tears stinging at her eyes before the second blow landed against her ass. She wanted to move, find a way to escape the pain, but already knew that would have made matters worse. Instead, all she could do was kneel there, accepting the two stinging blows with only her cries, her tears and the whimpers that followed both as any form of protest.

"Now you know what you will feel if you disobey me in this, or perhaps you will feel it anyway." The Devoted smirked, using one bare foot to nudge Alayna's knees apart. "Is that understood, little beast?"

Alayna whimpered, nodding as she watched Isabella through lowered lashes. Her mind reeled at what she thought might be expected of her; revulsion mixed with a need to conform, obey and avoid any further punishment.

"Good, though before we begin, I think a little extra decoration would be in order, don't you agree?"

No, she didn't, but disagreeing really wasn't an option.

Isabella leaned across the bed, taking hold of a small wooden box from the nightstand. Her smile, the pure coldness within her eyes, they all warned Alayna that what the box held would not offer any comfort to the kneeling woman. The box opened, the Devoted's slender fingers lifted a thin silver chain from within the dark wood. Clips hung from the ends of the chains, three clips with small sharp teeth at the end. "I believe these will look very nice hanging from your body, don't you agree, beast?"

Another mocking question she had no choice but to ignore or be punished for answering. The woman enjoyed taunting her with words, blows, pain, humiliation, where would it end?

Better to keep her thoughts hidden, her face schooled behind a mask of pale obedience than to let her catch a glimpse of something that would only give Isabella a reason to punish her further.

The small clips opened under pressure, metal brushing against the tips of Alayna's nipples, time taken to let her mind grasp the pain that would follow the bite. Then it hit, the teeth closed on both her nipples at the same time, digging into her skin, claiming a tight hold. Her body stiffened, the chains behind her back pulled taut, her hands jerking apart with the pain that forced free a cry. Burning, the teeth burned small points into the base of her nipples. She could have sworn she bled, but felt no trickle of moisture down her breasts.

What had been a cry turned into a scream. The small teeth of the third clamp closed on either side of her clit, trapping it tight. She squirmed, fighting not to move from her knees, tears tracking a path down her cheeks, her hands clenched becoming fists as she struggled to keep the sharp pains from taking control. Slowly they eased, needle burn points becoming heated throbs, the blood denied access into those tender portions of her body.

"Interesting sensation, isn't it, slut? First pain, then pressure, a numbness that makes no sense...you know it hurts, but the lack of blood takes some of that away. Now we add a little more." Isabella had been holding the chains that connected the three clamps until that point. Now they dropped against Alayna's body, tugging at the small teeth, a new moment of pain, a fresh reminder that her body was no longer her own. "These offer me another way to control you, slut. But I am sure you already figured that one out. You wouldn't want me tugging on these chains, would you? What would that do to you?"

She couldn't help but whimper. The thought of the sharp new pains such an act would bring only had her pleading for some form of mercy.

"Now we put your mouth to good use." Isabella parted her robe, dropping it to the floor.

Heat burned in fresh points over her cheeks as she looked at the naked woman. Small scars marked a pattern over her body, ranging from tiny nicks to long slender slices into her otherwise pale skin. The intricate mark over the woman's heart drew Alayna's gaze. A circular pattern, with small points, like a saw of some sort, had been carved into the Devoted. In the center of the circle lay something else, an ornate letter T with swirling curls.

"Yes, I am sworn fully to Traven. The very God you would spurn given the chance is the one I would happily kneel before, offering my life if he would but ask it of me." Isabella's hatred shone within the woman's eyes. She tugged on Alayna's hair, forcing the kneeling woman closer until she was between the Devoted's now-spread thighs. "Now I will do my part in other ways, training you, keeping you in the manner he desires. So we begin with this, slut; lick me, kiss me, I want to feel your tongue pressing within me, suckling at my clit. You will please me in this, or I will use the buggy whip on you."

Her throat dried at the order. She couldn't, wouldn't... her gaze moved to the whip that lay within easy reach on the bed. What choice did she have except to obey the woman?

Isabella grasped her hair, urging Alayna closer until she had no choice but to touch her lips to the woman's exposed sex. Even before she felt the soft skin under her lips she had smelt the other woman's arousal, felt the heat rising from her shaven mound. Had the control had affected Isabella just as much as the thought of Alayna's lips against her sex?

"Begin," she growled.

Nervously Alayna licked over the soft lips before her, trying not to taste the woman's need that already coated her sex. It was impossible not to taste her, though, and with the grip the other woman had on her hair she found herself forced to press even further against her mound. Swollen lips parted beneath Alayna's tongue, a low moan reaching her ears as the Devoted gripped tight into her hair.

Wrong, this was wrong to do. Serving the God was one thing, but another woman, what perversion was this?

"Suckle, bitch. I want to feel your lips about my clit, your tongue buried in my cunt. I'm going to fuck down on your face and you better not bite me, or I will pull your teeth out one at a time." The words were hissed from between clenched teeth.

She tried not to fight as she let her lips close on the throbbing nub. The chains between the clamps were tugged, sending shards of pain through trapped flesh. Her breath let out in a low gasp against Isabella's sex. Her tongue pressed between those needful lips, wriggling into the entrance of her clenching pussy, only to be caught, sucked within as the woman's hips began to rock.

Her tongue pulled free, lips closing on Isabella's clit, suckling it into her mouth as she brushed over the heated nub. The taste, she'd never experienced it before, now she drew another woman's clit into her mouth, suckled on it, filling her senses with the woman's taste, her need, her heat. Fighting the order was impossible, giving in and pleasing Isabella was the only option. So why, if this were nothing more than a way to save herself from pain, did her body now spring to life with a growing heat of her own? Her thighs clenched, the small pains throbbed into her body, a slick coating forming on her own vulva.

"More," growled the woman, her grip remaining tight on Alayna's hair, tugging her deeply against her mound, her hips rising as she ground against Alayna's lips. She wanted more from the kneeling woman, needing the delight that Alayna now offered and not just for the reasons of teaching or training her. Even though nothing else but the occasional order was spoken by the Devoted, Alayna knew that desire now fueled the cruel woman's grinding hips.

The heady scent flooded Alayna's senses, her seeking lips and tongue now delved eagerly into the woman, lapping against her skin, trapping her lips, suckling deeper, whimpering into the tight nub. Her tongue plunged into her rippling core, trapped only to be released and then grasped again by Isabella's needful sex. Each rock of the woman's hips pulled on the chains that linked the clamps on Alayna's body, sending a new shard of pain into her being, pain that tightened her own thighs. It left her fighting to control a thrust that gained life within her hips. She wanted to feel something against her cunt; fingers, lips, tongue, a cock, it didn't matter.

Alayna groaned into the woman's heated mound, drinking from her sex, her own body left squirming as she held position on her knees.

Serving did this to her?

Shock brought her lapping devotions to a halt.

No, no, this was wrong. She couldn't be enjoying it. Wrong, this was all wrong.

The knot of the whip snapped against her ass. "Get back to it, slut, I have no desire to stop now," Isabella demanded as the second strike added a small welt on her bare ass.

"And what of my desires, my Devoted?" The familiar voice of Traven sounded within the elegant room. "I have some other plans in mind right now. Though I admit you make an interesting sight. How are her skills coming along?"

"She has a potential talent at this," Isabella replied, though her words had a breathless quality. "My Lord, if I might continue." She shifted on the edge of the bed, keeping her grip tight within Alayna's hair.

"No." He walked towards the two women, though Alayna did not dare to turn and see what Traven would do.

"My Lord," Isabella protested. "I beg of you, don't leave me hanging like this."

"I have something else in mind for you, my Devoted. Something you have dreamed of all your adult life." His hand removed Isabella's from Alayna's hair. "But first we need to place this pretty pet in the corner, where a good beast belongs."

Relief flushed through her body; for whatever reason, Traven had saved her from service at the woman's sex. He had other plans for her, perhaps for later, but now his focus appeared to be on Isabella, a fact that left her confused with the warring emotions that sprang to life. Despite the mercy his appearance had granted, Alayna now listened as both relief and jealousy growled for dominance within her mind.

"Crawl over here, little pet, I have a nice place for you, where you can watch as I put my Devoted through her paces." He tugged hard on her hair, pulling her towards a small pole in the corner of the room. "That plug looks good on you, beast, as do the clamps, but I believe something is missing."

Missing, what could be missing?

A chain hung from the pole, one he locked to the collar she wore, his hands running over her body once he had forced her to kneel in place, a second chain linking the cuffs to the pole as she was positioned with her back against it. His foot nudged her thighs wide, parting them under his dark gaze. "Yes, something is missing. You need a little extra addition to those delights on your body."

The walls of her pussy rippled at his words. No matter the protests that gained a brief life behind her closed lips, she knew that her body craved what he offered. Somehow he was changing her, forcing her down a dark path of pain and humiliation. Her protests, silent or spoken, remained a falsehood and that frightened her far more than anything Isabella might do to her

He stepped away from her for only long enough to take a slender piece of wood from the nearby dresser. A fake cock, carved from dark wood. She'd heard of such things before, toys widows might use to enjoy the pleasures of the flesh denied to them with the loss of their mate. "I know this would fit well within your cunt, little beast. You'll writhe on this as she moans beneath me, your body filled fore and aft by toys that it pleases me to see you wear. Perhaps you will cum on those toys, just as she will scream and cum beneath my body."

No, she wanted to be the one that he pressed against the bed. Instead, all she could do was moan when he parted her thighs further, pressing her against the pole until her hips rose. A dark chuckle rang in her ears, the tip of the phallus pressed between her slick lips. Without warning or care he pushed it within her body, filling her pussy just as her ass remained stretched from the ever-present plug.

His hand claimed her shoulder, pushing back onto her knees, his growl mocking her already arching form. He wasn't quite done though, despite what she had hoped he still had plans before he left her to writhe. A band of cloth fastened about her eyes, stealing her vision, adding to the helplessness she already felt. "Stay on your knees, slut. I have business to attend to." Without another word he strode towards the bed and the waiting woman, leaving Alayna fighting to control the waves of need that rocked through her body with each tight clenching of her filled cunt.

"Now, my Devoted, we have a little business together."

The first cry teased Alayna, her body tightening on the phallus, her hands clenched tightly behind her back. At the second one she squirmed openly, trying to find a way to shut out the sounds, the soft slapping noises, the dampness that she recognized just from one night with Traven. A night she now replayed in her mind, images fed by the new noises, soft mewls, cries, screams.

Her teeth bit into her own lip, the bright taste of blood flushing across her mouth. The twin bite marks he had left on her neck now flared into life, a heat she had not expected. Those marks should have healed, yet now they ached, itched and left her wanting to claw at them even as she sucked on her own blood.

Isabella screamed, the bed creaking with the violence of

Traven's demanding thrusts. It wasn't right, she, not Isabella, wore his collar; it should have been her he now put to use.

Her body arched against the pole, the chains rattled with her drive to rock down onto the phallus, yet still she couldn't find a way to reach release. How could she without his permission, his touch, his bite? The memory of that cruel feeling as his teeth had sunk into her throat; that above all the memories of the past few days remained at the forefront. Three bites was all it would take, three bites she now craved the ability to claim had been inflicted upon her. Three steps into a life she now wanted above all others. One bite to mark, the second to light the drive, the third to damn her into eternal slavery.

"My Lord," Isabella whimpered. "I hope I pleased you." Her voice held a weary, sated tone. That shouldn't have surprised Alayna; how long she had knelt in the darkness as they had sported, she didn't know. Her inner thighs were soaked with the heated need that the sounds and phallus had inflicted on her bound body. Even now she waited, still chained next to the pole, her body alight thanks to what had occurred. Forgotten and untouched, she remained on her knees, squirming from time to time, her thighs aching from kneeling, her feet threatening to go to sleep, offering an odd counterpoint of sensation to the deep, clenching desire.

"Very, and I wish you to have the worst of those marks tended." The bed creaked as someone rose.

"As you wish, my Lord. Your presence this day has honored me more than I can ever put into words. I hope you will grant me such a time again," Isabella almost seemed to purr. "What of the beast?"

Beast, slave, slut, a thing, piece of property. The taunting words echoed within her mind, a new wave of need brought to life. She was all that and more, she needed to know what he could and would do to her. She wanted to tear free of the chains, pull the cloth from her eyes before she then crawled to his feet to beg for his touch.

"She has a task before I take her from your chamber." He chuckled, walking across the room towards the pole. "Open up, little beast. Open that sweet mouth wide."

She tried to see beyond the blindfold, seeking him out though she could feel him standing close to her, the scent of sex lingering on his body. Without protest she opened her mouth, trembling softly as she waited.

The tip of his cock brushed against her parted lips.

"Clean me, completely," he urged and rocked forward, his cock pressing between her lips.

She didn't hesitate; the drive to please him, to find some way of drawing his attention, however painful, back to her and away from Isabella left her with no desire to refuse. Her lips parted fully, welcoming him into her mouth. With a soft whimper she wrapped her tongue about his cock, teasing it, tracing it over the head as she began to suckle. She could taste it, him, her and their release on his flesh, a release that she had craved to be a part of. It drew her on further, sent a tight rock through her wicked hips as she began to dance on the phallus buried within her cunt.

"That's it, my slut, clean me, enjoy it and worship your God." His hands moved into her hair, holding her head in place, though she would not have drawn back without his order now. She drove on with the need to please him, sucking him harder within her mouth, wrapping her tongue tight about him, releasing only to re-wrap around his still-hard shaft.

"So needful, aren't you. I can see it, feel it. Each time you suck, your own sinful body then tightens, sending you further into that need," he mocked her. No, not mocked, she could hear pride in his voice. "I claimed the right woman for my new toy. Such a depth of passion burns within you, untapped until a few days ago, now you feel it. You want to deny it, but that denial fades a little more with each beat of your owned heart." He pulled from her mouth, his fingers trailing down over her neck, touching the bite marks that now felt as though they had only just been inflicted. "Soon you will experience a second bite, but already the affects of the first bite have begun. You can feel it, can't you, the way your skin itches, that burning sensation? Should I make you wait for the second, little slut?"

"Please, Master, no. I want it, need it." She craved the feel of his teeth in her flesh, that brilliant pain before a liquid pleasure claimed her body. Why did that need to be bitten gain such a drive within her? She didn't know, didn't care, it was simply accepted this time.

"What if I tell you such a bite will doom you to a path from which there is no return. That it will turn the taste of food into sawdust in your mouth, that you will begin to feel a thirst no water or wine will sate?" His touch moved slowly from her neck up to her face. "Would you still beg for that feel of my teeth on your throat?"

"Yes, my Master." She leaned into his touch, shivering. "I beg for it. Bite me, claim me, pull me into the darkness you command. I want it, need it."

"Are you sure?" His smile offered neither light nor hope.

"Yes, I know what you are. I accept it, crave to be a part of it and you." She knew the stories, however hidden they were, whatever damnation her words then pulled her into.

"So be it." His grip tightened on her face as he lowered to one knee, pulling her as close as the chains would permit. Panic rose, choked her voice, silencing her words. She wanted to scream no, beg yes, plead and have that plea denied should her words speak of mercy. Her cunt rippled on the phallus, her hips rocked, her body arching as she tried to press towards him, seeking the claiming bite that she desired above all else.

Darkness, there would be only darkness after the third bite. She knew that, accepted it and no longer cared what his touch would turn her into. A willing concubine of Vampyre Lord, bound for eternity should he permit it. Who, in her place, could ever deny such a chance as now lay before her?

One hand claimed a tight grip in her hair, the other smoothed over her skin, capturing a tightly clamped nipple, tugging on the chain between her breasts. His teeth scraped over her shoulder, tracing a path to her bared throat. There, above the simple band of metal he had locked on her but a few days before, his teeth sank into her skin. Twin points of pain pierced her skin, his grip firm on her body as she arched with a scream that offered him her soul...

Chapter Seven

With the clamps, plug and phallus still decorating her body, Traven had unchained her from the pole, clipped a leash to her collar and led her out of Isabella's room. She could still taste the combined juices from the two within her mouth, and crawling down the hallway only added to the torment on her body. Each step tugged at the painful clamps and rocked plug and phallus within her body. Pain, desire, she couldn't tell where one ended and the next began, she only knew she paraded through the temple, wearing his collar, attached to a leash he held.

A pride she had not expected took control of her movements. Her hips swayed with a deep roll, her head lifted as she looked up at those she passed, the tail caressed her inner thighs, no longer feeling like a strange thing to be wearing, a smile claiming her lips as she saw the way their gazes played over her flesh. She belonged to him, they did not, at least not in the way she did. The new bite had changed her; she could feel it, even if it was in a way she didn't yet understand.

Even her skin felt different. The low breeze--more of a draft than anything else--that passed over her body as she crawled through the corridor felt like a hundred fingers teasing at her skin. Leather, she could smell the leather of his boots, and then there was the way even her hearing had changed. Each person she passed by offered a new sight, new smell, new sound. It was almost as though she could hear their hearts beating. She was alive in a way she had never dreamt of.

She could see everything, each glimpse of emotion that passed over their faces. A slight twitch of lips here, the narrowing of a gaze on another, the way the color drained, then flushed back into cheeks. Each small move, the change of emotions across their faces, no matter how minute only expanded her understanding of the people she walked past.

"You did well, my beast." He didn't look her way as he spoke, but continued to lead her towards the bathing house. She knew that the smell of the oils, the soaps and the people had not been so strong the last time she had been there. "I am pleased with your progress, with your acceptance that being mine in all ways is what you were meant for."

She whimpered, leaning against his leg for a moment as he stopped before the doors of the bathhouse. A week ago this would have seemed like a nightmare to her, a situation that she might have fought to the death in order to escape. Now she embraced it with a willingness that marked her as little more than a whore for his delights.

"You will be bathed, tended, re-oiled and fed. I have no doubt that the food they offer you will taste odd, but you need to eat before we step into my chamber again. Tomorrow you will take your last step into eternal service with me. I will grant you an honor no other living soul within this temple has been permitted. It will be time for your acceptance, to take part in a right of passage not seen in over a hundred years. When the time comes, Isabella will bring you before me and the Blessing will take place." His hand lingered for a moment within her hair as the door opened. "Now crawl, my beast. You are granted permission to walk again, to speak. Indulge whatever pleasures you desire with the attendants, let the calling that has grown within you be granted life."

A knot formed in the pit of her stomach, a knowledge she wanted to deny. Something was within her; she could either embrace it fully or remain torn apart inside. Traven trailed a light finger down her spine as she slowly rose from her hands and knees. After so long crawling, it felt almost out of place to stand. Her legs felt heavy, her balance uncertain and she fought against the urge to reach out towards the wall and find a way to steady herself.

"Give in to it, my slave. You want to, you need to, fighting it will only bring you distress. Accept everything about the woman you are quickly becoming, embrace the changes, relish in each new sensation." She had no words for him yet; after two days of fighting to keep silent, her mind was reluctant to permit her speech in case it was some form of trick. "Now go, do as I have commanded. I will send for you when I am ready."

"Yes, Master." Her words were little more than a whisper.

The door closed behind her, leaving Alayna shut off from her Master and in the care of the attendants. Warmth wrapped about her form, welcoming her within the bathhouse. No members of the Devoted were present, no guards, just Alayna and the attendants, one of whom she recognized.

Bruised, her lip split, welts marking her back, ass and thighs, Lily still presented herself at Alayna's feet along with the rest of the women within the room. Each woman wore little more than a strip of linen about her loins, and a second one about her breasts, each one knelt on the tiles before Alayna, their gazes lowered in the same level of respect they might have shown one of the Devoted.

Had she become something more than a slave?

For a moment Alayna didn't move further into the room, but instead brushed her fingertips over the collar that had been locked about her throat. Still there, it continued to mark her as his property yet they knelt, waiting on her word.

"Honored Chosen, how may we be of service to you this night?" A soft female voice inquired.

Ten women, each in their early twenties, now awaited her pleasure as if she were the highest of women within the temple. It felt odd, to be addressed like that when the clamps and plugs still remained on her body.

"My Master has declared I am to be tended, the clamps, plug and phallus removed. He wishes me bathed, oiled and for food to be brought to me." Her inner walls rippled about the fake cock that remained buried within her body.

"Your every wish, voiced and silent, will be our pleasure to tend," a familiar voice responded. Lily, out of all of the women, she was the only one who bore visible signs of mistreatment. The livid welts attracted her attention far more than those whose skin remained unmarked, offering her a glimpse of how she herself had looked to these women but a few days prior.

"Perhaps the clamps should be removed first?" Lily suggested. "If you would lie down upon the cushions, Chosen, we can remove them along with the plug and phallus. And should you permit it, we would be honored to help ease the pain such a removal might cause."

In silence Alayna walked to the soft pile of cushions, easing herself down onto her back. The twin insertions into her body now left an ache she needed an answer to, and she needed them removed.

Soft fingers smoothed over her skin, teasing with gentle touches as they sought out the clamps. "This will hurt, Chosen, but we will do what we can to ease the passage of your body into a more relaxed state."

Of that she had little doubt.

The tiny teeth released from her nipples and clit. At first there was nothing but a sense of relief, then it hit. Blood rushed into what had been trapped flesh, sensation returning in a wave of pure pain, but before she could cry out, three sets of lips lowered to her body. Warmth and soft tongues covered her nipples and clit, suckling her abused flesh into their mouths, turning pain into pleasure.

"Did he bite you again, Chosen?" She barely heard Lily's words over the soft suckling sounds.

"Yes," she murmured, her hips pressing upwards towards the woman whose lips now remained about her clit. Her thighs parted further, welcoming the touch. Wicked, she had been taught this was wicked. It didn't feel that way, though. Her body loved it, welcomed it, her heels pressed into the floor as she lifted upwards. Fingers grasped the base of the phallus, rocking it deeper within her body, matching the pace that her own hips set. Wicked it might have been, but her desire had grown to a point where she no longer cared what another might say.

"You accepted this, the bite, I mean?"

Her jaw clenched. Why would Lily need to know? Couldn't the woman just be silent for a time and let her enjoy the pleasures being offered?

"Yes," she whispered, her eyes drifting closed under the lips of the other women. She arched, pressing upwards into the touch of the woman between her thighs. After so long denied, the cage, the pain of the clamps, feeling that soft touch against her clit was sheer bliss. Her hips rocked upwards, thighs parting wider under her tongue, the phallus sliding within her body, drawn out only to press once more within her clenching sex.

"Damned, you're damned, Chosen." Lily spoke softly, but there was no anger in her words and only pity in her eyes. "We will give you what pleasure and care we can, but for the bite and what it means you are condemned to, there is nothing we can do to help."

Didn't Lily understand she didn't want to be helped? Maybe a few days ago she would have, but now she welcomed the bite and everything it now meant. Thought fled under the gentle touch of the woman's lips.

So close. Pressure built in her body, a slick heat coating her inner thighs. The sounds of the phallus slipping in and out of her tight pussy should have left her cheeks crimson; instead, the slapping sound only urged her higher. Shame had no meaning.

Higher.

Further.

Faster.

Her thighs tensed, lifting her ass from the cushions, her nails dug into the soft fabric beneath her body. Now, it had to be now.

Enslaved By Blood

A cry, torn from the back of her throat, marked the release that she had craved in the past few hours. Sweat beaded across her naked body, pearling across her breasts, adding to the slick passage of the phallus. Her mind fled before the wave of delight, a crashing sound filling her ears, then it eased, the wood slipped finally from between her thighs. Gentle pressure rolled her now semi-limp form onto her belly, her cheeks parted as oil was added to the outer edge of the plug. Only when they were sure it could be removed without any pain did they remove it slowly from her ass.

Her limbs felt leaden, a weariness she had not expected claimed her body. At last she could rest without the pressure the plug and phallus had caused. With a sigh, she gave up fighting to stay awake, letting her mind slip into the welcome comfort of a much-needed sleep.

"Chosen?" Lily's gentle voice led her back into a state of wakefulness. Her dreams had been odd, compelling but confusing at the same time. Bodies had lain strewn before her, she'd walked through her home town, staring at the devastation, hunting for something. A hunger had burned out of control; she'd turned body after body over, searching for a sign of life, for a pulse, only to find each corpse had already been drained of blood. Out of all the bodies, one and one alone that she had searched for had been missing: Isabella. Such a dream should have had her screaming in terror.

Instead, she awoke hungry and disappointed that the images had faded with the opening of her eyes. Not even the knowledge that she had wanted to find the dead body of the Devoted at her feet appeared to cause her any problems. Isabella deserved to die.

Were the others who served in the temple any better?

It didn't matter, Isabella had earned her death. The others could wait their turn.

"Chosen, is everything all right?" Lily touched her shoulder. "You were dreaming, I could see your eyes moving in your sleep. Your hands, they kept clenching, then you started clawing at the cushions."

"I dreamt of such odd things, Lily. Blood everywhere, bodies, just strewn over the ground and no one cared," she murmured, rising from the soft cushions, her gaze shaking free of the last of the images. "But it was just a dream, nothing more than that."

"They say that the one bitten by a God will walk through realms of blood and chaos whilst they sleep." Lily spoke in a hushed tone. "I wish there was a way I could take the darkness from you, Chosen."

"Why?" Alayna inquired, her gaze turning from the well-marked attendant to the steaming bath. He wanted her bathed, cleaned, ready for whatever his plans for that night might entail She had neither the desire nor will to deny him that. Not only that, but the bath would ease the remaining aches from her time in the cage. Though the plug had been removed, she could still feel its ghost-like presence buried deep into her ass, a reminder of what she had been through and what she might yet endure.

"No one should have to enter that life, Chosen." Lily answered, following her to the edge of the bath. "Darkness. Blood. Pain. You'll lose yourself to his desires. You have to find a way to pull free of this, for the sake of your soul."

"What if that is what I now want?" She slipped into the bath, sighing in contentment as the silken liquid smoothed over her skin, enveloping her within its warm embrace.

"No, I don't believe that of you, Chosen." Lily shook her head as she sat on the edge of the marble bath. The young woman's gaze held an unfounded hope. How could she understand what it was like to feel the touch of a God? The way his teeth had scraped over her skin, that brief but wonderful searing pain. No, unless she found herself in his grasp, she would never understand.

Alayna watched the Attendant closely, her gaze moving over

the marks. They stood out on her otherwise pale skin, a living path of welts, bruises and small cuts. Something about them called to her, beckoned Alayna to reach out and touch them. She itched to run her fingers, perhaps even her tongue over the beautiful pattern that had been laid into her skin.

Had she screamed? Or simply pleaded for the torment to stop?

The marks on her neck burned, so why was the pain such a welcoming sensation? She didn't fear it, or crave for it to stop; instead it called to a new part of who she now was, offering her a chance to look within herself and see a side of her heart she had never believed could exist.

"Those marks look good on you, Lily." She smiled, seeing Lily flinch at the comment. "Perhaps when he has granted me a little more freedom I will be permitted to add a few more of my own." Maybe she didn't have to wait for that, though. He'd said she could indulge herself. Did that include marking the attendants?

What would it be like to be the one causing the screams?

To feel the whip in her hand and bring it down onto the back of a woman, or a man, just to hear them cry out?

"Please, no, Chosen. I beg you not to allow the darkness life within you." Lily moved to her knees at the edge of the bath, lowering her gaze. "It's not part of you, please fight it. You are better than this, better than those here who love to cause others to scream."

Her jaw clenched. How could the woman work within the temple and view things in that way?

"Alayna, you are a good woman, I know you are. I heard what the others said of you over the years, from before you entered the temple. How you didn't really believe in the Gods, but still kept yourself untouched. How you were pious in heart, your soul free to wander, your mind willing to explore so many new concepts," Lily continued, her voice trembling. "Giving into him, to them, would be granting them a victory they do not deserve."

"What did you just call me?" It had been strange how little time it took for her to be used to not being called by a name.

"Alayna," Lily replied.

"Why did you call me by that name?" Her hands tightened under the water, forming fists on her thighs.

"It's your name, the one your mother gave you," Lily protested, her gaze rising to meet Alayna's.

"And the one my Master took from me. I have no name until he decrees otherwise. I am his beast, his Chosen. Nothing more than that. Calling me by that name is defying his wishes." Alayna rose, water pearling over her skin to fall into the bath in a soft waterfall.

"What of your wishes?" Lily spoke quickly. "Do you not think you should have a choice in being able to use your own name?" The other attendants had fallen silent, their gazes showing only too clearly how they hoped not to be drawn into the fight. She didn't blame them; just one look at the beating Lily had taken would have been enough to silence most. Unless one within their number craved the pain the way Alayna now did.

Lily didn't crave the pain, she could see that about the other woman, sense it. She loathed being within the temple, so why was she acting so foolish?

"Ah, you don't think I will punish you, do you?" Small droplets of water formed on the tips of her nipples, spilling into the bath. With soft, easy steps she made her way out of the bath, her gaze fixing on the kneeling woman. "You believe I will put myself at risk by letting you speak this way, that I will be weak and let you get away with such behavior."

"We are alike," Lily declared.

"Maybe once we were, but no longer." She reached out, grasping Lily by the hair. "I am his Chosen, his slave, and I will not permit you or any other to speak against him or his commands in this manner."

"What are you doing?"

"I'm correcting your behavior." Alayna tugged her towards one of the benches, sitting down as she pulled the squirming attendant over her damp, naked thighs. "I will not permit you to speak this way about my Master or his decrees. He rules here, his wishes will be respected even if that means I must turn your ass bright red in the process."

"Don't, please…"

Alayna watched as Lily began to struggle over her lap, the memory of the spanking she had been given before entering the temple returned in full force. Now she would be the one administering the correction. Her hand rose, cupping before she struck against the other woman's upturned ass. The crack sounded out through the room, coloring Lily's ass and her hand at the same time. It hurt, smacking someone actually hurt. She'd never thought it would, though the sharp cry of pain made it worthwhile. Lily must have been in more pain than she was from the way she squirmed on her lap, kicking from the first blow.

"Have mercy, don't do this," Lily pleaded as she tried to struggle free.

Alayna smiled. Between the plea and the sound she had made at the first blow, it had awoken that dark part further. More. She needed to hear more cries. A need to know that she caused the woman pain had sparked into life. Wanted to see Lily's skin redden beneath her strikes. Three times in quick succession her hand struck against Lily's ass, sharp snaps followed by cries, a moan and a struggle to get free. Despite her drive to hold Lily in place, that was quickly proving impossible without help. Heat rose between her own thighs with the punishment she sought to put Lily through, a cold drive centered about her heart that spoke of the pain she might be able to inflict. So many images, ideas offered. Guards that would hold the woman still as others then used her, until she could scream no more.

Her hands knotted into fists. No, she wasn't ready to do that just yet, but she still could not let the woman go unpunished. A handful of sharp slaps would not rectify her behavior. Yes, she could do this on her own. Twice more her hand lashed through the air, snapping against Lily's upturned ass, and still the woman struggled.

Alayna frowned and shook her head. Unless she was willing to focus all of her attentions on holding Lily in place, then this wasn't going to work. If the servant had just remained still and accepted her fate it wouldn't have come to this, but now she also needed to be punished for defying Alayna.

"Bend her over the bench, hold her in place." Alayna nodded at the other women. They moved quickly, grasping Lily by the arms, tugging the struggling woman over the wooden bench. "And fetch me a crop. It would appear that a mere spanking will not be enough. I suggest you all watch this and take note. Just because I am only his Chosen does not mean that I am afraid to enforce his wishes."

The sight of the woman now held helpless over the bench by those eager to see her punished, if only for the sake of avoiding such treatment themselves, only added to the cold need within Alayna's being. The crop she was handed sat easily in her grip, lightweight, flexible, enough to strike with pain and she hoped, precision. It wouldn't take much work to add to the welts the woman already carried. A few blows, three or four sharp strikes, would be enough.

No, who was she trying to fool? A mere handful of blows wouldn't be enough. Lily needed to be taught the true consequences of her defiant behavior. Alayna hefted the crop in her hand and smiled.

"Mercy, I beg you have mercy, Chosen," Lily cried out, no longer able to struggle. One woman held each arm, another held her by the hair, holding her in place over the wooden bench. "I meant no disrespect."

"Yes, you did." The crop snapped out against the woman's ass, the leather leaving a small square mark. Despite everything

Enslaved By Blood

Alayna had once believed about herself, the cry the woman made; the sight of the mark, the way Lily arched even held in place, it all combined into a compelling delight. Two, three, four, five more times the crop snapped against Lily's ass. It wasn't enough, there needed to be more in the way of cries. Lily hadn't cried out enough.

Was this how Isabella viewed things as well?

What of Traven?

The rod of the crop lashed out, laying a deep welt across both ass cheeks. Any cry Lily had made before paled before the scream that tore free with that strike. "You're wrong, Lily, I am like them. I am far more like they are than you could ever have imagined. I wanted that second bite. I want what will follow the third. I'm his. Maybe once I fought, but that would have been a lie. I won't lie to myself any longer."

"Mercy," whimpered the weeping woman. "Have mercy, I will not do such again. Honored Chosen, have mercy on me."

She reached out, tracing the new welt with the tip of her finger. It felt hot, enticing beneath her touch. For a moment she nearly gave into the compulsion to lick at the mark. Then it was gone. She wasn't that far into the darkness, not yet at least. In time she would be just as others where. That time hadn't arrived though. Isabella, Traven, the others of the temple would have done far worse to Lily, of that she had no doubt. But this was enough, this time it was enough. "Get her out of my sight before I change my mind."

"Thank you for your kindness, honored Chosen. Thank you."

Kindness. Did that have a place in the temple? The images of the cruelties she had seen replayed in her mind. The cage, whips, plugs, not a single sign of kindness. Even the one that had escorted the waiting men and women into the rest chamber on the day before Traven had declared that she belonged to him. It had been nothing more a ruse to lull her into a false sense of security.

"Halt, hold her back in place. She has reminded me this is a house of devotion, and one who speaks out against the Gods must be forced to recall their place completely. I have been lax in doing so with Lily." The other women forced Lily back over the bench as the pinned attendant screamed in terror.

Six sharp strikes lashed through the air in quick succession. Six new raised welts formed a pattern across Lily's ass, the woman's cries mingling with gasps, her body pinned in such a way that all she could do was accept the blows. By the third strike, Lily had lacked even the strength to kick out.

Each new line doubled the desire that rose within Alayna's body, reminding her of the way she had writhed under her Master. Pain. She knew pain only too well now, yet even with that thought came the acceptance that she too had much to learn. "Release her."

The grip on Lily vanished, letting the woman stumble to the floor in a sobbing heap of pain.

With a cruel grip Alayna pulled Lily to her knees by her hair, shaking her hard before speaking. "I am his. I will obey him and mold to him in every way he wishes me to do so. I will be his for as long as he desires, until the last sunrise should he so wish. Is that clear?" Alayna spoke in a voice she barely recognized as her own.

Terror shone from Lily's gaze, a whimper of fear spilling from trembling lips. The young woman's face had drained of color, her eyes widened and she shook violently in Alayna's grip, but still couldn't speak.

"That wasn't the answer I required from you." Her free hand snapped out, striking openhanded across Lily's face in a blow she had never dreamed of committing. "You know far better than that, you have been in the temple long enough to know what is expected of you."

Blood marked the woman's lips, her eyes dazed, a stunned, fearful look claiming Lily even as she spoke. "Yes, Chosen. I...I understand. Please forgive me. It won't happen again."

"Good." Her gaze fixed on the thin trickle of blood as it traveled down Lily's chin. Hunger springing to life, the heady scent that surrounded Lily was one she could not ignore. With her fingers still tangled in Lily's hair she leaned down, licking at the small, rich brook of life. Only when her tongue traced over Lily's trembling lips did Alayna realize what she was doing.

The taste should have made her ill, instead it only made her desire more.

With a cry she struck, pushing Lily to the floor, her teeth seeking the woman's throat. All she wanted in that moment was to sink her teeth into her neck, tear into the skin, taste the rich blood that pulsed just out of reach. She could feel it, taste it, that rich path of life throbbing under the thin covering of skin. So close, all it would take would be a single bite.

Hands grasped her arms, pulling her from the woman, their combined grips far stronger than she had the ability to fight. A cloth, one that carried a spice-like scent to it, was pressed over her face, forcing her to breathe in or pass out from lack of air.

"Not yet, Honored Chosen. It's not time for that yet. Sleep until he calls for you. Sleep," a calm voice whispered in her ear. Whatever was on the cloth allowed her no other choice but to sleep. Her eyes rolled upwards, her legs turned to lead as she dropped, held only by the many hands that had prevented her from claiming Lily's life. Her mind fled into the darkness, taking with it the rich taste of blood and the knowledge that she wanted more...

Chapter Eight

Soft rays of sunlight bathed the garden in warmth as she watched. If she were right about the full effects of his blessing, this would be the last time she felt the sun on her skin. No one had told her, officially, just what taking that last bite would cause. Few beyond the temple had read the legends, at least from what she understood. Just the looks her tutors had given her when she had devoured a path through their books had spoken volumes. Now she held onto that knowledge.

No more sunsets or sunrises after this day.

Could she live in darkness for the rest of her life--an eternal life, if the legends were true?

She could see the changing of the colors across the sky, pink, orange and yellow, they melded into a rainbow display. A private performance for a willing audience that didn't know if there would ever be the chance to witness a sunset again.

"It's time, Chosen." The now familiar voice spoke. "He is waiting for you."

"I know." She turned, speaking calmly to the Devoted. "I feel as though I should have always known that this was to be my fate."

Isabella growled, her fists visibly clenching at her words. The woman shook her head, the tiny lines around her eyes crinkled, her lips pressed into a tight thin line. It would have taken a blind man to miss the emotions that played across Isabella's face. Still, for now the Devoted kept silent and turned instead to lead the way back out into the hallways. The anger the Devoted felt was palpable and only grew as they were told to wait outside the carved double doors. How long would they then wait until he would permit them entry into his chamber?

"One day he will see he has chosen the wrong woman. When

that day comes he will turn to me, to one who has always obeyed him, to a woman who knows her place at his feet and understands just what it takes to serve him fully." Isabella scowled, keeping her voice low enough that the guards would not hear. For his own reasons, Traven had seen fit to send the Devoted to be the one to escort her to the ceremony. Perhaps it amused him to send the one woman who wanted to serve him to this level to escort Alayna to her final blessing.

Blessing.

An odd word for it. Lily had seen it as being condemned into eternal darkness. It didn't matter; even if he gave her a choice to walk away now, she couldn't. The thought of his bite, what she would then be able to experience, tossing that chance away, it wasn't even an option any more.

"It is his choice to make, Devoted. Not ours." Not yours, is what she really wanted to say. Alayna fought to keep the smug comments under control. If she spoke that far out of turn, it could well put the blessing on hold. Isabella wasn't worth that, she wasn't worth forsaking the new life that had been offered.

"Indeed, and even a God can make a mistake," the Devoted hissed. "And in your case he has. There were others here, women like me who would have slit the throats of their families down to the last child in order to have the place you have been granted. That time in the cage, you hated it. I would have been thrilled to spend such a time for his amusement. But no, it went to you. A stupid little slut who still knows nothing about pleasing a man, let alone a God. You have to be shown every tiny little detail and it will take a lifetime to teach you. What a waste."

"Then I am sure you will make sure he is aware of your feelings on this matter." A smile played over her lips. "You would not wish to keep any further secrets from him, would you? You do recall how he reacted the last time." Nothing would have pleased her more than to see Isabella denied a part in the ceremony.

No, that wasn't quite the truth. Seeing the woman dead at

Traven's feet would have been ideal. Not that she could see her master wasting his time on killing the woman.

"You cannot even control yourself long enough to receive his blessing, slut. I heard what you nearly did in the bathhouse. I know the lack of control you have. You came too easily into the darkness, into his service." Isabella turned. Hatred shone within the other woman's eyes. Hatred, jealousy and rage at the path being offered to someone other than her.

Alayna smiled, keeping her focus on the double doors. It did not matter what the Devoted said, the choice would be Traven's, no one else's.

"A true Chosen would not have sought the blood of another without the permission of her Lord. You proved yourself unworthy of the blessing," she hissed, taunting Alayna with the weakness that she had shown. "I will witness your screams should he continue with this path. I will drink from your body before the night is through and prove myself to be worth a thousand of you. Stupid slut. Do you think that collar keeps you safe from me? It doesn't. You're nothing more than a momentary pastime to him. An amusement until he chooses the right woman, or man for his servant. It won't be you that will spend the rest of eternity at his side. No, no matter what you may think, you're nothing but dirt beneath his feet."

"Do I believe the collar protects me? No, not at all. It marks me as his, nothing more or less, Devoted." She would not let herself be goaded any further into a fight. That would solve nothing. Hadn't Isabella learned that? Or did she hope that such an outburst would have Traven rethinking his choice?

Whatever her reason, the opening of the doors silenced any further comments.

Soft light beckoned the within the chamber. As with the first time she had been brought there, not just Traven waited within. Thirty or more robed Devoteds lined the walls of the chamber. At the far end sat his throne, where Traven already watched them.

Enslaved By Blood

His gaze moved to focus on Alayna, giving barely a single glance towards Isabella.

"Come to me, Chosen," he commanded, his voice liquid velvet.

In silence she moved to the floor, naked save for the collar on her throat. How else would she reach his feet but on her hands and knees, as the beast she was? She felt no shame this time, instead there was a joy that built within her core, a desire to please him that she would not try and fight. Her breasts swung with each step closer to him, her thighs rolled, her head lowered towards the floor. She growled softly under her breath, fingers clawing at the stone floor, shivering as her own hair brushed at her skin. A hundred fingers, a thousand, they all lingered against her naked flesh. The twin puncture wounds ached the closer she drew to him, an ache that vibrated through her body, down between her thighs and deep into her clenching sex.

He watched as she crawled. She didn't have to look up to know that. His gaze buried into her, tugged at her in way no others could. The call that she felt was a silent one, yet it still urged her ever closer.

She'd lied to Isabella and not even been aware of it at the time. The collar did far more than mark her as his property. She belonged to him, body, mind and soul. Her body craved his touch; her inner walls rippled and ached to feel his touch deep within. Isabella would never understand just how deeply he now owned her.

Even without his touch, she was ready for him.

The leather of his boots now lay beneath her lips. Without hesitation she brushed against them, licking over the smooth leather, tasting it, cleaning it of dirt. Grit, sand, she tasted it, but that did not stop her devotions. A deep shudder passed through her naked body, her thighs parting wider as she kissed a soft path over both boots, pressing her cheek against them. Desire slipped in liquid form over her lower lips, a pulse throbbing within her exposed core.

Behind her, from one of the watching Devoted, she heard it; a low gasp of appreciation at the sight they witnessed. Her ass, her sex, it was all clearly visible to the robed men and women, just as it had been the first time she had crawled to his feet. Now she parted her thighs further, offering them a better view of her coated sex.

"Well done, my slut." He reached down, tangling his fingers in her hair, arching her back onto her knees with the harsh grip. "You have come a long way in so short a time. You have become a willing whore of darkness at my feet, seeking that which only a God can offer you. I will grant you eternal bondage, slavery until the end of days. Pain, pleasure, all of this and more will be yours. You will die a thousand small deaths, only to regain new life before each dawn, stronger every time. It will all be yours with one final bite this night."

She didn't move; the grip on her hair held her in a near-helpless arch at his feet, her thighs parted wide. Without being told, she moved her hands to cross in the small of her back, as if they had been bound in place.

"I ask you this formally, my slave. Do you wish to become mine, knowing that in order to do so you must pass through the crucible? Walk through the fires and scream your last breath into my mouth as your life force leaves your body? You will change, know pain, die and be reborn under the lash. If you take this offering from me then you will be condemned to a half life, yet one that many here would give their heart, or their soul, to enjoy. Nothing will be the same again. No more sunlight, no lovers beyond those I grant you, no children or husband. You will be nothing more or less than the lowest of creatures at my feet."

"Yes, Master. I accept this and more." Her gaze met his, only to find herself lost within the darkness of his eyes. How could she refuse him? All the doubts, the questions she had asked over the years, they all seemed foolish now; the actions of the child she had been. Now she knelt at his feet as a woman, one collared and owned, waiting to take the final step into the nightmare of his service.

"So be it, my slave." He smiled fully; for the first time, she saw the sharp teeth that had left their searing mark on her flesh. "Tonight we finish it. Open up the shutters, let the light of the moon touch my chamber," he commanded. "Open it and leave us to this matter."

"My Lord!" Isabella protested, her words bringing the sudden flurry of movement to a halt. Never before had someone openly protested or interrupted Traven. Nor could Alayna imagine that many others would have the nerve to try again. "Have I not earned the right to bear witness to this claiming, to the marking of your Chosen?"

Silence claimed the room to mortal ears. Even with her newfound senses, she struggled to hear anything but the beating hearts of those present. They even seemed to fight not to breathe, lest they turn his attention from Isabella to themselves.

"And what happened to make you presume such a thing, Devoted?" His grip remained in place on her hair. "What makes you think I should share this moment with you, or anyone else, for that matter?"

"My chamber. My Lord, did what we shared in that moment when you granted me your touch mean so little to you?" Isabella's voice grew closer. "I beg you, my Lord. Let your favored one be your witness to the coming event. Such a blessing as you will grant your Chosen has not been seen in generations, there should be a witness to this. Who better than one you have favored above all others?"

"Ah, yes, my favored one." Alayna caught the undertone of mockery in his voice, though it appeared she was the only one who did. "You may stay, favored Isabella. Stay and become a part of the ceremony."

One by one the others left, until only Isabella, Traven and Alayna remained behind. The vast overhead shutters had been opened, what light had been offered by torches and braziers had been extinguished. Now the only light that touched the room came from the full moon.

"Take yourself to the altar, my Chosen." His grip finally released from her hair. "Kneel before it, let the moon's light touch your flesh as you wait for my blessing."

Alayna rose, looking at him once before turning to the stone altar. He could send her into the darkness eternal or the darkness reborn when she took her place there. The choice would be his, as it always had been.

"What may I do to aid you, my Lord?" Isabella spoke as Alayna knelt down before the smooth rune-carved stone.

"Now you wish not just to witness, but to also aid me. Do you accept the consequences of taking part in the ceremony, Isabella?" Consequences. It seemed that life was filled with them. Each action or inaction offered one.

"Yes, my Lord. I accept them freely." She spoke without hesitation.

"Then fetch me a rope, the slender one from the wall." The sound of his passage through the room at least gave her warning of his approach. He said nothing more to her now, not even when the rope encircled her frame below the curves of her breasts. She tried not to move as he bound it in place. Her nipples hardened when he grasped one breast, lifting it so he could wrap the cord about the base of that claimed breast. His breath felt warm against her neck, her other breast then captured within his strong hand, bound tight with the cord.

The skin of her breasts grew taut under the new pressure, the ends of the rope then bound behind her neck, lifting her mounds upwards. She had never imagined that having her breasts bound in such a manner would result in such an intense sensation. Her trapped mounds throbbed; nipples throbbed as the blood was forced into swollen nubs. Each breath she took added to the growing pressure of her bound flesh. Whatever he planned on doing to them, she already knew would feel far more intense that it might otherwise have.

His hand grasped her hair, tipping her head backwards so he could look directly into her eyes. Without warning his free hand snapped out through the air, connecting with her face in a loud, soul-searing slap. Before she could finish crying out, a second landed against her other cheek in a near casual backhand. His grip tightening in her hair, the third blow dazed her fully, gasped cries echoing in the small room. She moaned, his grip remaining in her hair, his gaze holding her dazed one. She wanted to press to him, find a way to prostrate herself before him, beg for him to part her thighs as he pushed within her heated core.

Blood, her own blood coated her lips.

"Bound soul, bound flesh, bound beauty," he murmured, releasing her hair before tugging the cords tighter. His interest in slapping her had faded as if it had never existed.

"She looks quite the delight this way, my Lord." Isabella smiled.

"Indeed she does." Traven replied. "Stand, my Chosen."

She pushed up to her feet, the ropes tugging on her flesh, biting deeply as she moved. Pressure turned her skin shiny. His hands grasped hers, securing her wrists in leather cuffs. His smile, the cold welcome within his eyes, held her tighter than the cords or cuffs that now encircled her body. She'd give herself a thousand times and more into his care, nothing could change that now, nothing *would* change that.

He tugged on her cuffs, lifting her wrists above her head, attaching them to a chain that dangled from a hook. Even though the overhead shutters had been opened, there still remained a network of support beams above them. Not enough to block the moonlight, but still strong enough to support her weight. He didn't speak when as he secured her in place, not even when he stepped back and hauled her upwards using a small crank. Her feet barely touched the ground, her body arched as she struggled to maintain some form of balance.

"My cat." He barely even looked at Isabella, not even when the woman handed him the knotted leather whip.

"You will dance in the chains, my slut." He stepped back, shaking out the tails of the cat.

Snap! The leather lashed out through the air, connecting across her bound breasts. A dozen knots hit her glossy skin, pain burning into life as she arched on her toes, unable to do anything but scream.

Crack! Knots struck her nipples, leather wrapped about her breasts, thin welts raised under the blow that knocked the breath from her body. Leather hissed through the air before each new wave of pain. Her knees buckled, leaving her hanging from the chains as the fourth and fifth blows landed in rapid succession. Her sex rippled, clenching on air, seeking something to fill it as heat, pain and need grew with each blow. It no longer mattered just why her body reacted this way to the abuse he offered, all she cared about now was finding that moment of release at his touch.

She sobbed in the chains, hanging there as four more blows landed one after the other, barely giving her time to think in between each strike. Then nothing. She blinked the tears from her eyes, seeking him out. He still stood in front of her, holding the whip.

"One more, my slut. Just one more blow, then we move on." Both hands grasped the handle of the cat, his eyes intense as he swung, the weight of his body behind the blow. Pain, waves of brutal, searing pain lashed across her trapped breasts, the knots slapping into her sides, stinging into her exposed armpits when the leather wrapped fully. He smiled, tugging the wrapped leather away, leaving her hanging from the chains, tasting as her tears mixed with the blood still staining her lips. Sweat and need had coated her inner thighs, each strike from the cat adding to that slick heat.

"The tray, bring it." His order sent Isabella moving across the room to return a few moments later with a covered tray. "My

Chosen, I have a delight for you, a form of pain that you will scream with. I want to see you bleed before I grant the last bite."

Bleed. The thought left her moaning in delight, her thighs clenching as she watched him pull the thin black cloth from the tray. There on the bright metal lay two slender needles. Traven selected the first needle, holding it up so it gleamed in the moonlight. The needle was nearly the length of his index finger, the point looked sharp enough to pierce leather, so what it would do to her skin was only too easy to imagine.

He grasped her left nipple between his finger and thumb, pulling it taut away from the body of her breast, leaving her unable to do anything but cry out. He didn't stop, continuing to draw it out until the skin threatened to tear. A sharp flare of white pain pierced her trapped skin, the needle pushing through at the base of her nipple, popping free on the other side before he let go of her nipple. Sweat beaded on her body, the metal pressed against her skin on either side of pierced flesh. The pain eased a little with each breath, but didn't change the presence of the unwanted intrusion.

Smiling, he leaned down, licking over her abused nipple. "Delicious."

"Master," she whimpered, arching towards the touch of his tongue.

"More?" His teeth grazed over her nipple.

"Please." More, she wanted far more than a single flash of pain.

A second needle was taken from the tray, her unmarked nipple caught between his cruel fingers. He twisted, tugging a sharp cry from her lips, pulling it further than he had her other nipple, drawing a near scream before he seemed satisfied enough to press the tip of the needle against her skin. Her hands clenched, her gaze fixed on the offering of pain as he waited. Waited for what? Why couldn't he just thrust it into her body? There was nothing she could do to stop him. She wanted it, needed it; the first had already left her sex rippling in desire.

He twirled the needle, but still didn't push it into her.

"Please," she begged. "Please, Master, do it, pierce me." Pain, brilliant shards of pain lanced through her trapped nipple, the needle breaking through onto the other side of her flesh. Thin trickles of blood spilled over her swollen mounds, gathering in a heavy drip only to fall from her body in two drops of scarlet.

"Perhaps later I will pierce you on a more permanent basis, my slut. Hoops of gold in these nipples would be a delight to see on you. One brushing against your clit each time you breathe might be an interesting addition. Can you imagine it, my beast? How it would move across your clit, teasing you even within your sleep?" He reached between her thighs, pinching her clit, rubbing his thumb across it in slow, easy circles.

"Yes, Master." She could only hope he would choose to mark her in such a manner. To go through the rest of her life wearing such permanent signs of his pleasure? What more could she ever want or need in life?

"Just two needles this time, next time it will be double that number. And then each time we use them I will add more, until your body can take thirty in total. Small ones, longer, some slender as a strand of hair, others thick enough to be a rug hook." He squeezed her clit, releasing it as his fingers brushed between the wet lips of her pussy. "What do you think, Devoted?"

"I believe that would be a fitting way to mark a beast, my Lord." Isabella replied. "Your collar is an honor to wear, one this creature still fights against."

"Is that true, my beast? Do you fight your fate?"

"No, Master, I've embraced it," she protested. Isabella, the woman wanted nothing more than to find a way to provoke Traven into releasing her from his collar.

"Then why does my Devoted say otherwise?" His finger pressed deeper into her sex, reaching in to tap against that hidden point of delight. She groaned, her hips pressing towards him, his pressure matching the beat of her heart. A beat that vibrated through her body into her clit, echoed in her pierced nipples.

"I tried to bite one of your Attendants, Master." She tried to focus enough to speak, the desire growing in her body making it ever harder to think. "She thinks I lack the control your Chosen should have."

"Ah, then there has been a little confusion. My Chosen needs no control, she should lack it, give into her desires, be a decadent beast of delights, as such a thing amuses me." He leaned in, touching her lips, licking across them. "Such a beast as this gives up her pain, her essence without hesitation. Control only brings doubt, the ability to fight what I offer. You are how I wish you to be, my slut."

She leaned into his touch, seeking the depth of his control, offering herself to him fully as the kiss deepened. His hands moved over her aching, welted flesh, kneading her bound breasts, twisting pierced nipples until she screamed into his kiss.

"You will be mine, fully, eternally." He pulled away from her lips, seeking out her throat. "Eternal slavery."

"My Lord!" Isabella protested, but it was too late.

His teeth sank into her throat, deeper than ever before, piercing her skin, her arteries and her soul in a single swift move. Pain flared, delving into her core, rippling across her cunt. She arched into him, seeking out his touch, welcoming the pain as it tore through her body.

Deeper he fed on her, suckling her blood into his mouth, his throat working as he swallowed her life in eager, swift gulps. Her mind tried to flee but the welts, the pain, the presence of his bonds all prevented that escape.

"Please, my Lord, not her...."

She couldn't breathe, couldn't think, her body felt no longer her own. No, too much, he was taking too much. Her vision dazed, even when he pulled away from her throat, she couldn't focus.

"Your last breath is mine, as will be your first," he whispered against her lips, then covered them in a kiss. Blood washed over her tongue, his blood, even without being told she knew it was his.

Fire exploded to life in her veins.

No! Her mind screamed a denial.

"Give it to me, that breath, that last breath as a mortal. Trust me to bring you back into the darkness, my Chosen," he urged.

She fought to hold on to that last breath, to remain as she was, struggling against the bonds, pain, the fire in her body until she had no choice but to let it go. She gasped into his mouth, darkness claiming her eyes, her mind calling out the word her body lacked the ability to cry.

Master...

Hunger.

She'd never known a hunger like it. It raged out of control, seeking an answer. It had since the moment her vision had returned, her body free of the chains, the cords, even the needles. He'd pulled them free in the moments since she had gasped for that first painful new breath. Not that it would have mattered if they had remained; she'd have torn free in her need to sate the drive that had now been given life.

"You know what you need to do." His voice, her Master, her creator. Yes, he was right, she knew. She'd always known.

The heartbeat pulled her across the room, her vision seeing the prey in a new light, a meshwork of pulsating points. Did it know she was hungry?

"My Lord?" The prey spoke.

No, it didn't know, it thought it was safe, protected by something else. How could it understand what would happen? After all, it was only food.

She darted across the room, her hands tearing into the robe it wore, yanking the prey to the floor. Her teeth sank into its neck.

**Enslaved By Blood**

Blood, bright, alive, heated, swept over her lips in a welcome offering.

It screamed, but she didn't care.

It pleaded as she drank, but she didn't stop.

It struggled, but it was only a source of food and had no true way of breaking free.

How long had it been since she had truly fed? She couldn't remember and now drank from the source the frantic creature offered her.

"My Lord, save me!" Isabella cried out, trying to claw her way free. "I have served you, been faithful to you. Help me, please!"

Her Master remained silent, leaving his Chosen to feed. Hunger had no mercy, and mercy had no place within the temple. That at least should have been something the prey should have known...

Chapter Nine

"They'll call you a goddess."

Funny, she didn't feel like one. She wasn't sure how she felt right now. Her body was no longer her own, her mind clouded by a heavy blanket that left it almost impossible for her to think straight. All she knew was something had changed. She had become something else. The hunger had passed, and a strange feeling of being sated had settled into place.

There were confusing images and the all-too-clear memory of the temple. Yes, she'd been made to attend the ceremony by her mother and there was the spanking that had taken place beforehand. Hadn't she been convinced that attending the service was nothing more than just another waste of time?

Those images surged into life, yet barely lingered more than a few moments before they were lost back into the recesses of her sluggish mind.

Why couldn't she think clearly?

A pair of violet eyes looked down at her, strong, unyielding arms wrapped about her body. It was the sort of protective hold that should have left her feeling safe. So why did her stomach knot?

Who was he?

She knew him, feared him and couldn't move from his grasp, but still she struggled to remember his name. Dangerous. Every instinct screamed at her to move, break away and run for safety.

Run where?

Her mother wouldn't take her back in, she'd been chosen by...

By who?

Something to do with the temple, the service she had attended. Statues. One of the statues had moved? No, that didn't make sense, no matter how she tried to force the memory to reveal a little more. Damn it, why wouldn't her mind relinquish the memories she so desperately needed?

Naked?

Why was she naked and in the grip of a man at the same time? This wasn't right. It went against the behaviors expected of an unmated woman. Her mother would have a fit, send her to the square for lewd behavior.

Unless she already knew?

Had this been arranged so she would no longer question her place in society?

He cradled her in his lap, slender fingers sliding through her hair, lingering for a moment on the collar that had been locked about her throat.

"My Chosen, my priestess in training, you have so much to learn. You'll never become used to the taste, no matter how many years pass, how many lives you take. The first life or the first thousand, it won't make a difference. Each life, each new surge of blood as it slips past your lips, coating your throat, granting you a glimpse into their futile lives, is a little different than the last one. Leaving you wondering about the next, craving it. For a time you can ignore it, then it becomes overpowering, demanding and you give in."

The fog eased a little more from her mind with his words. Alayna whimpered. She could taste it, the blood coating her lips, feel the slick covering on the inside of her throat as it slid down into her stomach. Taste it, and want more. Even now that the madness of the moment had passed, the drive to take it again remained; subdued and caged, but ever-present.

A thing of the temple, this man, this being with the violet eyes, he belonged here, so did she now. Gods, what had she done? The dead woman, there had been a woman and she had died, no, she had been killed. But by who? Her neck throbbed, twin points from the bite. A bite she had begged for? Her mind refused to comply, holding the answers back in the depths of her mind. She shuddered, licking across her lips, trying to ease the dryness that coated them.

No, they weren't dry, it was something else. Blood on her lips, the dead woman...

No.

"I killed her?" she murmured, a cold sweat coating her nude form. "I killed her, and drank from her. You've turned me into a monster." She tried to push away from him, pressing her hands against his chest, struggling to break the hold he had on her body. Teeth, small, sharp and deadly, had formed in her mouth, replacing the incisors that had been there before. She was stronger, her muscles corded under her pale skin, but not strong enough to break free.

"Easy, my pet, you've still got a lot to learn about your new status in life." His grip shifted, one hand moving to the collar on her throat, fingers sliding into it to grasp it tight. "But never forget, you are my slut, my pet, my slave until the day the world ends. I've given you the gift of eternal life, the pleasure of blood, but that does not change your status at my feet."

The marks had healed, all but the ones in her neck, the change leaving her body whole, untouched. Even the small points of pain from the needles had faded, but she could remember it all. The way she had squirmed for him, begged, pleaded for his touch and then embraced the new life that he had offered her.

"Kneel." His grip tightened on her collar, forcing her down to her knees at his feet. "This is where you belong. You're no longer a human, but you are still just a slave to me."

Alayna fought to hold back a low mewl of fear, the stones cold and hard beneath her knees. Everything had changed. The darkness of the room no longer hindered her vision. She could see into the shadows, the corners of the chamber where the light of the candles failed to chase away the darkness. Her skin tingled, the smells in the room assaulted her senses but more importantly, the blood drying on the floor called to her.

She knew the dead one, or thought she did. The robe of a Devoted covered much of the corpse, but still there was something familiar about her. A memory that refused to take shape in her mind long enough to make sense.

"Of course you know her," he chuckled, brushing the backs of his fingers against her cheek. "She tormented you and thought she should be able to take your place at my feet. She wanted to serve me, and begged to take part in the ceremony that brought you into the darkness. Strange, she truly believed that I would welcome her into my life. Some humans still don't understand that in serving in my temple they offer themselves, their lives and of course, their deaths, to me in any way I see fit."

Isabella. She'd killed Isabella.

She'd deserved it.

Alayna shuddered, clutching her arms tight around her body. She'd killed a woman. Why?

You needed the food, and she deserved to die. She wanted to take your place at his feet. She had no other purpose but to feed you. Accept it. You're a monster like he is. Accept it.

Her stomach rolled, threatening to free itself of the blood that still coated the walls of its protesting form. No, she couldn't be sick, not like that. She needed the blood. He'd changed her, corrupted her, and she had been a willing convert.

Blood, she could smell it, drying on the floor, offering her images of living bodies, her gaze drawn to the pulses that throbbed in their necks, lips parted as they danced, spun, pleading with her to sink her teeth into their flesh. They begged her to partake of the life that throbbed through their mortal bodies.

What had she done?

She was a monster, not a goddess. A creature of the night, the darkness, everything she had claimed did not exist, and now she was a part of it. Worse than that, she had become a willing member of it.

"I can't think straight." The room moved, walls blurring, shifting around her.

"Focus." His grip tightened on her collar. "You will focus and not let this overwhelm you. Remember, you are my creature. You have my strength flowing through your veins and you have just fed. Do not let such human emotions weaken you now. Those petty problems are behind you. You need not pay them any attention unless it amuses me."

"Odd, everything feels so odd." Breathe, she had to breathe, not let it get to her. But the world spun around her even as she leaned into the grip on her collar.

She glanced back at the unmoving corpse. Isabella. Cruel, hurtful, spiteful, but she hadn't deserved to die like that, had she?

Her skin crawled. A thousand tiny fingers of sensation edged their way across her body as she found herself unable to look away from the dead woman.

"Don't lose control," he insisted as he picked her up from the floor, enfolding her in the circle of his arms. "Focus on me."

"I'm evil."

"No, you're not." His fingers tightened in her hair, tipping her head back, arching her neck. Her nipples crinkled, vulva heated as she squirmed on her lap, meeting his violet gaze, searching for answers in his terrible eyes. "But you will be, in time."

Reason fled, shadows spinning around her, wrapping about her body, taking control as they rushed her into the darkness at the back of her mind.

Chains held her in place, hands clawed at her flesh, tearing off small pieces as she whimpered, thrashing in the grip of pain. His eyes, those violet eyes that had followed her through the past few days now seared into her soul, mocking her, urging her to enjoy the pain, give into it and let her body sink willingly into the depths with him.

Braided cat, the knots lashed into her skin.

Needles slid though her nipples.

Fingers probed into her tight ass, parting her cheeks, probing. Another set opening the soft, heated lips of her cunt. She burned, thighs tight, a rippling warmth washing through her sex.

Trapped, helpless little toy. He'd changed her into a thing to scream and crawl at his whim. His nameless and helpless pet, she was nothing more than a slave in all things to him.

No! This wasn't what she had wanted. So why did her sex tighten in blatant need at the thought of him?

Corrupted. He'd taken her, drawn her into the night, the darkness, holding her in place there until she had no choice but to bend to his will and beg to become just like him. A slut sworn to serve the night.

Chains vanished, but she still couldn't move; walls enclosed her, holding her in place. Trapped. She was trapped.

Alayna reached out, hands pressing to the stone walls, feet bumping the bottom of the small chamber. No, not a chamber, a coffin. Sarcophagus, she'd been locked in one, buried alive. A punishment for killing Isabella.

Nails dug into her palms, fists striking out at the stone above her, someone had to hear her, help her out. No one would be cruel enough to leave a woman to starve to death in a stone deathtrap like this.

Of course they would. Pain, humiliation, death, they were all a part of the life she had seen in the temple. Traven had taught her that. Isabella had delighted in showing her just how low those who served him would sink. The depths she had crawled to in order to be with Traven should have taught her that all too well.

Had she displeased him? Or was this just a lesson in his control?

"Please," she pleaded, clawing at the stone, one nail shattering, tearing down to the quick. "I don't want to die this way. Please let me out. Master!"

Stone scraped against stone, a piercing sound that etched into her memory. Violet eyes glared down at her, soft torchlight flickering behind him. "Foolish girl, did you not understand? You cannot die now. Not unless I will it."

She hesitated, flinching back against the stone beneath her. "Master, I'm sorry. I thought you had decided to be rid of me, that I had done something to anger you."

Traven snapped, "Out, now," taking a step back as he held out his hand to her.

Her fingers caught around his as he pulled her free from the tight confines of the coffin. "I'm sorry, Master, truly I am." Her stomach rolled, cold sweat covering her back as she stumbled free of the terrifying stone coffin. A cell would have been easier to handle than the coffin. Those tight, confining walls pressing on her limbs, holding her in place, the lid locked down. A prison. "Please, why was I in that thing?"

"It's how we sleep. Our kind prefer such things instead of beds, these help protect us through our rest. You will become used to it in time. Sleeping in other places, where the sun might touch us, is dangerous. You'd have been able to manage it for a few days, then the problems would have begun. I simply decided to push the matter and make sure my property was kept safe." He shrugged off her concerns, pointing to the floor at his feet. "You've been asleep for a full day, as will become a habit for you to do. When you are older, more used to the changes that have taken place, you will be able to stay awake during some of the daylight hours, but only if you keep to the darkened chambers of the temple."

Alayna eased down to her knees at his feet, her gaze lingering on his boots instead of daring to look upwards. The collar still remained about her throat. The way he treated her; the words, the tone. She was still his slave, a piece of property. But did she have a name yet? He'd stripped that from her at one point, just a beast to crawl and plead at his feet.

"Something bothers you, slave?" His fingers tangled in her hair, tipping her head upwards to meet his gaze. "I can sense it. You're my child, a creature of my creation. Your emotions vibrate through the air whenever I am near you, so speak."

"Do I have a name yet, Master?" She spoke quickly, instantly regretting the words.

He smiled, laughter bubbling from a dark place within his soul. "Ah, the little beast wants a name, craves a way to identify herself beyond the collar on her throat. Is that it?"

She nodded, meeting his gaze, trying to fight the tears that burned in her eyes. She was a creature of the darkness like him, but her human emotions, the needs that went with them, still lingered. "Please, Master."

"The collar and the gift I gave you, that step into the darkness to walk eternally at my side, wasn't enough?"

"No, Master. I didn't say that."

"Yet you still want more, don't you? You want something to mark you above your station." His eyes narrowed. "It seems you still need to learn a little more about your place in my life."

Her stomach knotted. If he had not had his fingers wrapped in her hair, she would have thrown herself on her belly at his feet, wept, pleaded, covered the leather with kisses until he accepted her apology. She could have done something, anything that might have eased the harsh look in his eyes.

"Please, Master, I meant no harm. Just my own foolishness, a curiosity." She tried to find the right words. "I'm your slave, your beast, the one you have taken to be your Chosen. I accept that, welcome it, but there is a part of me that is still human, still remembers what it was like to be another type of being."

Did he understand? Did he remember what it was like to be a human, or had he always been one of these dark walkers, a vampire?

"That is something you will overcome in time, little pet. You have a lot to learn, rules, the way your life will be, the duties that you will assume." His grip eased slowly. "You will take your place here as my Priestess, my voice when my travels take me elsewhere."

"Your Priestess?" Her throat tightened. He would leave her? What then? She was a slave, his slave. Without him, who would she answer to?

"It will not happen overnight. You have a long way to go yet. A very long way." He shrugged, taking a step away from her into the low-lit chamber.

She didn't recognize the room. Torches flickered along the walls, casting a low light in soft orange and yellow circles across the stone floor. Two coffins, both stone, lay side by side on the floor. The one she had slept in--a blank, unadorned sarcophagus--and one that had been carved with elaborate symbols, ones she felt she should know from somewhere.

Ancient tongues. She had never been the student her mother had hoped she would be, but the markings had to be one of the ancient languages.

"You'll learn what they mean in time, my Chosen." He followed her gaze to the markings. "You've more than three thousand years of lore to learn."

Three thousand? She had never imagined it would be so much. Had the legends about his kind even hinted at how long they had walked the world?

"You will be leaving me, Master?"

"Soon, for a short while, but one of my kin will be looking over you. I am not foolish enough to leave one newly come to the darkness alone, without guidance." He settled down in the large, padded chair on the other side of the room. Stone, covered in velvet drapes of dark red, almost the color of dried blood. "And Isabella will be replaced easily enough; her kind are disposable. Little more than a higher grade of cattle, though they at least offer a small amount of entertainment during their brief lives. There are certain things that I can do with a human that I cannot with an animal."

"Is that all we are to you, cattle? Walking sources of food?"

"We?" One eyebrow arched, vanishing under his dark hair. "Have you forgotten what you now are?"

"I mean them, humans." Her neck throbbed, a reminder of the bites. "Are they just sources of food for you?"

"No, they are also sources of pleasure, pain and of course, delight." He smiled, tapping his fingers on the arm of the chair. "I hunt them. I don't just wait for them to be brought to one of the temples. I move among them, seeking out the ones that will be of the most use to me, feeding me in the way I need or want at the time."

Hunt? "Like beasts, animals."

He shrugged. "You don't understand it yet, do you? The craving, the need...but you will. When the drive to hunt one down, seduce them, take their life calls to you until you can no longer ignore it, then you will understand. You killed last night, fed, hunted in a primal, simple way. You screamed in joy, her blood dripping down your throat, coating your breasts, your body, and yet it was nothing to what you will eventually come to enjoy."

Alayna shuddered, her gaze moving to the floor, stomach rolling at the memory. She'd taken a life, and loved it. Killed, and would do so again. Isabella had been but the first. What if she let that need loose on the temple servants? Or worse, escaped the temple and hunted amongst the people she had known, even cared for before he had chosen her amongst the robed men and women in the temple? "I'm a monster."

"No, you're my Chosen." He pointed to the floor. "Come here, now."

She lowered to her hands and knees, crawling slowly to his feet, her breasts swaying softly, nipples crinkling into small, hardened points. Just being near him left her wanting more, wanting something she feared at the same time. His touch, the pain he had given to her in the hours before she had taken that last step away from humanity.

"Good, you've learned to crawl very well, my pet. Steps still to be taken, but there is improvement. I do not regret turning you into one of my kind. You had better pray you never cause me to change my mind." He tapped against his thigh lightly. "Here, put your head to my boots."

She glanced up for a moment before lowering her head to the black leather boots, her dark hair sliding over her face, veiling her eyes. This is where she belonged, though a part of her still screamed no, begged and pleaded with her to find a way to fight it. But it would have been easier to fight the need to breathe.

Had she given up on her life, her real life, so easily?

Yes, I ran from it. Embraced the darkness. So tempting, delicious to feel the blood of another human being slide down my throat. Cattle, yes, he's right, they're nothing but cattle.

Alayna shuddered. No, they were people, not food. Friends and family she had grown up with. Treating them like this would only condemn her further into the evil she had allowed herself to be caught up in. There were good people in this world. Ones like Lily.

A woman she had punished. Dragged over her lap, then held in place whilst she had beaten her and for what? To prove she wanted to give up her soul to the creature who now stood over her?

What have I done?

"My little slut, you have only just been brought into the darkness." He shifted one foot out from under her feet, pressing it into the back of her neck instead. "You will be worshipped as a goddess, becoming a Priestess at first, my voice, the voice of my kin. But in time you will take your place amongst us, if I deem you worthy of such a step."

She whimpered, the pressure of the boot forcing her to flatten along the ground. Nowhere to run, or hide from his touch. Even if there had been, she no longer knew if she would have taken that option.

But why would she even want to? This is where she belonged. "Master, all I can say is I will try to be pleasing to you. I know I have much to learn and I beg your forgiveness for my display of human weakness."

"You will do more than just try. You'll be pleasing, or you will be punished. I don't accept half measures." He ground his boot down further into the back of her neck. "A day has passed since you were turned, a day since your first feeding, and you now seek to find a way to claim your humanity. You don't have that option open to you, my slave. You are mine now. A slut to pain, pleasure and blood. Accept it, and rejoice that you are no longer one of the cattle."

Part Two: Priestess

Chapter One

"They're waiting for you, Milady."

Alayna glanced towards the door and the waiting woman. Long blonde hair, gentle green eyes and pale skin would have made her attractive enough, but the rapid pulse that beat in her slender neck called Alayna's attention more than the woman's appearance did.

No, it wasn't time to feed, but that didn't stop her mouth from watering. Taking just a small bite wouldn't be such a bad thing. A tiny taste of the fresh blood that surged through the woman, not enough to kill her, though, but still, it...

Alayna pushed the urge back under control before she spoke to the young woman. "Is the moon high?"

"Not yet, Milady. Another candle mark before it reaches its zenith."

"Then they can wait." What need did she have to scramble to serve them when they lived to obey her in the absence of their Lord? Too often they pushed, tried to find a way to manipulate her. That ended tonight. "And they had best do so without uttering a word of complaint. I am in no mood to deal with their petty little attempts at whining."

"Yes, Milady." The blonde servant bowed her head.

"Has the discipline of the temple been overseen?" Discipline. Strange how such things went in cycles. A month ago, two at most, she might have enjoyed overseeing this side of her duties, but now instead of exhilaration, she felt--what did she feel?

Empty.

No, not that. It didn't make sense to her, not entirely. But there was something missing now. The thrill of ruling over the temple had faded.

Everything does in time, and how long has it been since he left me in charge of them?

"Not yet, Milady. The Devoted who strayed from the path waits without." She nodded towards the door. "Should I have her sent in?"

"Yes." Such a correction would not take long. Better that she dealt with the matter and moved on to other things. "Then go to the chamber and let the others know I will be there when the time is right, and not a moment before."

The maid bowed quickly, backing towards the door without offering a single word of complaint. The woman knew better; all the servants in the temple did. Arguing with Alayna brought swift punishment or worse, a prolonged one. She would never be as strict or cruel as the one who had turned her, but even without that, they still feared her.

Good, such a fear might help keep them alive during the days she stalked the temple, seeking for that one person to take out her anger on. Not that she let that side of her out too often. A dozen times maybe, since he turned her. Each time, she regretted it. The guilt ate her up inside until she tossed restlessly in her coffin at night.

Only one death had not left her torn with guilt. One face could she call from her memory and feel some measure of satisfaction at the way she had drained the woman. Isabella. The Devoted who had taken part in Alayna's training.

Not before or since that woman had she known one who was capable of such cruelty, though Helena, current head of the Devoteds, came close. Now she had the chance to think about it, the two women had a lot in common. Their smiles matched, the drive for control, the need to try and be seen by Traven, perhaps be chosen by him as more than a passing moment of pleasure or a release point for his seed.

If they truly knew just what it meant to be chosen, then maybe they wouldn't have tried so hard to catch his attention. There was no peace for one such as her. No place she could rest without the faces of the dead lying in wait for the moment when she closed her eyes. And love, passion shared with a warm human being, that had been denied to her with his final bite.

So much had changed, yet it couldn't have been more than a few hundred years since he had picked her out of those gathered for the presentation. She was no longer the frightened woman that had wanted to find a way free of his touch, or the eager slave desperate for his attention. She had become something else.

A creature of darkness?

No, the phrase did not do her any form of justice. Perhaps she had been forced into the darkness but she was not of it, no matter what others of her kind might be like.

Her kind. It hadn't taken her long to accept she was no longer human. Strange, looking back she would have expected a fight, a denial of the beast she had become, but it had never come. She'd fled willingly into the seductive embrace Traven had offered her. Her skin tingled, nipples crinkling beneath the thin robe, thighs tightening in the memory of his touch.

Damn him. Even now the need affected her, no matter how hard she tried to shut it out. She had wanted to fight him, fight the dark desires he had brought to life. Instead, she had embraced them.

The door creaked opened to admit the trembling figure in the robes of the Devoted. "You sent for me, Milady?"

Slight, dark-haired, deep brown eyes. The woman would have been better off with a husband and children than entering the service of the Temple. She simply wasn't suited for the life here. But once the oath had been given there was no way back, no way out, save death.

"You broke the codes of the Devoted, Kareena."

The soft brown gaze lowered quickly to the floor. "It was a slip, Milady."

"Nevertheless, such must be dealt with. Discipline is vital

to the running of the temple. If those within are not held to the highest standards, how can the people who look to us for guidance then be expected to obey our laws?"

What little color remained in the woman's face drained away. "Milady, it was nothing more than a little food."

"For a man under public punishment."

"I showed him mercy." The young woman trembled, hands tangling into her robes. A pretty little thing. In many ways, it was a pity she had broken the codes. She would have squirmed well under Alayna's lash and perhaps learned to enjoy the mix of pain and pleasure that ruled here. Strange how it worked out, those whose faces hinted at innocence blossomed fully when introduced to the painful ways Alayna knew by heart. And now the woman faced a very different fate.

"Which is forbidden by the codes of the Devoted." Alayna's heart hardened against the young, trembling woman. "Discipline, obedience, such are the ruling forces behind those who take this path. You showed weakness, public weakness. By doing so, you disgraced not only your vows but your God."

"Milady, please." Kareena took a step closer before falling to her knees, head bowed. "I could not see him go without a little food and water. He would have died before his sentence was completed."

"And that was his lot." And by the standards of Traven's rules, it had been an almost merciful fate. Far worse would have been to give him small amounts of food and water every couple of days to drag out his death. Or subject the man to the death of a thousand cuts.

"Cruel, too cruel. He did nothing that deserved that."

She has no idea what real cruelty is.

"And you believe you have the right to overrule the sentence of the temple?" Alayna frowned. "By placing yourself above the laws of the temple, above the teachings of Lord Traven, you have sealed your fate, Devoted Kareena."

"Milady?" Small lines tightened around the woman's eyes, her brow furrowed, gaze narrowing on Alayna.

"The public brothel."

"Please, no, Milady. I beg you, not that." Tears streamed down her face, fear alive in her soft, warm gaze. "I could not live with such a thing. My life is sworn to Lord Traven."

"Then you should have remembered that before you ignored the laws of the temple." How would she look naked and bound to a pleasure rack, spread out for the use of any man or woman with a copper to spare? "Strip."

"Mercy, Milady, I beg you, show mercy."

Alayna moved without warning, grabbing the woman by the hair as she yanked her to her feet. "I gave you an order, slut." Her free hand reached for the robes, ripping them free from the woman's body. Cloth tore, shredding quickly under the harsh yank, baring the shaking Kareena to her view.

"I can't do this, Milady. I'd die in the brothel."

"No, you might wish that you could die at times, but after a while you'll come to enjoy your time there." Attractive, soft, round hips, full breasts, a gentle innocence that would call to those who frequented the brothel.

"I'll do anything you wish, Milady. Just not the brothel. Temple slavery, death, exile." Kareena squirmed in the grip, desperation burning in her gaze.

"And if I desired you as my plaything, something to scream when I wish it, a nameless little pet at my feet?" Alayna's held Kareena's gaze, fingers tightening in the woman's hair.

"I would do it, Milady."

"Even if I wish to throw you to the temple guards when the time came?" She twisted her grip, pulling her closer, her lips a breath away from Kareena's. "All those men and women using you in front of me, for my amusement."

Kareena let loose a low moan of terror as Alayna claimed her lips, forcing a kiss on the trembling woman. Sweet, so very sweet.

Kareena whimpered, arching close, nipples hardened points that brushed against Alayna's breasts. It wouldn't have taken much to force the woman to the floor and enjoy her completely. The darkness she fought to control every day surged into life. Images of the woman bound, helpless, stripped and beaten at her feet flashed through Alayna's mind. Blood and sweat coating her body, desire filling the air, it was almost too much to bear.

So very sweet. The woman tasted of honey, innocence and need all rolled into one.

With a slow, shuddering breath Alayna broke the kiss, nipping at Kareena's bottom lip. "Do you think you could face that, day after day?"

Kareena struggled to keep silent, shaking her head quickly. The color drained from Kareena's face, her eyes wide, lips pressed together as she swallowed and regained control of her voice. "No, Milady. I couldn't do that."

"Then you will go to the brothel, where you now belong. Better that than end up as my personal plaything. What happens to you in the brothel, at the hands of mere mortals, will still be easier to bear than my touch, my needs, my version of amusement. Remember that."

The fight died in the woman's eyes, her shoulders slumping, shaking as she fought to stay on her feet. "Yes, Milady. I understand. Thank you."

"Guards!" The door opened, two of the temple guards entering within a moment of Alayna's summons. "Take the brothel slave Kareena to her new home. She begins her five-year sentence today."

Five years. It might as well have been a lifetime to the sobbing woman as she was dragged out of the room. They knew the penalty for breaking the codes of the temple, understood the consequences and it was her duty to oversee the keeping of the laws. Duty, nothing more, yet she had enjoyed the terror she had caused, drank in the soft, seductive scent of arousal the kiss had brought to life.

No matter how much she tried to deny it, she had become the very beast Traven had claimed. The darkness lived in her soul, growling at the bars she tried to force around the being in her core. She was the creature, the beast that stalked the temple.

"Of course you are, my slut. How could you ignore something that powerful?" He stood in the moonlight, bathed in the soft caress of silver white light. Living alabaster, just the way he had been that night in the small chamber.

Chapter Two

"Mast…" The word died as she clamped her lips shut, taking a small breath before speaking again. "My Lord, I was not expecting you for a few more months. I thought you would still be traveling. I received no word of your arrival."

What was he doing here?

He hadn't been due to arrive yet, had he? She couldn't recall any messages stating he would be returning ahead of schedule. He should still be out traveling, though calling it hunting would have been closer to the truth. Sampling the bloodlines of other areas, tasting them the same way a human might have enjoyed a collection of fine wines. What was he doing here now? He had no reason to return to the temple at this time, did he?

No, he wasn't supposed to be here. Not yet.

"You almost called me Master again, my pet." On a normal man, his smile might have been a welcoming sight. "You shouldn't fight that desire. You'll always be my little slut, the hopeful young woman I turned into the sobbing, pleading slave at my feet just a short time ago."

"That was years ago, my Lord." A small frown crinkled her brow. Violet eyes. No matter what she did, she could never forget how his gaze made her feel. Intense and cool they were, but able to turn a look her way that could sear her to the core. How could he lack emotions one moment, then appeared to burn with them the next?

She would never understand him. She never truly knew what he was feeling. That alone left her unsettled.

"Years ago for mortals, perhaps. Not for our kind. You'll always be my slave. That's why I brought you into this life, and why I permit you to exist." A slight smile tugged at the corners of his lips, his gaze trailed over her body searching beneath the robe as if the cloth didn't exist.

The years stripped away. Her heart sank down into the pit of her stomach and for a moment she felt his touch afresh. The feel of his lips against her throat, his teeth piercing her skin as she sobbed and clung to him. Then it was gone. Over. Pushed back into the dark recesses of her mind where it belonged.

Her jaw clenched.

No, she wouldn't return to that place.

"No longer, my Lord. You raised me up from that point, set me high in the temple, your voice, your Priestess." Her jaw tightened as she pushed up to her feet. Hitting him would have done no good; he was still the stronger and faster between them. Even if she had been able to land the blow, any damage would heal before he so much as turned back to look at her.

All the training she had been through, turning from being a mere slave, a plaything, into the feared leader of the temple. How could he ever believe she would crawl back into slavery again? Not now that she had tasted the power of the darkness he had given her.

"And I can bring you low again, if I so wish it." He leaned against the wall, tracing a slender finger along his chin. Those damned violet eyes of his. All it took was just a single glance from them and she was fighting the urge to drop down to the floor and lick the dirt from his boots.

No. She wasn't that creature any longer and wouldn't take the step into that darkness. She had learned to rule others, to turn them into whimpering creatures at her own feet. The time to crawl was over.

"You looked so pleasing when you would crawl to me on your belly, and you enjoyed it, didn't you? You can try and deny it, but you loved every painful, humiliating moment of it." The words purred from his lips, each syllable calling to her, beckoning her closer. A soft tug on an invisible leash that she denied even existed.

"I've changed."

"Perhaps."

"I'm not that pitiful creature anymore."

"You are if I wish you to be. If I want you back at my feet, then that is where you will be. Crawling, licking and pleading for my attention."

"But I have a life now, duties."

"And I can change all of that on a whim."

"Is that all I am to you, something that can be pushed from one role into the next on your whim?" Her hands clenched tightly at her sides.

"Of course, what else did you think you were?"

"Your Priestess, of course, your Chosen. Just as you set me up to be. You wished me to rule in your place when you left and that is what I have done."

"And have you learned nothing since I claimed you? As my Chosen, I can do what I want with you, when I want. Regardless of what you desire."

"I see no need to upset the balance of the temple." She tried to keep calm as she forced her hands out of the tight fists they had become, looking away from him rather than meeting his gaze. "They have come to rely on me."

"What you see or believe is not relevant, my slut. I rule here, not you." He closed the distance between them, fingers pressed under her chin, forcing her gaze upwards, his lips brushing against hers only to vanish again as he took a step away. "My sweet little pet. You never truly have accepted your place at my feet, have you?"

Alayna tensed, turning away from him, fingers returned to their fist like state, nails digging into her own palms. Bastard. He knew exactly what to say in order to get her to react. "No."

"Stubborn creature, but I enjoy that about you. You say no, want to fight it, but when I show you the way, you dance willingly into that place of pain with me." He chuckled openly.

"You're mocking me."

"Of course."

"Why?"

"It amuses me, and you live to provide me with entertainment."

"Is that all?"

"What else would there be? Don't tell me you still hold on to some hope that I might actually care for you? Even love you?"

"I have a ceremony to oversee." She turned, stalking across the room away from him, cheeks flaming. "Your Devoted ones have assembled in the main chamber and await my arrival so that we may offer you the correct sacrifice."

"And you were planning on making them wait, so why the change of heart? Don't tell me you're afraid of being alone with me?" His mocking words followed her towards the door. "After all these years, you're still afraid of me."

"Do I have any reason to be?" She turned, meeting his gaze, muscles knotting across her shoulders.

"Yes, you do." He moved without a sound, clearing the distance between them, fingers tangled in her hair. "You've forgotten your place, my pet, the depths I can take you to. You've welcomed their worship, the fear in their eyes and thought that took you out of my reach. Ah, my dear sweet creature, you have forgotten the joy of being on the other end of the lash. Perhaps I should take the time to remind you of how that feels. How you squirmed for me, begged for more each time we played. Such an insatiable little slut you turned into after the right persuasion."

She growled, turning in his grip, lashing out towards his face with her nails. Anger blinded her, fury's fuel added to her strength as she struck out, small, sharp nails biting into his face for less than a heartbeat. Not that it did her any good; his strength surpassed hers a hundred times over. Yet still she struggled.

He wouldn't do this to her again. She wouldn't let him. Not

this time. She'd become stronger. She knew what he enjoyed, how he preferred to treat humans and--and she wasn't one of the cattle any longer!

"Foolish." His grip tightened, pulling her onto her toes, free hand closing on her throat. "Very foolish indeed. You've forgotten everything I taught you. All those times I punished you for such pitiful attempts to attack me. Perhaps you need a little alone time with me? Time in my chamber, exploring the darkness together?"

Her breath caught in the back of her throat, a cold chill caressing her flesh. Memories flooded back, all those nights spent under his control, a helpless pet for his amusement. She couldn't go back to that, wouldn't go back to that again.

Not even if the cost was her life.

"You're mistaken," she hissed, trying to fight free of his grip. "I don't have that in me anymore."

"You've missed those times with me." His lips brushed over her neck, the hint of fang scraping into her skin. Nothing much, just enough to turn back time if only for a moment, sending her mind running back into the memories of pain and pleasure combined. He smelled the same; that odd scent of blood, power and lust all rolled into one. "You still crave that darkness."

"No, I haven't. Not in a long time." Cold, his touch was still cold, little more than shards of ice that threatened to cut into her skin. No warmth in his eyes, or his heart. "I've learned to fulfill the duties you set upon me instead, and one of those duties is waiting for me out in the main hall. They are your devoted followers, ones that see me as your voice, your Chosen, and a creature that they bow down to in your absence."

"And you believe that takes you from my grasp? Do you truly believe that in acting as my servant for such events that you are now free of my hold, my desires, my touch?" His fingers tightened on her throat, releasing it a moment later. "I've been lax, then, in my control. Something I will have to correct after the ceremony, don't you think?"

Enslaved By Blood

Lax. If hunting, spending time away from the temple and leaving her to her own devices could be looked on as being lax then yes, he had been. The time without him had been something she had cherished and now that he had returned, fear threatened to lock her in its harsh embrace.

The last thing she either wanted or needed was to end up under his control again. Not now, not when she had finally placed herself on a level footing, put herself in a position where she no longer jumped every time a door opened or a whip crack split the air. What was she now expected to do?

Drop to her knees in submission and crawl to his feet, begging to be touched?

It wasn't going to happen.

"There is nothing to correct." The door. If he gave her even a chance, she would be through the door and out down the corridor. "I'm a Priestess now, no longer the slave, the slut or pet. I oversee their devotions, their prayers and sacrifices to you. You raised me out of that low status, and I see no need to correct that situation."

"Oh, I think there is, and you know there is." Traven smiled, folding his arms across his chest. "Go, little slut, attend them, enjoy the gifts they offer you this night. When you return, I will correct the balance between us before the matter causes any further problems. It would not do for another of our kind to see how ill-trained you appear to be."

The claw marks had already faded and ceased to exist before she fled through the door. Unless he willed it, any marks her body endured quickly faded before even a fraction of a candle mark had passed. This time he had done nothing to prevent them from healing, another sign that he was pushing her, testing to see what her reaction would be to his presence. He had his choice of a dozen or more young women in the area who would throw themselves at his boots and beg to become his new Chosen, his new toy of the moment. Why would he waste time trying to bring her back into line?

It made no sense.

Did he enjoy pulling her back down, only to see her struggle out of the darkness again when he left?

There had been times he had left her alone before, but none of them had come close to the extent she had known this time around. A few months, even as much as a year, long enough to set her off balance, yet this had been different.

Years had gone by.

She had first struggled with her life, looked for a way to try and settle her raging emotions, and then finally closed the door on being a slave. He'd even removed the collar the last time he had been here. Why else would she ever think that it was all right to act as a full Priestess?

No one had corrected her.

No one remained who would have dared.

They looked to her for guidance, discipline, the cruel cold hand of judgment in the place of their dark god. Why risk feeling the wrath of the Priestess by suggesting they had the right to correct her behavior? Not even Helena had dared to try such a thing, no matter how hard the woman had fought for power and position in the temple.

The ceremony, those waiting for her. By the time it was done he would have found another to keep him busy, a source of entertainment in the form of a new mortal. It didn't matter who he picked from the temple servants or if he stole a woman from the street, just as long as he played with someone else.

His kind hunted where they wished to, so why wasn't she permitted to leave the temple?

Because she was still nothing more than a slave?

The knowledge irked her. Despite the work she did in the temple, the way she watched over them, all for him, she still had not been granted even the basic right to leave the temple when it pleased her.

Enslaved By Blood

She deserved more than this, more recognition than he had ever granted her. Instead, she remained limited by the offerings within the walls. Yet here she was, unable to hunt beyond the courtyard, the servants and slaves who were bound by their oaths or chains to the temple.

Oh, she'd tried to leave, but the runes, the magic that he had placed on the boundaries of the temple had kept her locked within the confines of the holy ground.

What would it be like to truly hunt? To sight a prey and track them down, seducing them, calling them until they willingly offered their throat to her? Not something she had ever known, and she doubted he would change his mind about that anytime soon.

The last time she had tried to step beyond the boundaries of the temple, she had known such pain that she had passed out and slept for close to a week. No marks, no sign of what existed in the temple to keep her captive, yet it had worked nevertheless.

Just the thought of the pain that had lashed its terrible course through her body was enough to leave her shaking, one hand pressed against the wall as she tried to support her body and regain some measure of focus. She could risk no servant of the temple catching her in such a moment of weakness. Not if she wanted to keep her status and control of those within the hallowed walls.

Slow, deep breaths, a moment with her eyes closed as she steadied her thoughts and pulled her emotions back under control. No matter what happened today, she would remain strong in the eyes of those who served in the temple. Despite being Traven's chosen, there were those in the numbers of the Devoteds who would happily try to kill or replace her.

Seeing her dead would be the first choice of Helena.

The thought of that woman gloating over her dead body was enough to push the last of the shaking back under control. Did she share a bloodline with Isabella? Her instincts said yes, but without a way to leave the temple or search down that information, she had no way to be sure of it. Still, there were similarities between the two women that had shaken Alayna to the core the first time she had laid eyes on Helena.

Power-hungry bitch didn't even begin to describe the woman.

How many of the servants had she flogged for just looking at her the wrong way, or by bringing up false charges against them? More than Alayna could count, and there would be others soon enough. It had been far too long since she had taken out her anger or frustration on a member of the temple.

Lights flickered along the corridor, torches that cast soft yellow and orange circles of light across the bare stone. No statues here, the ornamentation stripped at her orders. She ruled here, not him, not any longer. He'd been gone for too many years.

Not one or two, but three decades had passed since he had graced the temple with his presence. And now he walked back into her life, expecting her to do what? Drop down on her belly, worship him and beg for his attention?

Too late. He'd left it far too long.

Neither he nor any of his kind paid attention to those of the temple unless they wanted something. It could be something as simple as a new ceremony, a source of food, something that would pique their interest for a short time. Traven's interest changed from one matter to another depending on his mood, or so it seemed, but it had been a long time since he had turned his attentions her way.

His kind? Did more than just Traven exist? If so, she had never met them. After a couple of hundred years she had expected to meet at least one more of his...no, *their* kind. A few bites, a tug into the darkness and she had been changed, become this creature that now stalked her way through the corridors.

Her jaw clenched and she looked back down the hallway. Did he even know how they now treated her, how she was expected to be perfect and the subject of their worship? They came to her, crawled to her feet, sought her approval and begged her for correction when the need arose. It didn't matter what she had once been, that she had been human and just as afraid as they now were. All that had changed. She held the power of life and death over them.

Everything had changed.

No longer the slave, the beast, the creature at his feet, she had become a Priestess, a woman with power and respect. Another could take her place in steel, another would writhe for him and save her from the shame he enjoyed inflicting on the women at his feet.

There were other delights for her. She had learned well how to make men and women scream, beg for her touch and plead for the right to worship her. No more the slave, now she had become the Mistress, and she would never again take that step into the past with him, or anyone else.

So why did her stomach knot at the thought of another at his feet?

Foolish. She should be welcoming the idea, pushing women towards him, not feel as though she would rip their throats out. Would he take another for his pet, his Chosen, the way he had claimed her?

In time, maybe. There must have been others before her, but she had never been told about them, and trying to ask him had resulted in either punishment or him simply ignoring the questions, dismissing them the same way he did anything else he had no interest in.

What had happened to the ones prior to her?

And what would her fate be when another took her place at his feet?

Her place. She barely stopped herself from biting into her bottom lip. No, it wasn't her place now. It hadn't been for a long time. Thinking like that was nothing more than a side effect of the training she had been through. A drive implanted during her early years with him, it would fit with what she knew about the man.

Man. Beast. Vampire. Who knows what he really was anymore? A creature who needed blood to survive, one that avoided sunlight unless he was freshly fed by a dozen bodies. Even then, he could only manage a short time in the early rays of the day, or the dying light just before nightfall.

Something she couldn't even manage, not even entering the small courtyard. The pain of daylight had been worse than the spell he had woven in order to keep her in the temple. She had tried to slip out during the time when the shadows had been at their longest, hoping for a moment that she could lay claim to the same powers, the same level of strength he did.

Her lips twitched into a smile. Yes, if she could grow into the power he owned, then she would never again have to worry about him returning to the temple. She'd rule, completely. No more jumping at shadows in case he appeared and tried to order her to his feet.

A foolish hope. He had lived this strange life for how long? Years? Centuries? A millennium or longer? She had no real way of knowing. How stupid did she have to be in order to believe she might have the same chance as he did to step out into the sunlight?

Not foolish, or stupid, but stubborn. And it had been that same stubborn strength that she had relied upon through the years in order to keep from going completely insane.

"Milady? Is everything all right?" Soft blonde hair, a gaze filled with concern, the sort of woman that did not belong in the temple. Gentle, like another woman that had once lived here, more years ago than she cared to recall.

What had been the name of the servant? Alayna frowned, struggling to recall her name, her face, but could bring nothing more to life than a soft voice, that moment of kindness at a time when she had been alone. She had been punished by Isabella, that part she recalled clearly, sent out to crawl and beg to be beaten. Or was she recalling another woman, another face? They all blurred one into the other over the years.

Was this what it was like for Traven?

Humans becoming just blurred images for the most part, the occasional memory, if the emotions attached to it were strong enough?

Lily. Sweet, gentle Lily.

She hadn't belonged in the temple, but once an oath was given, it bound the mortal for life.

"Milady?"

"Yes, I'm fine."

"You look a little distracted."

Alayna's gaze focused on the hypnotic throb beneath the young woman's chin.

Throbbing pulse, pale skin, the offering of life beneath a thin coating of flesh beckoning to her with each beat of the young woman's heart. *Control it and keep the need under the lock and key. Don't give in to it.*

She growled softly, tracing her tongue over her lips, licking softly. Would the woman growl, scream or beg for more? Each meal was a little different, their reactions unique, the waves of emotions adding their own delicious flavor to the blood Alayna now craved.

It would only take a moment. All she had to do was reach out, grab the woman, tip her back to bare her neck. Her teeth could pierce that soft, delicate neck before the woman would have the chance to cry out.

The maid wanted to serve her, Alayna could see that, read it in the way the young woman moved. If she craved it, then it couldn't be wrong to take the gift being silently offered to her. She would be serving the temple, serving Traven and following the very codes those of the temple forced those in the town to follow.

Take it, spill the blood, take the woman's life. Such a simple thing to do. She'd only have to sink her teeth into that sweet, tender flesh. With little more than a simple bite, she'd allow the woman's blood to trickle down her throat, right here, right now, in the middle of the corridor.

She had every right to, as his Priestess. It was expected of her to take what she wanted from the men and women here, as long as Traven did not wish the human for himself. Those who served here were hers to do with as she wished. If she desired a virgin, then they would hunt through the houses around the temple to find one suitable for their Priestess. If she wanted the blood of a dozen men and women, they lined up to beg to be the one under her blade.

She ruled here, so what would be so wrong in enjoying that power?

No. She had more control than that. Or did now.

A memory; flash of blood on a slender throat, a scream, that plea for mercy carried by the same soft voice that had been the source of comfort.

Name, why couldn't she keep hold of the woman's name?

Lily, remember the name. Lily. Don't lose it again. She meant something to me. I know she did.

But what? Lily had been nothing more than another servant in the temple, why would a mere human mean anything to her, other than as a marker through the years?

Damn him. Damn him for turning her into a creature that thrived on blood and terror. For denying her any chance of a normal life, friends, companions and family. He'd taken all of that from her.

Yes, I did, my pet, and you wouldn't change a single moment if you were honest with yourself, his voice whispered in the back of her mind. *I'm always with you, I always have been. Every thought, every emotion, I've known them all and I know it is time to return you to my feet.*

"You just looked a little pale. Did you need to feed, Milady?" The woman smiled shyly. "You were licking your lips."

"Soon." Very soon. The more he pushed his way back into her life, the harder it became to keep control of her needs, her drives. "I'll need to feed soon, but I am fine for now."

She had grown stronger in the passing years. He would not be able to push his way back into her life so easily. She only fed when she had to, took enough to survive and little more. On rare occasions she had let that control slip, sated herself on the blood of the willing and unwilling alike. Just for that moment, she became the dark creature he had tormented her with.

Yet she had always regained her control afterwards, and the time between her loss of control grew longer with each incident. No matter how tempting the maid was, or how great her need, she would not lose control again. Not now, or ever. She had changed, grown stronger than before; the blood called to her, but she remained in control.

Who are you trying to convince, you or me, my slut? His voice mocked her at the back of her mind. *I know you better than you could ever know yourself. I feel the hunger in you, the drive to kill, to hunt. Why else do you think your gaze moves constantly to that low, throbbing pulse in her neck?*

"I would be honored if you chose me for that, Milady Priestess. I had hoped, dreamt you might one day turn your attention my way." Did she even know the maid's name? Not that it mattered. They were all just sources of food when the hunger hit.

No, she mustn't give in like that.

She had to ignore the throbbing pulse and the way the woman's lips parted. Shut out the soft lights playing over the soft upper curves of her barely covered breasts. A caress of shadow and light that beckoned to her, making them attractive, soft and so very delicious.

What would her throat taste like?

Would she moan as her throat was pierced?

Arch into the touch, the painful embrace, her soft fingers clawing at the one who held her in the painfully tight grip?

It would be so easy to just take her and find out. Push her to the floor, bare that neck and take everything offered.

"You don't know what you are suggesting," she snapped, struggling to push the images back under control, to not reach out and grab the woman, tear into her throat and sup until the life drained from her slender form. Focus, control it, don't give in, that's just what he wanted her to do. Become the beast, the creature craving blood, ready to do anything just for a taste of sweet life.

"Yes, Milady, I do. I've seen others taken. The delight, the way they are welcomed into the temple fully as a member of the Devoted afterwards." She smiled shyly, raising her gaze. "I would be honored, Milady Priestess, if you would take me in that way. I have tried to find a way to serve in the temple beyond cleaning or fetching fresh food, new linens and avoiding those members of the Devoteds who would use me and toss me aside. But this, this moment where I can truly serve, it is what I have always wanted. I'm strong, Milady, I've worked hard in the temple, and I know I would be all right if you granted me that dark kiss."

"Some do not survive." Stupid, warning the prey to be afraid of the hunter, yet after all these years she had only lost control of that need a handful of times. "They die from the blood loss, their throats torn out, or because they become addicted to the pain and pleasure that serving can bring."

How well she knew about the addiction to pain. Not that the woman would listen to her. Few who offered themselves in such a manner were ever ready to heed such warnings.

"No, Milady, they die because they seek something for themselves, not to simply serve. I wish to serve you. You're eternal, a Priestess, some say a goddess. Who would not wish to beg at your feet?" She moved softly to her knees at Alayna's feet. "I have watched you for so long, Milady, and beg you to take me."

"Anyone with a grain of sense would stay clear of me, girl."

"But--"

"You try to walk a dangerous path. One that would end your life, or condemn you to eternal damnation." Did she have the ability to turn a human into one of their kind? She'd never tried, not in the years since he had left her alone in the temple.

"It is one I crave, Milady." She lowered her head to Alayna's feet, pressing a soft kiss to bare skin. "I offer you my blood, my life, if you so desire it. They are yours to do with as you wish."

"No, when I feed, it will be from someone who deserves the darkness my touch offers, not a woman whose heart is pure." Alayna explained, waving the nameless young woman away. "Attend your duties and leave me to tend mine."

"Milady, please."

"No. I will not discuss this any further with you. Go now."

Shaking, the woman pushed back to her feet, turning on her heels. With a low sob and hurried steps she ran down the corridors, bare feet slapping against the stone. The woman cried as if the greatest of gems had been taken from her.

She'd escaped death, couldn't she understand that?

Of course not. She wanted the dream, and refused to accept that the dream was a nightmare.

Foolish, you still don't understand the creature you have become? I know, I'll watch and wait for that moment after the ceremony, perhaps I'll even take the girl you've just turned away. Her blood feeding my need instead of yours, her life taken by me when she offered it freely to you. Will you let that happen?

Chapter Three

Fifty men and women turned their attention fully on her the moment she walked into the room, each one wearing a mask of sheer devotion and love, that sickening mix of obedience and lust for power she had come to expect from those called Devoteds. Only a rare few ever escaped that craving, keeping themselves free of the darkness by some measure of will she had never understood. Not when they remained in the Temple, regardless of the cruel actions they witnessed.

Something felt odd even as she entered the room, a tension she had not expected from a simple rising of the moon ceremony. Had something happened that she had not been aware of?

Alayna glanced around the room. The altar had been prepared, the robes worn showed the trimmings of a high sacrifice, and Helena stood at the head of those gathered holding the ornate dagger that only saw use in the most powerful of ceremonies. Her gaze narrowed on the cold-faced woman, trying to read the glittering greed she saw clearly in the gaze.

"Is there something amiss, Helena?"

"Milady, we have been anxiously awaiting your arrival." The senior member of the Devoted moved to the altar. "I had feared you would not arrive in time. The moon has risen, the light is at the right angle for the prayer and offering."

"Offering? I sanctioned no such occurrence today." She frowned, looking towards the altar. There, kneeling by the side of the white marble waited a young man. Blond hair, blue eyes, his gaze lowered to the floor and wearing little more than a loincloth as he mumbled his quiet prayers.

A very small loincloth that barely covered a very large package. It seemed a pity to waste such a delicious-looking young man on a sacrifice that shouldn't have been taking place.

Had she seen him before in the temple? Her mind scrambled through the assorted images of those that lived and worked within the stone walls. No, she couldn't recall seeing him, not that it mattered now that she beheld him. Sculpted thighs, well formed chest, tight buttocks, a body better suited for the pleasures of the flesh. Her thighs pressed tightly together, lips parting with the thought of the delight that lay hidden under the small scrap of cloth.

No, a man such as this was not wasted on a simple spilling of blood.

Damn the woman and her desire for power. This time she would try to gain more through the death of the man kneeling at the side of the altar. Had he angered Helena at some point? Or crossed her?

It could have resulted in something as simple as the wrong look at the wrong time, knowing that woman.

"Lord Traven has returned, has he not?"

"Yes, but…" Alayna frowned as the woman continued on.

"Tradition dictates an offering. Surely you know this, being his Priestess?" The woman's dark gaze narrowed, her frown deepening. "I find it hard to believe you would not wish to celebrate his return."

Just what she needed right now, a member of the Devoted pushing matters, forcing the issue. No, Helena wanted to do far more than push, she wanted attention. Traven's attention. "I would have preferred time to choose the right offering for our Lord. Such a young gift, with such obvious signs of sensuality in him, seems an ill-fitting choice for one such as Traven. He prefers them with a little less fire in their souls, not ones who would be better served through pain and pleasure combined."

"But, I don't understand. He wishes to be given to Traven." The woman shifted her gaze from the kneeling man back to Alayna, then to the altar. "And I see no point in turning him down. Is it not said that it is better a gift be given freely then ripped from the unwilling?"

"Helena, since when did you dictate what makes the right offering to our Lord? Have you been raised above the position of a mere Devoted into that of his Chosen, or a Priestess? Odd, I felt sure I would be notified of such a prestigious event." Pride, power, that need to push for a better position in the temple. She'd seen this play out a dozen times and more. "I am also well aware that few are brought to sacrifice without them having crossed you in some small way. Though I have every belief you would deny it outright, so do not waste either my time or yours with the lies you now burn to spew forth."

The kneeling offering didn't wait to see the outcome of the discussion. Instead he looked up, giving Alayna a grateful look before he fled on bare feet out of the room, the door slamming shut behind him.

So much for him being eager to offer his life, and the dark look that Helena shot his way spoke volumes.

"I have not been raised..." Helena turned her attention back to Alayna.

"I see. Then did you perhaps speak with Lord Traven himself about this matter?" She was tempted to fold her arms beneath her breasts, an old habit. One she had tried hard to be rid of in the past hundred years or so. "I would think he might have mentioned that to me, as I left his presence to attend the service."

"You were with him?"

"Yes, and he mentioned nothing about a desire to see a high ceremony. Or are you trying to tell me you know his wishes better than he does?" Good, if she had not spoken of being with him prior to the service, then Helena might have attempted to convince others she had been in the presence of Traven herself. If the confused glances she caught out of the corner of her eye were anything to go by, Helena had already tried to suggest that to a couple of the Devoteds in the chamber.

Somehow that didn't surprise Alayna. Power-hungry woman. One day she would push too far, if she hadn't already.

"Well, no." Helena took a step back, lowering her gaze as she folded her hands demurely in front of her robe. The image of the humble, devoted servant. With someone else, that portrayal might have worked. Not with Alayna. She'd seen better performances before Helena had ever been born. "Please forgive me, Milady. I meant only to serve our Lord in the manner I know best. I truly thought our Lord would desire such an offering."

"Indeed." Alayna nodded slightly. "Have the man returned back to his quarters. He fled the chamber, but he needs to be assured he is safe and may relax in his chambers, giving thanks to Lord Traven for his reprieve. However, you are correct in one matter, Lord Traven does desire an offering to celebrate his return, but I find the choice lacking. However I believe there is one in the temple who, above all others, would be fitting to offer their lifeblood to our Lord." Time to be rid of the woman once and for all, before Traven took it upon himself to turn her. Or offer her a higher place in the temple. Not something to be risked.

Interesting idea, pet. Hurry now, before I find my way down into the chamber and turn this Helena into your darkest nightmare.

"Speak their name, Milady, and I will bring them in myself." Helena's eyes glittered.

"You."

Color drained from the Devoted's face. "You can't mean that, I have other duties I could perform instead," Helena faltered, casting a quick pleading glance around the chamber. "I am needed here, my death would be a loss to the temple and our Lord."

"Perhaps, but I believe this is an honor you well deserve, or are you refusing?" Ignore the pleas, the voice of mercy at the back of her own mind. She deserved no mercy, no thought of leniency. How many had she sent to their deaths?

Ten, twenty, closer to a hundred, and those were just the ones

Alayna knew about.

Every gaze turned on the now trembling woman. "No, Milady. I just…have had no time to prepare my soul."

"You are one of his Devoted, are you not? Your soul is already well prepared to be used as such an offering." Alayna stepped closer, savoring the terror that now emanated from the woman. "Or have you spent years lying about your devotion to his service?"

"No, Milady, I have not lied." Helena drew herself up a little, forcing the signs of fear from her face quickly. "I am a true servant of our Lord. But I beg you to reconsider your choice. I haven't had the chance to truly prepare for him. This male has. He has been through the rituals as dictated in our teachings."

"And as one of his true Devoteds, you spend hours each day cleansing your soul, preparing yourself for whatever he might desire?" Good, the woman was caught in the web of her own making. Odd how those with too much greed were so easy to trip up just at the right time. In the long run it was better this way, far better than letting the darkness loose on the woman.

Are you sure about that? Don't you want to make her pay for everything she has done?

"Yes, I do, just like all others in his service." She spoke quickly, her gaze flickering about the room, seeking some sign of help, respite from the fate that now faced her. "But it is not the same as preparing for the final sacrifice. You above all people know this."

"Ah, but I am sure Lord Traven will accept your offering…unless you have betrayed him in some way?"

Helena shook her head quickly. "I would never betray him."

"Then there is no problem, is there? You are prepared to serve him in this final act. I will drain your blood in the proper manner and then present it to him myself. Is it not said that the second greatest honor a Devoted could be granted is to feed the Lord with their life essence?" She could taste the fear, that bittersweet smell on the air, coating the other woman's skin in small beads of sweat. The same scent that pulled on the beast she knew growled in her own soul, the one that wanted to taste sheer terror on the air, savor every moment, each cry of pain as she squirmed and pleaded for her life.

Such a delicious image, and a fitting end to a woman whose heart remained shrouded in darkness.

She had let the matter of Helena go on far too long but now, yes, now the woman had pushed too far. Her death would bring an end to the petty attempts at manipulation that had threatened to overrun the temple in the last year.

There were other scents now and emotions that carried in from those present in the room. Need, fear, arousal, excitement and eager anticipation for the spilling of this woman's blood. Cruel, she had been cruel to most in the room at some point, forcing them through harsh levels of training, devotions that had been forgotten by many, hours spent in prayer instead of enjoying their status.

They wanted her dead. Every single man and woman in that room wanted Helena to suffer through the death of an offering. Well, they would be granted that pleasure soon enough.

And you want to kill her. She reminds you of the first life you took, that woman who controlled some of your training. What was her name again? Not that it matters. Humans, all the same at the end of the day, just another source of food. Well, then, take her life. Take a few mouthfuls for yourself, you're looking far too pale, my slut, and you will need your strength before my family arrives.

Family! His kin, the ones he had warned her about in the past. Did they exist, or was this nothing more than another of his mind games. He enjoyed those, twisting her expectations, leaving her wondering what would happen next.

Yes, just another one of his tricks. Prince of Lies, Master of Deception, those were the titles he should have laid claim to. Why should she believe him this time?

You've been wondering if we were the only ones left. Well, you will find out soon enough. Another reason to bring you back into line, my pet.

If she didn't growl, didn't let the others in the room see the way his whispered words affected her, then she might gain a little extra time to prepare. Helena first, then him, she'd need blood, enough blood and power to face him, stand up to him and finally make him see that she had changed.

My, my, the pet is going to challenge me. That should be interesting indeed. Well, then, little one, I will leave you to your preparations and wait for you in your chambers. Take all the time you need, at the end of the day the outcome will be the same. You'll be back on your belly at my feet, groveling, pleading to serve me. Exactly the way it should be.

No, not if it meant killing every member of the Devoted in the temple in order to be sated and ready to face him. She would not return to his feet. Not again. She took a long, slow breath, steadying herself as she turned her full attention on those in the chamber.

"I'm not ready to take that step." Helena whimpered, edging backwards towards the door. "There are others who are better suited to be offered to him. Men and women here in the temple who would plead for such an honor. I have duties I must attend to, devotions to oversee, younglings to train in his name. He would be better served by my life, not my death. I am sure he would agree with me."

"Are you claiming to know the will of Lord Traven better than his Chosen?"

"No, Milady. I just wonder if this has been thought through to the bitter end."

"Then you are either refusing this honor or suggesting that I do not seek to serve him? Perhaps you believe that you would be better as his Chosen than I am? That you would know how to serve him, or perhaps you believe that I am targeting you in some petty human need for revenge when you are nothing more to me than another of his Devoteds, a woman sworn to his service in whatever manner either he or I see fit?"

"No, Milady, I am suggesting that another, more worthy, take my place. One whose loss in the temple will not be missed. Perhaps one of the younger Devoteds?"

"It sounded as though you were making excuses." Small tremors ran through the Devoted's form; her nipples hardened beneath the thin robe, pressing against the rough material. "It would be a pity if you proved to be unworthy. You might not have the hope of a new life after you give up this one to his thirst. You know the fate that befalls traitors to his temple, don't you? You should, you've overseen how many executions before now?"

Helena paled fully. Being found to be a traitor, one who lied to gain power in service, would mean a death the likes of which had not been seen in several years. A death that meant days of slow torture, brought to the brink time and again before the last of her blood was finally drained from her body. Better the honored death of a sacrifice than a traitor's fate. "I understand. I just thought that another might better serve him this way."

"Ah, then be thankful that I have found you to be of worth, Devoted Helena. Or I might now look at questioning your reasons for serving in the temple. It would be a pity if it turned out you only served him in order to further your own desires, wouldn't it? A traitor's death is quite painful, and something of a rarity these days. Didn't you oversee the last one?"

"Yes, Milady." Helena nodded, her voice little more than a croak. "I would be honored to give my life to the Lord Traven in this sacrifice. And beg your forgiveness in how I addressed you earlier. I was caught off guard by the honor you have gifted me."

"Of course you would be, I never doubted it for a moment." Alayna smiled calmly, nodding towards the waiting altar. "You are, of course, a loyal servant of our Lord Traven."

Helena looked back over the assembled men and women one last time before she turned and walked to the altar of her own free will. "I will give my life to our Lord and know that the reward that awaits me in the next life outweighs all that I lose in this."

A slow smile tugged at the corners of Alayna's lips. Reward. They really believed in that. In all the years she had been in the temple she had never seen any return from such an offering. A small amount of blood they could survive, but a draining of this nature, no, that wasn't possible.

Pity Helena would not learn that until it was too late.

"One thing from you first, Devoted." Alayna reached out, tangling her fingers in the other woman's hair. "A kiss, to show that I send you to his embrace with my blessing."

Lips met, parting under Alayna's touch, a low moan vibrating in the back of Helena's throat, that moment of hope that such a kiss could not be given if death was to follow. Her tongue slipped into Helena's willing mouth, stroking, seeking, probing the depths of the trembling woman's mouth, the inside of her tender lips, learning each part of her. Such a soft, pliant mouth. A pity it belonged to a woman who made a serpent look like a warm-blooded creature.

The Devoted pressed closer, arching into Alayna's embrace, hardened nipples pressing against the robe. Alayna could feel the heat rise between Helena's thighs under the soft caress of her hand down the woman's back before the Chosen cupped Helena's taut ass cheeks.

Low murmurs filled the room at the sight those gathered now witnessed. Few had seen Helena like this, her sexual nature, the side she struggled to keep hidden from the others in the ranks of those that served Traven. Now they watched in rapt attention, fascinated by her reactions.

Alayna moaned, tracing soft, nibbling kisses down the woman's throat, licking over her throbbing pulse, capturing it between her lips and suckling a circle of warmth to the surface.

So easy, so tempting. A simple layer of skin between Alayna and the blood she could taste through the red mark. Just one small, quick bite.

No.

Alayna shuddered, breaking contact, pulling back from Helena and letting go of the woman's hair. "It is time, Devoted Helena. Time to receive the reward you so richly deserve."

Chapter Four

Rich, seductive and filled with life, Helena's blood slipped down her throat in a warm caress. She groaned, pressing back against the wall, thighs squeezing together, her need urged into life.

Screams. She could still hear the woman's screams. Urging her to cut deeper, delight in the death she granted the woman. Fear had turned into hope, only to crash into terror as the last of Helena's life had flickered in her eyes.

Delicious.

Gods, she had forgotten just how it felt to have her arms coated in the blood of another, their life ended at her hands, blood so rich that it fueled her body, mind and spirit in one brilliant burst of delight.

It still hadn't been enough.

She needed something else.

More blood.

Pain. Not hers, though, something from another source. The screams of another living soul. To feed from. A body squirming beneath her. Soft touches, low moans. Those delightful little noises they uttered at those interesting moments under the control of another living soul. Humans, they could become such delightful creatures when they were in the throes of sexual ecstasy.

She craved that now, the time with one of them as they lost themselves in the maelstrom of emotions and sensations such a time would create. Male. Female. It didn't matter. Not right now. Did it?

Maybe it did. How often did she choose one just for her needs? Not that often, less than a dozen times since she had first been permitted to wander amongst those of the temple with the full blessing of her creator.

Strange, she could still recall the first man she had chosen. Full lips, soft words, a cock that had filled her, stretched her body in such delightful ways. Her nails had left their mark on his flesh, his voice had carried her name through the temple in a tender worship she had never forgotten.

How long ago had that been?

Not that it mattered now. He was dead, like so many others. All the men and women she had known in her youth had long since turned to dust. Just as she should have if Traven had not taken her from the fold and turned her.

Her jaw tightened, anger burning bright for a moment only to fade into the dark craving she knew not to ignore. Shutting it out when it had already reached this point would turn into a hunger that would rage out of control and might cause the deaths of twenty or more men and women in the temple.

Too many lives to quickly replace in his service.

Yes. A male. She enjoyed those more. Women were sweet, but she had never truly been able to rid herself of the memory of Isabella. Not even when the women she had sported with had come to her without a trace of evil in their hearts, wanting nothing more than to please her however they could. The price she paid, no doubt, for feeling no regret at the woman's death. What had her mother said so many years ago? For every deed done or path ignored, there followed a price to be paid. This was the nature of the world, the way of the Gods themselves.

Funny, she hadn't noticed anything of that nature ruling Traven's life. He seemed immune to the ways of the world around him. Did he not even care just how they looked at him, how they craved to be like him or the lengths they would go to?

No, he just ignored it and went on with his own path.

Why would the top of the food chain be bound by the same rules as the very pack animals we feed from? Foolish little pet.

So much of you still thinks and reacts the same way as the herd beasts. A pity, really, I had such hopes for you. When you tore out Isabella's throat all those years ago, you showed me a glimpse of the real you. And now you've spent so much effort hiding that side of your nature.

Bastard. She had to find a way to shut him out of her mind once and for all.

"Milady, you wished something?" The door had barely opened enough to let the young woman in. The same one she had run into before the ceremony. Had she actually called out?

Not that it mattered now.

"Yes, fetch me the one that Helena picked out for the offering." She nodded, the answer coming before she had the chance to truly think it through. Still, it made sense; she had at least seen what that one looked like.

"Jason, Milady?" The young woman inquired.

"I don't care what his name is, just bring him." He would do nicely, and the relief he had felt at being saved from the altar, well, no doubt he would be suitably grateful once he arrived in the room. Yes, that worked, a willing male eager for her touch, joyfully pleasing the woman who had saved his life. His body...she recalled how pleasing it had been to the eyes and the way he had moved out of the chamber--even with his hurry to flee the room that had almost been his death--had held such promise of sensuality.

"Yes, Milady, at once." The young woman fled just as quickly as she had appeared in the room, her steps echoing down the corridor with the speed of her flight. Yes, after today very few of them would think twice about arguing with her, or even giving her the wrong type of look.

Every now and then it did them all good to learn just who held command here when Traven wasn't present. Too soft with them. She had been lax in her control of them. They were just humans, cattle, food sources, not the delicate creatures she had tried to protect for a time. If she had been stronger, kept a tight rein on those in the temple, then Helena and those like her would never be able to climb into any real form of power again. Nor would Kareena have stepped out of line and offered food to a man under punishment.

Not that Helena herself would ever be a problem again.

She'd seen to that.

Jason. Young. Well built. Nervous. Filled with a life energy and drive that would sate her, at least for now. He'd squirm well, and scream. After today he'd do almost anything he could in order to please her and repay her for the new chance of life.

Her heart raced, breath catching in the back of her throat. Not even in the room and she could feel him, taste him, enjoy the sensations of his skin pressed tightly against her own body. Heat built across her body, pulsing through her core, every inch of her skin alive, excited as she watched the door for signs of his arrival.

She needed to control herself, though, or it would be far too easy to take his life and not just the energy she now craved. Control, self-control, just another one of those things that Traven had hated her learning.

Of course I hated that, it took you further out of my control. Or so I thought. But now I begin to see that it just offers me another challenge, a way to enjoy forcing you back into your place. Enjoy your snack, little pet.

Pet. She'd show him. No longer the pet but a woman in charge of her life, her destiny and one strong enough to take her place at his side fully as his equal, not a slave, a pet or anything else. She had the strength to keep the urge to eat under control. The blood cravings would not be permitted to strip away her focus the way they once had.

By the time his kin arrived, she'd be a force to be reckoned with.

Others of their kind arriving. When? He hadn't said, of course. Trust him to leave that useful piece of information out of the conversation, if his voice in the back of her mind could ever be classed as conversation. How many would there be? And what would they be like?

Where there others like her? Ones who had been human at one point and then turned on the whim of their lords?

What about the females? She had studied the statues of his kind, yet the ones of the women had been vague, lacking power. Like other questions about her status and the world around her, she had tried to ask him about them, only to be brushed off. He had granted nothing more than a small nod, a slight hint that there had, at least at one point, been females like him but if they still existed, she had no idea.

Damn his arrogance.

Arrogant. The word fitted Traven well. And one as stubborn or perhaps blind as he did not see the need to hold in-depth conversations with slaves and beasts, or food sources such as those in the temple. Just once, she wanted to be able to truly hurt him. Lash out in a way that he could not heal instantly and make him feel even a fraction of the terror she had known under his control.

It would take a miracle in order for that to happen. She lacked the strength needed. Even if she fed for a hundred years without stopping, she still would not be able to match him blow for blow. He created her, turned her, but there had to be a way that she could finally break free of his control once and for all.

She just had to find it.

Perhaps the answer would come with the arrival of his kin?

And what if the answer you seek carries with it more danger than you are ready to face? Have you thought about that, little pet?

Yes, she had, and for that reason she hesitated even bringing the matter up as more than a random thought.

Good, I would hate to lose you due to rampant stupidity. There are worse things in life than being my pet. Live long enough, and you'll find out just what they are. Pray you make those discoveries through watching others and not being forced into those positions yourself.

A small sound; the door opening up again to the young, wary face of the man who she had sent from the altar only a few candle marks ago. His gaze widened, then lowered, softening as he realized who had sent for him. Had the maid not informed him beforehand? Not that it mattered. He was here now and would serve her very well indeed, or there would be hell to pay. "You sent for me, Milady?"

Chapter Five

Her gaze moved over Jason, taking in every inch of his well-formed body. She hadn't been able to take the time to examine him fully in the ceremonial chamber, but now Alayna enjoyed every inch of his flesh. A soft shiver of delight playing through her form at his entrance, each step he took flowed through his body with a catlike grace. He was delicious, just the way she had hoped he would be.

Could he see the blood on her lips? Not that it mattered if he did, he knew what she was, what Traven was. Such things were not hidden from those who lived in the temple. Word of the sacrifice would have spread through the temple. Had the story grown to a point where she had bathed in the blood of the dying woman yet?

No doubt it would do so before the setting of the moon. By the time the story had been finally retold, the simple but long and painful sacrifice would have turned into an orgy of blood, sex, pain and pleasure, which suited her well at this moment in time. If the exaggerations saved one foolish soul from offering themselves to Traven or the temple, then it would be worth the looks of horror that might turn her way.

But then she'd be denied a delicate meal when the craving hit her, or the chance to turn an innocent into a squirming toy at her feet.

No, she'd not lose her entertainment. How could she? All she had to do was send out a group of the temple guards or walk through the Devoteds to find one she found amusing. Or one like Jason.

"Yes, come, kneel before me, pet." She gestured to a spot on the floor, fixing her gaze on his well-sculpted form. How had she missed seeing him the temple before today?

Helena. No doubt the woman had taken pains to keep him hidden. Until the time he had crossed her one time too many.

His gaze flickered, fear touching soft blue eyes. The first of the stories had reached his ears. Yet behind the fear lay something else, a need, a desire that he took no pains to shield from her gaze. He wanted her. Even knowing what she was capable of, he craved to be near her, touch her, serve her.

So much the better.

"Yes, Milady."

She watched, barely able to refrain from licking her lips as he moved to his knees in front of her. Candlelight played over his well-built form, his skin slick from the oil that he had been prepared with for the ceremony, and he still wore nothing more than the loincloth she had seen him in by the side of the marble altar.

"You offered yourself to Lord Traven, or so Helena proclaimed. Is that true?" Her gaze lingered on his chest before playing a slow path down his taut and the white linen loincloth covering his groin.

"No, Milady." He didn't hesitate, shaking his head quickly. "I did no such thing, despite anything the Devoted Helena might have said about the matter." His voice was soft, cultured, as if he had been taught how to speak in a way that would attract attention from men and women alike. Something he had learned in the temple? Or in his life before then? She had lost so much in being locked behind the temple walls, missed small changes in the way lives now were lived.

Customs had changed.

Dress codes.

Even the way men and women were raised had altered in some subtle ways. When she had been chosen, no man would have been seen dead wearing any form of make-up. Now she saw men enter the temple for worship wearing kohl about their eyes, color on their cheeks, even tinges of it over their lips.

Such strange advances in the society she had been ripped from. But the cost had been worth the extended life she had been granted. No one knew for certain if she had the immortal life Traven laid claim to, but she had already outlived not only her mother but every single member of her family line, if the reports the Devoteds had been accurate.

"Then what happened?" Interesting, though not all that surprising, that a lie had been told. Helena and her twisted little games were well known in the temple, though no longer. No more games to play. No more men and women finding their lives ending in misery just because they looked at the woman the wrong way.

The death, however much she might regret it later, had played some purpose already if Jason was to be believed, and she saw no reason to look for lies hidden behind those perfect white teeth.

"I refused her advances, Milady." He shifted a little on his knees. "Several times over now. I don't believe she appreciated that."

"Why?" Interesting, not many would turn Helena down. "You prefer men? It is not against Traven's laws to enjoy your own sex, or prefer their company." He had to have known the danger of refusing a woman with Helena's mean spirit and power in the temple. Dangerous to say no to a woman like that, yet he had done so.

Courage, or just stupidity?

"No, Milady, not that." He shifted a little on his knees, heat burning in twin points across his cheeks. "It was nothing like that at all. She tried to see if I would be interested in serving her intimately in many ways, including offering me the sweetest of men to sport with."

"Then what was the problem?"

"It feels a little strange discussing it now, Milady."

"And I wish to know, so speak. Or are you ashamed?"

"No, not ashamed, I just did not wish it to come across the

wrong way. I would not wish to cause offense."

"I see. Then speak from your heart, Jason." Her gaze lingered on his chest before she dragged it back slowly towards his face and those full, soft lips. Long lashes, why did men seem to have such long, thick lashes when most women would kill to have them and did everything they could to find a way to make theirs look longer, thicker, fuller.

She almost chuckled at the thought. No matter what happened she still remained, at least partially, human in her tastes.

"She did not appeal to me, Milady. Her desires were blatant and they left me feeling ill. She wanted nothing more than to use me because I found her company distasteful. I refused, and when I continued to refuse, she had me dragged out to be prepared for the offering." He glanced up at her, his gaze soft, tender. "When you came in, I thought that if I could be granted one kiss from you before dying, then it would be worth it. You're his servant, his Chosen, as cruel and dark as he is, but you don't frighten me the way he does."

"Or the way Helena did?"

"Yes, Milady."

"Why is that?"

"I'm not sure. I know you're just as dangerous, if not more so. That you have spent so many years learning from Lord Traven. You could kill me without a thought, move before I had the chance to defend myself. You have more power at your command than Helena ever could dream of, yet I am not afraid of you."

"What do you feel, then?"

"Desire." Heat touched his cheeks in twin bright points. "I feel desire every time I look at you, or think of the chance I might have to serve you. I've carried your image in my heart since the first moment I was fortunate to lay eyes on you. She knew that, Helena. I believe she kept me from you in case I blurted something out, and it ate into her. I was something she could not touch, not fully."

"Interesting." She leaned back, struggling to keep focused instead of giving into her desires. It would have been so very easy just to take him, force him to the floor, taste him fully as she took his hardening cock into her body. "Yet you would serve me, knowing just how dangerous I can be?"

"Willingly, Milady, with all my heart. You could take my throat or my heart and I would accept that, embrace the death you offered me, knowing that I had pleased you. I just hope you would grant me a kiss before you took my life."

"You've not changed your mind since you entered the room and saw the blood on my lips?"

"No, Milady. Not at all. If anything, the craving has grown further. You are more beautiful than I had hoped."

"Pretty words."

"The truth, only ever the truth, Milady."

"Why should I believe you?"

"I have no reason to lie." He smiled softly.

"Don't you? Perhaps you seek a form of power in your own name, and see me as the key to that?" Her jaw tightened. How many had tried such games with her, tried and failed, then died beneath her teeth? Yet it didn't stop others from trying again. It never would. There'd always be some newcomer who thought that the rules didn't apply to them, or that they were too smart to be caught. Yet this one, this Jason, radiated sheer joy at being in her presence.

"No, never, Milady." Honesty. It vibrated from him. He didn't even think to lie, or hide his intentions.

Such a rare gift.

"Strip." Foolish, she needed to put a stop to this, send him away. If he remained she'd corrupt him, mark him for the rest of his life.

Yet he didn't care. He wanted her. Needed her. His gaze fixed on her face and each exhaled breath carried with it the sweet scent of desire.

He smiled, a light touching his young eyes. Humans. Twenty, thirty, even forty seemed young to her now. How old was he, twenty-five at most? Young enough to still think he was immortal, old enough to fear the brush with death he had endured, yet willing to take the risk again.

His gaze never left her face as he stood up, the small loincloth falling to the floor, his cock springing into life, hard, throbbing, the head already glistening with the first drops of pre-cum. Full, thick, eager in every way. "I would serve you, Milady. In any way you desire of me."

"Are you sure of that?" Why did she keep testing him, keep offering him chances to change his mind and leave?

"Yes, Milady. I have never been so sure of anything before in my life."

"And if I desire to hear you scream?"

"I accept that, willingly," he answered without a thought. "Do you wish me to kneel again, or crawl somewhere?"

He had perfect skin, unmarked and flawless. It would be so very easy to mar that perfection, taste his pain and fear combined.

"Fetch me the whip." Each room like this had them hanging from the walls. Toys waiting for use, sometimes barely repaired from one session before they would be snatched up for the next. "The single tail."

"At once, Milady." He turned, eager to obey, the fear she had witnessed earlier long since gone. He meant it. He would give his life if she desired it. Better one like him squirming under her touch than an unwilling victim.

Traven hadn't managed to corrupt her that far. Not when it came to her own personal pleasure.

Not yet, at least.

Never, if she had her way.

You've come close to it. You've been lucky that those you have summoned to serve you have wanted to please you. One day that will change. You'll call for entertainment and they will plead with you for their very life. Then what? The darkness is within you, my sweet slave. One day you'll accept that.

No, she'd never let herself be pushed that far.

Jason stalked back towards her, hips rolling with each step, his head held high, the whip resting across his open palm. Candlelight left a warm, glistening glow across his oiled form, his cock jutting out from the neatly trimmed patch of dark curly hair. Toned thighs, well-formed chest, taut ass; before he had come to the temple, he had taken good care of himself. From the way he walked, his work must have involved some form of hunting as his steps, when he was not running for his life, were almost silent.

She rose slowly, setting the now empty goblet down, small beads of blood collecting in the bottom of the simple pewter form. Had she drunk only one cup of blood? No, there had been more, two, perhaps three, the rest sent to Traven as the gift he had every right to enjoy. "Give me the whip."

Jason pressed the handle into her hand and stepped back. "Do you wish me bound, Milady? The pole or at the ring?"

"The ring." She smiled, curling the single tail in her hand, fingers playing over the braided handle. The ring that hung from the ceiling along with the chains she could attach to his wrists would work very well right now, giving her the chance to walk around him, passage to every part of his body, no matter what delights she decided to put him through. "I wish access to all of you."

He smiled, turning as he walked to the hanging metal ring. No fear, no doubt in his eyes. A strength that called to her, summoned her attention fully, fed her desires before she had even begun to grant them life.

How often did she indulge this part of her nature? Once, maybe twice a year? So why do it now?

Traven.

His arrival had changed everything.

Enslaved By Blood

If nothing else, this would show him she was no longer a submissive little pet, that she had taken that step from being a slave into being a Mistress. She ruled here, not him. She controlled her emotions, her drives, and would indulge them only when she wished to. Traven had failed to intimidate her.

Chains fastened quickly onto Jason's wrists, the wheel then turned on the wall, pulling Jason's hands above his head, forcing him onto his toes, his body pulled taut.

"Your last chance, little pet. Ask to be granted mercy, and I will let you go and send you back to your quarters." There, again she offered him a chance to walk away, to pull back from the danger he so willingly gave himself into. Would he beg, plead, ask for a reprieve? A part of her wanted him to, hoped he would realize just how dangerous it was to submit to a being like her, one touched by the darkness.

Touched by it, is that what you think has happened? Oh, my dear little pet, you are far more than simply touched by the darkness. You have become a part of it. A willing slut, an eager beast to writhe beneath my touch and now you seek to enjoy another. Good, build your pride, your strength, I will enjoy the struggle between us all the more. You gave in far too easily when I first claimed you. That fight died even before it began. Now you have the means to fight me at your fingertips. Take it, embrace it, enjoy the moments you have.

The presence, his voice, spirit, the feeling of being watched, finally eased for the first time since she had heard his voice earlier in the day. Damn him. Did he seek to provoke her further, push the control she had?

Of course he did.

He wanted her off balance, out of control, easier to reclaim.

It wouldn't happen. No matter what, she refused to take that step into being his, the helpless pet he had created. She ruled here, and with this life, this willing participant for her darkness, she would prove to all just how far away from the path of submission she had traveled.

"Milady, I want this, need this with you. You saved me today and I beg you, please, use me as you wish. If you want me to scream, I will. If you desire my blood, my soul, I give them to you freely." His soft, cultured voice brought her attention back to Jason.

"And if I wish your life?" She walked slowly around him, halting in front of him, meeting his gaze calmly. "What then, Jason? Would you offer me your life?"

"Yes, freely."

"Think carefully, I will ask this of you again." She lifted the whip upwards, stroking across his chest with the braided black leather. Light touches, a barely-there caress of the leather as it traced over his chest, the curled whip circling about his nipples. "Do you offer yourself to me of your own free will?"

"Yes, please, yes, Milady."

He had been given all the chances she was prepared to offer. Far more than most would think she needed to, but this way she had an unblemished heart. Without another word she stepped back, snapping out the whip with a flick of her wrist, leather snapping into the air with a loud pop.

His cock throbbed at the sound, a low moan of pleasure escaping his lips. She hadn't even touched him beyond the light caress and already he arched towards her. Interesting. Had she reacted the same way with Traven?

No, this wasn't the time to think about it.

"I'll make you scream," she promised, stepping a little further back from him, curling the whip through the air, the small knot at the end of the tail biting into his left thigh, urging a cry from his form.

"Yes, Mistress!" Jason moaned, his cock trembling as a hardened rod that beckoned her touch. "Please, do with me as you wish."

Snap! Leather bit into his skin, a bead of blood forming in

the middle of his chest, calling to her before she stepped around him, tracing the curve of his ass with the soft curl of leather. Taut buttock, well formed back, both would mark so well under the whip, leaving him carrying welts into the coming days, a memory of his time under her control.

The whip hissed through the air, leaving a line of fire across his upper back, his scream urging her on to the next blow.

Sweat, pain and blood mingled in the air, his breath a ragged sob for air in between the harsh blows. Welts raised on his body, lines that began as white then turned into an angry red, tinged with small, bright beads of blood.

She groaned, fighting the drive to run her tongue over the welts and taste the offering that beckoned to her with every beat of his trembling heart. Had he known it would be like this? Not that it mattered, he had been given the chance to leave, to find a way out of this. Instead, he had pleaded to stay.

Foolish little human.

When would they ever learn to take the chances to run when they had them?

A little more, just a little more pain and he would be ready.

Sweat beaded across his buttock, blending with the blood until it traced soft patterns down his calves. Sleek, powerful, he could have had almost any woman in the town he wanted as his mate. Not that he had that choice now, but she could see why Helena had desired him so much.

Not that the silly bitch would have been able to handle him.

A hiss, his scream, a new welt forming across his upper thighs, the leather wrapping about his legs, binding them in a circle of fire-touched pain until she tugged the whip away from his trapped form.

"Who do you belong to?" she asked.

"You, Mistress," he sobbed, no longer able to hold himself up on his feet, each new breath being released as a shuddering gasp. "I belong to you. Now and always."

"And who will you serve until your dying breath?" She cupped one taut ass cheek, brushing her lips along a welt, tasting him.

"You, my Mistress, only you, if you will have me."

Her vulva tightened, inner walls slick at his words. Hers. He begged to become hers. "I choose you, take you for my own. My pet, not my Chosen yet, but soon. Yes, soon." Her lips fastened about one bead of blood, suckling it into her mouth, tasting him. So young, rich, full of life and passions. Yes. He was the one.

Gods, she could almost come there and then from the taste of him. *Hold back. Keep it under control until the moment is right. Then enjoy him fully.*

"Yes, please, my Mistress, make me yours, to walk with you eternally."

"Soon," she whispered, forcing herself away from him. She needed him inside, his cock pressing into her core, filling her, his eyes wide as she rode him, claimed him. Then she could bite him, taste him as their passions soared.

The cuffs released from his wrists with nothing more than a thought. Traven had taught her that much in how to control the gifts his change had given her. Slowly she had learned more, trial and error during his time away from the temple.

Damn him. Even now, when she had a willing servant crawling to her feet, his body marked from the touch of the whip, every thought and desire focused on her, even now in that moment of control, her thoughts returned to the one who had made her.

Bastard.

He had no control over her, she would grant him no more thoughts.

"On your back, my slut," she snarled, dropping the whip to the floor, the soft silk of her robe following, pooling about her ankles with little more than a seductive whisper. "I want you now. I plan to take you, use you for my pleasure and if you please me, then I will grant you permission to enjoy yourself at the same time."

"Let me please you, Mistress." He moved onto his back, hissing in pain as the welts reacted to the pressure. "I beg to please you, to feel you closed about my cock, to rock up into your body. Your sweet, wonderful body."

Sweet. Had she ever been sweet?

Spoiled at times, headstrong, stubborn. Those words described her far better than sweet ever had.

"And why do you think I am sweet?"

"I look at you, Mistress, and I feel a need, a peace I have never known before. I knew it before today, long before today. I just never had the chance to speak to you. Helena saw to that. I think she knew about how I felt, what I wanted. That's why she became so angry when I would not serve her." He reached up towards her, hips thrust forwards. "Please, my Mistress, let me worship you."

How could she ignore a plea like that?

"Cross your hands above your head and do not move them until I give you leave." She lowered down over his hips, settling on her knees above him. "You are my pet to use as I wish, and helpless you will be in this moment."

Helpless, just as she had been.

His cock brushed against her inner thigh, thick, throbbing, needful with his desire to please her. Each welt burned across his back, thighs and ass, yet still he lay there, waiting for her touch, her pleasure, not moving, his gaze fixed on her form.

"You want to be able to touch me, don't you?" she whispered, cupping her own breasts, brushing her thumbs across her nipples. "I can see that in you. That craving burning in your eyes."

"Yes, Mistress, please let me touch you."

"Not yet." Her fingers closed on her firm nipples, pinching them, pulling them into tight buds before his eyes, her hips rolling, lower lips teasing across the throbbing head of his cock.

"I beg you, Mistress, just let me touch you for a moment."

"No. You will wait," she murmured, lowering a little more over his cock, feeling the head slide in between her lips. "I set the pace here, not you. Perhaps I will bring another man in here, have him fuck your sweet ass, would you like that?"

"Yes, my Mistress," he whimpered, arching upwards, hips pressing towards her. Even the threat of a man using him, something that would have made many a male blanch, had not changed his desires. What he offered her was so rare, so potent that she could no longer ignore it. True submission. A drive to please her, serve her, that carried far beyond his own desires for safety or well-being. A dangerous gift that would be easy to abuse. He knew nothing beyond his will to serve her. Perhaps it was only for the moment, perhaps it burned in him long enough to carry him through endless days and tormented nights, but only time would be the judge of that. "I know, I understand, I just crave to please you."

"And you will." In more ways than he would ever understand. What had she done to deserve this gift of a man's life and service? Nothing that she was aware of. Still, she would have to be a fool to turn him down, to refuse the offering he made of his own free will.

"Yes, my Mistress." He groaned as her cunt accepted him into her body, clenching about his hard, tight erection. Her walls rippled along his cock, images of him being ridden by another man as she felt him thrust into her body danced through her mind. Maybe not now, not this time, but in the future. Oh, so many pleasures they would share. He world would be opened before his eyes. A life of torturous sensations until he screamed her name with every breath. "Oh, Gods, yes!"

"You like that, don't you, little slut?" Her hips rolled, circling his cock slowly. Her body clenched on his erection, slick walls welcoming him, encircling him as she groaned, fighting to keep what little control she still owned.

"Yes." More a hiss of delight than a word. "You're my goddess, my Mistress! Everything I have ever wanted and so much more besides."

"Good," she groaned, rocking a little faster, feeling him press against her slick inner walls, forcing them wider. How long had it been since she had been with a man? Too long, close to a year. Self-control had become her life. "Yes, that's it, push upwards into me."

His heels pressed into the floor, arching deeper into her body, pressing him against that sweet hidden spot in her core.

"More," she moaned, her thighs tight on either side of his hips, one hand resting on his taut abdomen. "That's it, give me more."

"Yes!" he screamed. Only then did she realize her nails were digging into him, leaving long, deep welts across his body. "Thank you, Mistress, thank you for this pleasure, this moment."

Blood tainted the air, heavy, beckoning to her as she rocked down on his cock, building the desires higher in her own body, no longer caring about his reactions. Her toy, her plaything, he lived only to serve her now, to please her in any way she wanted him to.

"Taste me," he begged. "Let me feed you, share with you everything that I am and more besides. Grant me the chance to give you all the pleasures you have ever wanted."

Why not, why not take what he offered?

Her sex rippled along his cock, taking him deeper with each thrust, each rock of their bodies. The welts fed into his pain, building his drive, adding to the delicious scent on the air, the need, his wants, his desires, she offered him the chance to enjoy it all and he took it willingly.

She needed a little more.

With a low cry she sat up fully, one hand pressing between her thighs, seeking out that small, tight nub as his gaze fastened on the movement of her fingers. She moaned, thighs tightening, inner walls clenching with each rock, one slender finger dancing over her throbbing clit as she urged her passions into a burning rage of need.

"Please, let me touch you, Mistress." His gaze never moved from the play of her fingers between her thighs. "Let me please you."

"You already are," she groaned, sweat beaded across her breasts, her body shaking with need as she rocked down against him. So close, so very very close.

His pulse throbbed in his neck, calling to her. That's what she needed, his blood to set her over the edge. No matter how much a part of her wanted to deny it, deny what she had become, she was like her Lord now. A beast who needed blood to survive, not just blood, but all the potent emotions it could carry.

No, fight it. She had to fight it.

Why?

Why deny what she had become?

Foolish after all these years.

"Taste me, Mistress, I beg you, taste me."

How could she ignore such a delicious plea?

She moved, lowering down over his chest, lips fastening on his throat. She could feel it, taste it before she even moved to bite him. Just a single bite, a small taste.

Her teeth pierced into his throat, his body shuddering beneath hers, cock throbbing, swelling as he lingered on the verge of his own orgasm.

Fresh, hot, brilliantly laced with his passions, his blood surged across her tongue, slipping down her throat in waves of delight. Such strength, all his desires, his fears and hopes wrapped up in the sweet force of his life.

Control, she had to keep control, not take too much, not end his life.

Yet he gave it freely, offered himself up as a living sacrifice to her desires.

Sweet, filled with power, submitting to her with every fiber of his being. How could she not take all that he offered her and more?

Pleasure rocked through her body, her vulva tightening, liquid heat coating the inner walls of her sex as she screamed, lifting her teeth from his throat. He groaned beneath her, arching upwards, pressing his cock deeper into her core, grinding, forcing her into a second release on the heels of the first. Her mind reeled, thought lost as her body took over, primal instinct in the place of controlled desire.

Chapter Six

What had she done?

Jason lay unmoving on the stone floor, drained of life and blood alike, her body still tingling from everything she had taken from him. His essence had been torn from his corpse, leaving little more than an empty shell. Even in the throes of her bloodthirsty passion, she had wasted little more than a drop of blood here and there. Strange how that worked, how she could be so locked in the drive of the hunter, the killer, a beast that knew no mercy, yet so meticulous in preventing the loss of her food source.

Now she had committed the worse sin of all. At least in her eyes.

Loss of control. After all her hard work, all the times she had kept it under wraps, she had still managed to lose control.

Why?

Gods, why?

There were no Gods, she knew that now better than anyone else in the temple. No Gods, just blood-drinking demons who kept the populace under their control. Creatures of nightmares who took their pleasure without thought for anyone else, and hunted whatever took their fancy. Just like she had done.

Reduced to nothing more than an animal, hunting the humans as food, unable to prevent her reactions, control her lust. She had become lower than Traven, lower than the predators that roamed beyond the town boundaries.

Because of him. All because of Traven.

It's time.

No.

You don't have a choice.

If that were true, why was she still within the chamber and not running to his feet?

Come to me, or I will find you and it will be far worse for you, my pet. She could almost feel his touch, the caress of his fingers across her cheeks, that cup of her chin in the moment before the blow landed.

No, she'd stay away from him.

Why, so you can kill a few more pretty boys? You've lost your precious control, my Chosen, my Priestess. It's long past the time for you to accept who you are. Come to me! Now!

She moved a step towards the door before she could stop herself.

"I'm not even dressed."

Foolish little pet, do you think that matters to me?

"You can't make me do this, not in front of them."

Can't I?

"But they will see me like this, and know I have been summoned." All the time, the work she had put into her position here could die in a heartbeat.

Pride, such a wonderful thing. You've grown so proud of your station here, haven't you? Perhaps you've forgotten the times you crawled naked through the temple, curled at my feet, bore the signs of my pleasure and pain combined? Perhaps I should remind everyone here just who rules before my kin arrives.

Kin, his kin. Others like them. Her steps took on a swiftness she had not expected as she hurried through the door. It didn't matter that others saw her like this. They knew Traven was here, that she belonged to him, and as Priestess, no one would think to mock her for how she was dressed--or not, as the case may be.

Or so she hoped.

You can move faster than that, my pet.

Bastard. The only reason she now hurried was due to her lack of clothing, or so she tried to tell herself. Why else would she now almost run to him?

She wanted nothing of him, no touches, no reminders of what

it had been like at his feet. No push to return to that place. Yes, the only reason she had run to him had been the chill from the lack of clothing.

"You've become more stubborn than I remember you being." Traven murmured as she entered the room. Her rooms, except he had taken them over. In the short time she had been absent from them, they had changed and taken on a darker appearance. White silk drapes had become black silk, trimmed with deep scarlet edges.

Her bed now sported chains.

Whips, canes, paddles and more now openly decorated the walls, hanging from hooks ready for her to use, or be used on her. Though in many of the rooms in the temple the open appearance of the tools was quite normal, she had chosen to keep them hidden in a chest in her private quarters.

Was nothing sacred?

"I've had plenty of time to settle myself into the role you had chosen for me." She spoke calmly, trying not to let the situation antagonize her any further. What else had he changed? Had he destroyed her clothing, the small store of books she had taken solace in over the passing years, her journal?

Not that it mattered, he seemed able to read her thoughts. No matter what she had written in the pages of her journal, it paled compared to the thoughts that she had presumed would remain hidden in the back of her mind.

"I see." He rested back in her favorite chair. "And you truly believe you can remain in that position, regardless of my desires?"

"You picked the role, my Lord." The door finally closed behind her and then locked. His whim, no doubt. She could open it just as easily as he had locked it, but the small show of power and his wishes added to her growing discomfort. No point in wasting what energy she had by getting into a battle over a locked door. "I simply accepted it and went on with my work once it was clear you had left for some time."

"And I now choose to change that role, for a brief time at least."

Brief. For their kind, brief could be several years. Not something she wanted to endure. "And if I do not wish to find my role altered?"

"I don't recall mentioning you had a choice in this." His smile sent a chill through to her soul. "And you have already seen for yourself that you lack the ability to rein in your desires. That young man--Jason, wasn't it? You wanted him to remain alive, a possible Chosen, a pet to play with when it suited you? Yet you failed miserably in that. How did it feel to take his life? To know he died with your name on his lips?"

Her hands clenched into fists, lips pressed into a harsh, thin line. "A momentary lapse in control, nothing more. One I shall be sure not to repeat again."

Momentary, yet it had brought about a death. One she wished with all her heart that she could undo. If she had a little more understanding about her powers, the strange gifts that the change had brought about in her, then she might have been able to bring him over into the darkness.

Knowledge Traven had kept from her.

"Are you so sure about that?" He gaze locked with hers, that same cold, uncompromising stare she recalled of old. "I'm not. I know you, I made you, remember. I know the darkness within your heart. The cravings you struggle to keep under control. If you simply accepted them as a part of you, it would be so much easier on you. The bites, the changes you accepted, embraced, all set you on this path and there is no turning back." One slender finger tapped against the arm of the chair. "You look good naked, my slut, though I don't think it is fitting that you stand in the presence of your owner, do you? Kneel. I am sure you recall how to."

Yes, she knew.

"I have no desire to kneel, my Lord."

He rose, moving without warning. One moment he had been

sitting in the chair, the next he stood behind her, fingers tangled in her hair. "I don't recall giving you a choice, my pet. Now kneel!"

She struggled, trying to fight the grip in her hair, pain lancing through her head and shoulders. Long hair, he had never let her cut it, and during his time away she had forgotten just what it felt like to have her hair grasped in such a manner. Pain shot through her scalp, pulling along her skull. Her neck ached, eyes watered, hands clenched at her sides. In that moment, she would have agreed to almost anything in order to stop the pain she now endured.

Her knees buckled as she dropped to the floor, whimpering.

"Better. So much better, don't you agree?" He tugged once more on the handful of silken strands he still held before releasing them. "Thighs apart, head high, you know the position."

Yes, she did, how could she forget it after the years of training she had been through? Reluctantly she forced her thighs apart, resting her hands on her thighs, fingers clenching tight. Caved, she had caved with just a yank of her hair.

What had happened to the strength, her determination?

Reality and pain had chased them both into hiding, at least for now. "I don't believe that you expecting me to become your slave again is a wise choice, my Lord. We have so much to work on, and you told me that your kin is due to arrive."

"Indeed they are." He walked slowly around her before returning to the chair. "And they are expecting to find you at my feet. If I have to force you back to your rightful place, so be it. But you will be my little beast when you meet them. It would be ill advised of me to raise you above your station whilst they are here, don't you think?"

She tried not to watch how he moved, but the soft steps, his silent stalk still reminded her of a predator. Fitting, considering that's what he was. The ultimate hunter. How many lives had he taken? Hundreds? Thousands?

Did he even keep track of the lives he had ended?

"Am I not like you now, like others of your kin?" She frowned, trying to put the scant pieces of information together. If she pushed the conversation, perhaps she would learn a little more.

"No, you are not like either myself or my kin."

"But you turned me." What was she? If she had not become the same sort of creature as he had, then just what abomination had she become?

"Yes, and we were born into this state. You are one of the rare ones that began life as a mortal. I have never known such a time, nor have my kin. Even should you learn every facet of the powers that come with this life, you will never even begin to be my equal. Foolish little toy, did you really think I could turn you into a goddess?"

"But you said..."

"I told you they would call you a goddess. Not that you would become one. I will always know your true nature. So will my kin. All it takes it one look into your mind, to see the lack of control you have over the need to feed, over your desires, and it is easy to see you are nothing more than a slut granted an immortal life for the pleasure of the one that owns her."

Fury built in the pit of her stomach, an anger she struggled to control. Lashing out right now would do no good. Be patient, wait and she might find that moment, that time of weakness where she could prove to him--to all of them--that she was far more than a pet.

A play on words. He'd dangled immortality before her by a simple play on words.

There had to be a way, a clue hidden amongst the ancient writings of the temple. Once he had left on his hunts again, she would begin to search for the answers. There had to be an answer, a clue, something she could use. It was just a matter of finding it.

Yet even as she planned to search for the information, she knew it to be pointless. If such had existed in the temple it would have been found by now, or destroyed by Traven. She doubted he would have permitted such damaging information to be left anywhere she might stumble across it.

"You want to deny what you are? Hope to find a way to become something more than just a turned human?" His gaze narrowed on her kneeling form. "Foolish. You are exactly what you are. You can no more become one of my kind than a bird can become a fish."

"There has to be a way, Milord," she probed, watching his face for any signs that she was on the right track.

He leaned against one hand, watching her intently. "And how do you believe such a miracle could be performed? You think I have some magic key, a power I have kept secret in order to change your very nature? I can and have turned you into a shallow reflection of my status. Be happy with that."

"You took my life." Her hands clenched into tight fists.

"I raised you above the status of the cattle around us. You should be grateful for that, not be fighting against your fortune."

"I could have had a husband and children." If she had actually wanted them. Had there been a man she could have settled down with? Not one she had noticed in the town, but she had planned on traveling, seeing a little more of the world.

"And you would now be dead, some hundred or more years ago." His smile remained cold, violet gaze locking with her own, giving her no chance to pull away. "Buried so long ago that only dust would now remain. Do you even think anyone might recall your real name? Those who live now simply know you as my Chosen. How many even think to address you by your birth name now? A handful of the Devoteds, perhaps? Or a rare one that has studied the old records?"

Yes, she would now be dead, but it would have been able to live an honest life. She might have enjoyed the chance to explore her dreams. A time amongst real people, a husband, love, children, grandchildren.

"My line, the memory of my name, my deeds, would have

been carried by my line." Great-grandchildren, kin to spread out across the lands, yet his touch, his claiming had taken all of that potential from her.

"You truly believe you could have been happy as nothing more than a brood mare for some grasping, sweaty man who took what he wanted, only to then roll over and start snoring? Ah, Alayna, you have deluded yourself completely if that is the case. I recall your pride, your desire to travel and not be held back by your family. Especially your mother."

"My mother. I had almost forgotten about her." Strange how it easy she had pushed the memories of that fanatical creature from her mind. The spanking just before the presentation, odd how she recalled the small things. Had that been a test arranged by Traven? "She died, didn't she?"

"Yes, many years ago now, but in a manner that she enjoyed. Her blood fed me one night. She offered her throat to me freely and I, being the benevolent creature I am, granted her wish. She clung to me, her nails scratching my back as she gifted me her last breath. An honorable death, in her eyes at least. These humans are so easy to manipulate, but you're aware of that as well." His soft tone and violet gaze mocked her. "After all, you've done the same with others like young Jason. He begged for the chance to serve you and you granted that wish."

"I'm not like that, not some heartless creature that..."

"Are you so sure?"

"Yes, I don't commit the types of cruel acts I have seen you enjoy. I'm not a monster!"

"You mean one that hunts, kills for pleasure and food alike? Oh, my dear child, that is exactly what you are. Pity you lack the ability to accept that. However, it goes to prove my belief that you would be far better off at my feet. If you had the chance to step beyond the wards that have kept you locked within my temple, then you'd have hunted as well. You've dreamt of being able to do that, of walking through the towns, the villages, leaving nothing but death in your wake. I kept you from doing that. You don't have the control needed in order to stop before you wiped out every living soul in your hunting area. Yet my wards, my spells offered you a shield to hide your hunger behind. A pity you never thought of that when you raged against their existence." He gestured towards his boots. "Crawl, my pet, and show me how much you have missed me."

"No." The words gained life before she could prevent it. "I'm not a beast to be ordered to crawl around any longer. You have no right to do this to me."

"Hm, and what happens to a slave who disobeys?"

"I'm not a…"

"I asked a question. You've overseen the temple servants and slaves for some time now, you know the answer. What happens to a slave who disobeys their owner?" Thick lashes brushed against the pale upper curves of Traven's cheeks, leaving his half-lidded gaze fixed on her kneeling form.

Looking into the eyes of a snake would have been more comforting.

"They are punished."

"Yes, they are indeed, and what happens when a slave is not punished?"

She shifted a little on her knees, hesitating a moment as she tried to find a way to form her answer without making things worse for herself. "They believe that the rules no longer apply and will seek to break them further. Pushing more with each chance they get."

"Indeed." He pointed to his boots. "Last chance, little slut, crawl to my boots and show me how you have missed me."

Would doing so prevent him from punishing her? Perhaps it would, and in doing so, grant her a little longer to try and find a way to break free of the situation. Something to distract him? The arrival of the others, if they even existed. She didn't put it past him to be lying.

Enslaved By Blood

She glanced up at him, then back to his boots, swallowing hard as a cold sweat formed across her body, clinging to her breasts and taut belly. Slowly she lowered down to her hands and knees, nails catching on the rugs. Soft strands of hair brushed over her shoulders, her breasts tugging towards the floor, nipples hard as she crawled slowly across the floor towards his boots.

"You're out of practice, slut. You used to be far more sensual than this," he growled. "You can do better."

She stalled, looking up at him beneath the soft veil of her own hair. Better. She had not crawled in years, perhaps closer to a hundred years. How could he expect her to just be able to show the same level of sensuality, the same grace that she had struggled to learn all those years ago when there had been no call to practice it?

Her teeth caught on the inside of her cheek. How had she managed it before?

She moved a little closer to the floor, her ass raised high in the air, nipples brushing over the floor as she edged towards the dark leather of his boots. Full breasts swung with each move towards his boots. This had to work. If she distracted him, then it would buy her time.

Gritting her teeth, she lowered her lips down to his boots, brushing them lightly across the toes.

"Is that what you think I called you over here for, a brief kiss? Oh, surely you have not forgotten that much?"

No, she knew better than that. Nervously she slipped her tongue between her lips, tracing a light touch across the smooth toes. Small pieces of grit caught on her tongue, a taste she had hoped she would not have to experience again now bringing back a hundred unwanted memories

Crawling across the rooms and through endless corridors.

The feel of a plug buried deep in her ass.

The cold, mocking gazes of the Devoteds as she crawled, whipped and naked, through the corridors of the temple.

Those images now came crashing down about her shoulders, pressing her closer to his boots.

A low whimper formed at the back of her mind, her tongue tracing over his boots, slowly licking them clean. Small kisses covered the leather, her ass raised high, her vulva tightening on air, seeking to clench on something, anything that would add to her growing pleasure.

A pleasure she still wished to deny existed.

"Now you begin to recall what it was like."

She glanced up, biting back the low moan. "Yes, Milord. I do. A little, at least." Forgetting had been painful to attempt, yet still she had tried. Anyone in her position would have done the same thing, and now all her hard work was undone at the first hurdle.

"Good. It will make matters so much easier in the long run, though do not think me to be a fool. I know you are not simply going to bend to my every whim without a fight. I have given you far too much in the way of freedom to expect that." He reached down, running his fingers through her hair. "I have been lax. I allowed my interests in hunting to draw me away from you. And in doing so, my control over you slipped."

Hunting. Better he should spend his time tracking down new sources of food than be wasting it here with her. She had other things to do. The temple to get back into order, the body of Jason to see to, and a replacement for Helena.

"Your duties can wait, there is nothing that urgent. Your little snack has already been cleared away, and the Devoteds will be squabbling amongst themselves to settle the new chain of command between them. If they continue beyond tomorrow moonrise, I will settle the matter myself." His grip tightened in her hair, pulling her up onto her knees. "But there is still the matter of your earlier disobedience."

"I corrected my behavior." No, she didn't deserve to be punished, it wasn't fair to even suggest it.

"And a slave who is not punished will continue to find ways to disobey."

"I tried to please you," she protested, heart pounding in her chest, sweat building across her upper lip.

"Yes, but only after you were corrected." His grip tightened, tipping her head back. "I cannot permit what is mine to be that lax. Not unless I wish to spend the next month retraining you and taking pains that you obey me in every tiny detail."

"I will do better in future." Her heart skipped a beat.

"Of course you will, once I have corrected you fully."

"Milord, please." No, she wasn't ready to face his wrath again. Even though it had been years since she had squirmed at his feet, she hadn't forgotten what he used as punishment.

"Please, what?"

"Don't punish me. I was lax, I admit that, it won't happen again." She squirmed on her heels, back tight from the arch he forced into it through the cruel grip in her hair. "I'll remember what it meant to serve you, if you just give me a little time."

"Time? Is that all you believe you need. Time?"

"Yes, Milord." Alayna nodded.

"I disagree."

"But I am sure..."

"If all you need is time, then why are you still making a very basic mistake?" His free hand snapped through the air, cracking into the side of her face, the grip in her hair vanishing in the moment the blow landed. Lights danced across her vision, her body sent crashing to the floor in a sprawled heap, blood pooling inside her mouth.

He'd hit her.

After all these years, he had hit her as if she were nothing to him but a disobedient slave.

"Kneel!"

"You...hit me."

"And I will do so again if you do not kneel, slut." His voice turned cold, words biting into her soul with the harsh blast of the north wind. "Kneel!"

Her hands pushed at the floor, body shaking and the taste of blood now heavy on her tongue. Her vision was dazed, lights floating in multicolors across her eyes. How hard had he hit her? Enough to rattle her senses and more.

"Position."

Her thighs parted, breath shaking in her lungs. Funny, for a long time she'd thought them dead. The vampire lords and their kin did not breathe, yet she still did. Now she understood why. A pale reflection of her maker. Not human, not truly his kind, either. Instead, she had been turned into a mockery that existed somewhere between the two.

"Better. Much better. You're missing something in your attire, however, and you are still forgetting something very basic."

What?

"What does a slave call her owner?" He spoke softly.

Her heart sank. "Master."

"Indeed, and what does a slave wear to show she is owned?"

"A collar."

"Correct. Something I decided you no longer needed to wear when I left on my last hunt. However, you appear to have taken that as a way of being released from my service as the beast you are. I granted you position, clothes, the return of your name, and you took that as permission to act as you wished."

"I thought things had changed, Master." She almost whispered the last word. It choked her, threatened to press down against her chest with a weight she couldn't bear. "I honestly thought you had given me leave to be this way. I never thought..."

"Did I tell you that you were released?"

"No."

"Did I indicate that you would ever be anything more than a low, meaningless beast, a toy, a source of pleasure when I wished it?"

"No, Master."

"Then why did you assume things had changed?"

"You removed the collar," she murmured, lowering her gaze back to the spittle-shined boots. "I thought that meant I had been released, raised above the level of mere property. When I was granted the control of the temple, I assumed that I had been right. What slave could ever be placed in charge like that?"

"Ah, I see where your misconceptions have gained life."

"Misconceptions, Master?"

"The ones concerning your status. If you were just human, then I would agree with you, however, you are not. You're a beast, half kin, a shadow of my glorious self," he purred, brushing one thumb over her cheek, trailing a light touch down to her throat. "You are my creation, that places you higher than mere humans, but always lower than my kind. No matter what you do, how things change, that status will remain. You are my creation and property until the end of your days."

Her heart dropped into the pit of her stomach.

"And I plan to remind you just how low I can take you before my kin arrive."

Chapter Seven

A circle of metal had been locked about her throat, the leash snapped to the ring at the front of the collar connecting her to his hand. Nothing more than a leashed and owned beast, led through the corridors of the temple down towards the bowels of the temple in front of anyone that happened to be awake at the time. Shame colored her cheeks, her wrists bound tight behind her back, breasts thrust forward as she hurried after Traven.

Why now?

After all these years, why had his kin decided to appear at this moment?

If there was a reason behind the timing she had not been told about it, and he seemed in no mood for polite discussion.

One door opened, another closing behind them, shutting them away from the harsh gazes of the Devoteds and servants alike. How many laughed at her, at the way she had been paraded through the temple?

No doubt just as many had wanted to take her place.

Idiots.

They had no idea just how dark his tastes ran. In the years he had been absent from the temple they had been blessed by her control, not the cruel, harsh touches of the being that now sought to reclaim her. By the time he was done setting his hand upon those in the temple, the walls would be painted red from the spilled blood, new skulls would decorate the assembly hall, and a hundred new entrants to the ranks of the Devoted then culled from those that lived in the surrounding areas.

All because the beast had returned home.

"You remember this place, don't you, pet?"

Torches erupted into life, flames dancing over the pitch-covered ends, smoke curling towards the stone ceiling. The chamber, the one she had spent so much time in, the place he had turned her into nothing more than a crawling, begging, whimpering piece of owned flesh.

She hated this place. The memories of it had filled her nights with a delicious, unwanted torture and now she was forced to return here.

Bastard.

"Yes, Master, I remember." Her hands tightened into fists behind her, wrists still caught in the cords that bound them in the small of her back. "I remember this place very well indeed."

"Fearfully, it seems. I can taste it on the air, along with your arousal."

Mocking words, the memories of her screams replayed through her mind, the pain she had endured for his pleasure. The needles, the whip, bondage that had forced her body into twisted shapes until her muscles had cried out in pain, all his dark desires had been realized in this chamber and played out on her helpless body.

"Kneel by the frame." He unclipped the leash from her collar, curling the leash up before attaching it to his belt.

"Master, why is it so important you teach me things before your kin arrive?" she asked quietly as she walked towards the frame.

"Your behavior is just one of the many factors that they will judge me by. If I am found to be weak in my control of this province and all under my rule, then I face the risk of a challenge and the possibility of being replaced."

Replaced? Was that even possible?

"How could they do such a thing to you, my Master?" Alayna glanced up at him as she eased to her knees on the floor. "Do they rule you?"

"Not in the way you mean, but strength is important to my kind, and if they see a weakness, then they will act on it. A challenge would mean a fight between me and whoever it is that they would seek to take my place in ruling this area." His voice remained cold, gaze unwavering. "Be warned, my pet, do not seek to aid them in being rid of me. If I am replaced, then you will be killed or given to the one that takes my place. You will never be free. Think carefully on this. You know me, know some of my tastes and what I expect of you. I have granted you some small freedoms. Do you think another will be as caring of you?"

Caring. Is that what he had been? Not a word she would have associated with his treatment of her. He had beaten her, used her, turned her into a sexual plaything for his pleasure and yet he used the word caring?

Her stomach turned, knotting as it threatened to be rid of the blood she had taken from her last meal. If this use, this training was classed as being caring, then what did his kind see as harsh treatment?

"I'm not sure, Master."

"Beasts of your nature are often used as little more than feeding points. Eternal sources of blood and pain. I use you as that, I don't deny it, but I also grant you other things. Time alone. Moments in control of the humans around here." He spoke quietly, his gaze never leaving her body. "Think closely on this, little slut. Do you truly believe my kind will take well to a mere source of food being granted the type of power that you were?"

She frowned, listening to him. Would another of his kind be worse than him? Such a thing was hard to imagine.

"You will find out soon enough, little slut, when they arrive. One of my kin has a beast of his own. Take a good, long look into her eyes when she is here. See if you can imagine living as the shell she has become."

"A shell, Master?" What did he mean? Broken? Beaten? She had been through that herself, and yet had not become a mere shell.

"You will find out soon enough," his voice softened, a near

gentle touch tracing across her shoulders. "Just remember when you see her that I do not tear the soul from you. There are worse things in this life than belonging to me. Far worse."

His grip shifted, fingers sliding under the collar as he pulled her up onto her toes, turning her about until her belly pressed against the x-frame. A swift kick parted her thighs, leather straps fastened about her wrists, ankles and waist, keeping her tight to the wooden frame.

"I can smell you, little pet. Your mind screams no, that you are being forced into this, but the cravings I awoke in your body are not ones that are easily forgotten. How many days have you tossed and turned in your sarcophagus, hoping for a touch, that spark of pain to send you over the edge? How often have you woken from dreams of being controlled, crawling across the floor, your body sore from use, only to find your nails scraping at the coffin walls surrounding you?"

Her jaw clenched, heat blazing a path across her naked body. Unfair.

How had he known just what she had endured in the times he had been away?

Speaking to her in the back of her mind whilst he was in the temple had been enough of a shock, but to think he had been able to ready her all the time? No. Impossible.

"I know you, I'm always with you in some form, little pet. You should have known that by now. I've known your dreams, shared them with you, and your fears. I knew long before Jason was called to your room that you would pick him for a brief moment of pleasure. And you did enjoy him, didn't you, slut? Almost as much as the first life you took." He cupped her mound, one finger parting her lower lips.

"Please, don't." She tried to arch away from his touch, shame coloring her body from head to foot. "Please, I don't want this."

"Strange how you say that, and yet you're damp, little pet, very damp. Could it be that despite your protests, you really do crave my touch?" His finger pressed a little deeper into her body, forcing her walls to react. "You're clenching on my finger."

A lie, she wanted to cry out that he was lying, but her body had other ideas. A low moan slipped from her lips, her body tight on his finger, hips rolling towards the frame that her body had been held tight to. "Please, Master, I beg of you, don't push me back into this."

"Whyever not, dear little pet?" he purred into her ear.

"I can't do this again," she whimpered. "Please, Master, I can't become that again."

"Yes, you can, and you will." He pressed against that small shell-like hidden spot in her sex, rubbing over it, teasing her body into a heat she wanted to deny.

She arched, trying to pull away from the frame, thighs clenching, his finger tapping in time with her heartbeat. Sweat beaded across her body, slick need rose, coating her inner walls until she could smell her arousal clearly. No matter what she told him, what lies she permitted breath, her body craved this, just as it had since the day he had first claimed her as his Chosen. Foolish. She wanted to fight it, scream out against the thing he had turned her into, yet there she was, moaning eagerly, pressing against his touch and seeking more with each passing moment.

"Now you're ready, my slut, for what I really want from you." His finger pulled from between her thighs. "I'm sure you recall the pain I enjoy inflicting on others? The way I would come to you after they had screamed their last breath, carrying my name into the afterlife." He wiped his hand off against her bare ass.

"Yes, Master," she said her voice little more than a low moan of need.

"Then you won't be surprised by what I have in mind." Leather cracked through the air, a dozen tails striking her back and ass. Small points of pain exploded, welts rising instantly as she cried out, forced tight against the smooth wooden frame. "You still mark well, and I will make sure those marks, each small flower of pain remains until I am ready to let you heal our way."

Fear merged with pain, her inner thighs growing slick with the need that still rolled through her tight, rippling walls.

"You used to enjoy pain, under the right circumstances. And I know you have learned a little about how it feels to inflict pain in return. Jason saw that. The way you made him dance under the single tail, did you enjoy that?" Leather snapped against her back, the blades this time, not just the knotted ends. "You'd bring him back to life if you could, but only to take him down again and again, forcing him through the darkness with every ounce of cruelty you could muster. Deny it all you want, my slut, but the desire to cause pain is alive in you."

She screamed, arching tight in the bonds, nipples scraping against the wood as she squirmed, sobbing for breath with the dying cry of pain. His words made little sense as her mind tried to flee the pain, only to find there was no escape. No option to slip free from his tormenting touches.

"Nice. Very nice. You'll be able to show off these marks when they arrive."

A game, nothing more than a matter of showing who was in control. But what if they could read her thoughts, see into her mind the way he could? Would her beliefs then cause him problems?

"No, they won't. If they do pick up on your misguided thoughts, they will just assume that I am all the stronger for keeping you under my control without completely crushing your spirit." He laughed, stepping back a little further from the frame before he began to strike out at her back, ass and thighs in sharp blows, barely giving her a moment to breathe between one wave of fire and the next. "It's considered bad manners to pry into the mind of someone else's property. As strange as it might sound, manners, the protocol that governs our kind, is vital for the survival of our species."

Welts rose, points of pain merged with lines that striped her body.

He knew when and how to strike, what parts of her thighs would hurt the most and how to temper a blow so it brought her to the point of passing out without pushing her that extra edge into the darkness, a respite he refused to grant her.

"You've missed the pain. Admit it, little pet." He brushed the tails over her throbbing back, caressing each line, each welt that now marked her skin. "You crave this just as much as I do, you can't help it. This is who you are now, what you are. No matter how much you try to fight it, or what you do, you will always return to this place, this need. The squirming, helpless slut willing to do anything I want."

Had he pushed her that low before?

Yes, and she had come to love it, even crave it. Just the way he had once told her she would.

"You'll be there again, and soon. Maybe not in time for the start of their visit, but by the end of it. You won't even be able to recall what it was like not having that control in your life. I left you for too long, but it's a mistake I won't make again." He lashed out with the whip between her thighs. "I will make sure that they only see the pet, the willing little slut who answers to my every whim. No matter how dark that whim might be."

Knotted tails bit into her lower abdomen, the blades wrapping against her cunt, thin white lines of pain biting deep into her most sensitive of skin until she screamed from the depths of her soul.

"Ah, you liked that, didn't you? Perhaps later I'll take the crop to your cunt, beat you with it until you come from nothing more than those strikes."

Alayna shuddered, hanging against the frame, held up only by the leather straps. "Please, Master, no more, I can't take this. It's been too long. I'm begging you, stop!"

"You can, and you will." He tugged the leather away from her body, only to strike twice more. What kept her from collapsing from the pain she didn't know, but still, despite the angry lines of white-hot flame that now burned a path through her body, she clung to consciousness.

Sobs wracked her body, need rippled through her core and still she knew there was more to come.

"Ready for more? I think so, don't you?" The whip dropped to the floor as he walked around the frame, reaching for her breasts through the frame. His fingers captured her nipples, twisting hard on the small, trapped buds as he tugged them. "These tight little pieces of flesh would look well being decorated, don't you agree?"

Decorated. What did he mean?

Clamps?

Needles?

She had felt both from him before now.

"Yes, a little decoration, but first, your breasts seem to be lacking a color." He leaned in close, growling against her throat, his teeth scraping across her tender skin. Just a moment in his embrace, his teeth sinking into her flesh, arms wrapped tight about her body as she shuddered in delight.

No. Don't think about it, don't give into the pleasures he had opened her mind to. There were other things to think about, the times he had not been in her life. Times she would enjoy again.

Cord wrapped about her chest, beneath her breasts. With the way the frame stood, her breasts were easily accessible through the upper V of the wooden contraption. He tied the thin rope off beneath her breasts before winding it around her left breast, the skin tightening, flesh forced into a balloon shape before he began the same painful process on her other breast.

"Such a delightful sight," he murmured, tugging on her tight nipples, the skin of her breasts taut, swelling under the pressure of the cords. "You remember what it was like to wear a harness like this, don't you? How every sensation heightened with the pressure? You almost came a dozen times from the play I used to do on your breasts."

How could she forget?

Needles, the cane, wax, cuttings. He had experimented on her bound mounds a hundred times over, delighting in each new reaction and eagerly seeking the next.

"I've missed this, these times with you under my control." His nails dug into her trapped nipples, twisting them hard, tugging on the small, tight nubs until she had no option but to scream. "And there is the sound I have missed so much. Your screams brought me comfort when I was away from the temple."

Comfort, why would a being such as him need comfort?

Thought fled with the fresh twist to her aching flesh, a cry torn from lips as she arched and pressed against the wood. Too long since she had danced for him under the lash, sinking into the pain that he offered. Her mind tried to reject it and embrace it at the same time.

"You've missed it as well. Be honest, my pet." His fingers released their grip on her nipples as he stepped back away from the frame. "I know you have, you just lack the courage to admit it openly."

Missed it?

Yes, she had. However dark and twisted that made her, she had missed his touch, the pain and humble place he brought her to. All the pleasure that crashed through her body as he forced her to a plane of existence few knew to be possible.

"Admit it, slut. It's not such a difficult thing to say. Remember, I've seen you at your lowest, watched as you crawled across the floor, begging for my touch, to lick my boots clean, to service every man and woman in the temple if only it meant a slight smile of my approval." Chains rattled, the clink of clamps dangling from his hands. "I know that dark, willing place in your mind."

"Please," she whimpered, twisting weakly against the wooden frame.

"Please what, my pet?"

"Mercy, Master. I beg mercy." Tears streamed down her cheeks, fear knotting in the pit of her stomach as the beast gained new life with each breath she took.

"Why should I do that when I know what you desire, truly desire in your heart?" He cupped one soft cheek in his hand, thumb brushing over her jaw line. "I've known you better than anyone else that has ever walked this world. I watched as you turned from a naïve young woman into an eager plaything at my feet."

Had she been like that?

Perhaps at one point she had been.

"You'll return to that place all too soon, and then wonder how you ever left it, how you were able to walk away from it." Metal touched her nipples, closing slowly on the throbbing points of flesh, pressing them, squeezing them tight between the clamps. Pain shot through her body, her teeth clamped shut, lips thinning as she fought to prevent herself from crying out.

"You want to scream. I can see it in your eyes, but that delicious little stubborn streak has kicked in. Don't you think that I enjoy watching you struggle?" The clamps turned a little more as he spoke, threatening to flatten her nipples completely between the cold, unyielding metal grip.

A long, slow hiss escaped from between her clenched teeth, hands tightening into fists as she squirmed against the wood. Her vulva rippled, inner walls slick and coated, thighs glistening with her growing need.

Shame burned in her core, adding to the drive as her hips rocked against the wood.

"Please, I don't want this."

"Yes, you do."

"You're wrong. I want to leave. I don't want to become that creature again." She twisted, shaking her head. "Please, Master. Don't make me walk that path again. I couldn't bear it."

"You could leave, walk away or fight me. But in order to do that, you would have to actually want to escape this, and we both know you don't."

"Liar!"

"Oh, am I?" The door to the chamber unlocked, leather straps loosening about her wrists and ankles. "Prove it. Walk away now, and I won't stop you."

She looked towards the door, whimpering, her hands moving to the clamps on her breasts, the cords that bound about their swollen base. "You would just let me walk out? Remove the clamps, the cords and never look back at you again?"

"Yes, why not?" A sultry smile played over his full lips. "We both know you won't be able to leave. You're addicted to the pain and control I offer you."

"I lived without it." She took a step back, away from the frame, her fingers lingering on the clamps.

"Yes, and now you have the chance to enjoy it again."

"Something I don't want."

"Yet crave with every fiber of your being."

"No," she whimpered.

"Then why are you still here discussing this with me instead of fleeing this room and all the terrors it holds for you? Why are you standing there, not even removing the clamps from your nipples, when you know I won't stop you?" He spoke quietly, watching her every move, violet gaze lingering on her breasts before moving down to the heated patch of hair between her thighs. "I can smell the desire on you, the need, hear it carried across the room with each beat of your heart and still you try to deny it."

"I..." she faltered, unable to move.

"Yes?"

"I don't understand." Why didn't she run, flee the room? She wanted to, had to desire that freedom he now offered her.

"Yes, you do."

"I'm not going to stay here."

"Then leave, the door is open, the only person stopping you from leaving now is you." He nodded towards the door. "So why are you still standing there, little slut? Should I help you? Aid you out of the door?"

Her shoulders tensed, gaze narrowing on him, a single forced step moving her back from the frame. "No, I can leave on my own."

"Go then," he murmured.

"You really want me to leave?"

"Ah, but this isn't about what I want right now, is it?"

"But you're the Master, not I." She tried to take another step towards the door, but her body refused to obey. "Why would my needs matter?"

"Because I choose to let them in this moment. Prove to me you do not wish to be here, show me by walking out the door here and now. You have the choice before you." He walked around the frame, watching her closely as he settled in place and leaned against the wood.

Alayna closed her eyes, trying to focus past the pain in her nipples, pain that had become a low, constant throb matching each beat of her heart. Something had gone wrong, she should have moved towards the door, fled and sought out the sanctuary of her room in the full knowledge that he would not follow her. He had given his word. Promised her if she left of her own free will the collar, the time serving him, would be over.

Finally over.

She had a choice, one that she could ignore no longer.

Where would she go? Her life would become what? One chore after the next as she remained trapped in the temple, lacking purpose and reason? What sort of life was that?

She turned, walking across the room, her mind reeling.

Slowly, without hesitation, she walked towards him, easing to her knees, thighs parting wide. Her mind screamed in protest even as she lowered her head down to his boots and pressed her soft lips to the leather.

"Please, Master, don't send me away."

He reached down, grasping her by the hair as he pulled her up onto her knees, deep violet eyes meeting hers, holding her gaze. "I never will, my pet. You are mine for as long as you continue to live."

Chapter Eight

She hadn't left. He had offered her the chance to leave and instead she had crawled back to his feet. All right, walked, but the result had been the same thing. She had bound herself back to him willingly, knowing just what it meant, the darkness that he would now expect her to embrace.

"Will you finally accept what you are?" His fingers slid through her hair, cupping her chin. "That you are my pet, a toy, a slut and can never be anything but that when you are with me?"

She wanted to say no, deny it, but the way she had moved to his feet had destroyed the majority of her ability to fight. "Yes, my Master."

"You missed it, didn't you? The control, the way I made you feel." He spoke in a soft, seductive whisper that teased an answer from her before she could prevent it.

"Yes, my Master, more than I ever thought I would."

"That is the nature of being a slave. Though a part of you now enjoys controlling others, you could never truly be at peace without the safety of being able to submit to me." He brushed a soft touch across her lips with his fingers.

Submitting to him offered safety? She frowned for a moment, trying to make sense of the words. Her stomach rolled, images flashing through her mind of the times she had curled at his feet, knowing that she belonged there, understanding that no matter what he remained in control. "I think I begin to understand."

"Good, it will make life easier for us both during my kin's visit." His hand dropped away from her face, and she found herself craving the contact the moment it was withdrawn. "They will be expecting you to be submissive, obedient and curled at my feet as the little pet you are. You'll not let me down now. I know that."

Alayna shivered, her thighs parted wide, taut ass resting on her heels. The clamps remained on her nipples, cords tight around her swollen breasts, heat burning between her thighs. She needed him. No matter how she tried to justify it, she needed what he offered.

"I've missed you, Master." Her throat tightened, the words difficult to say at first. "I waited for you to return for a year, maybe longer, then started to wonder if you had found someone else to replace me. I won't let you down when they arrive. I swear to you that I won't."

"No, I allowed myself to be caught up in the thrill of the hunt. Time has little meaning to my kind, so I forgot how long it had been since I had enjoyed the presence of your company at my feet." He shrugged slightly, dismissing her concerns. "Now I have returned, and the matter is ended." He reached down, taking hold of the chain between her clamped nipples and pulling sharply on it.

She whimpered, squirming on her knees.

"Ah, you used to scream so nicely." He lashed out with one hand, knocking her to the floor with a crack that blossomed across her face. Her vision dazed, breath turning into a ragged, sobbed scream as she struggled back to her knees.

"You remembered the rule about positions, good." He nodded, looking down at her.

"Yes, Master." Blood coated her lips, teasing her with the growing need to feed.

"I should toss you out to the guards. I could let them take you, just to see if you remember how to please a man in the guise of a slave."

Alayna shuddered, thighs tensing, fighting the urge to close them and hide the arousal that she could feel coating her lower lips. "If that is your wish, Master."

"You'd crawl to them and beg to please them for me, wouldn't you?"

Heat claimed her cheeks, a dozen unseen hands playing over her body, teasing with light touches. A caress stroking over her clit before the mental hands vanished, leaving her squirming on the floor.

"Such a pretty little slut." He moved slowly to his knees, grasping her by the shoulders as he pushed her down onto the floor. "You used to squirm well beneath me. Do you remember how to do that?"

Alayna tried to resist, but only for a moment. The stone floor, cold and hard dug into her back, his knees parting her thighs, fingers pressing into her shoulders. "Yes, Master. I think so."

"There's only one way to find out." His teeth grazed her neck, nipping into her flesh, enough to scratch but not bite. A sharp point of pain as he settled between her thighs, one hand tight in her hair, forcing an arch into her back. Even now, when he wanted to take her, there would be no doubt on which of them ruled here.

"You missed me, Master?" she whispered against his neck, feeling her own sharp teeth, the desire to sink them into his neck building. But she didn't have permission to bite him, and that had been a mistake she had made only a handful of times.

Dangerous. He had warned her just how dangerous it was for her to try and bite his neck without consent. To take the blood and power for her own.

Blood and power. They combined as one in so many things in her new life.

"You have your uses," he admitted, his free hand releasing his cock. "You're my slave, a beast, a pet. It is not unheard of to feel something towards a pet."

She arched towards him, hips raised, seeking to welcome his cock into her body. It didn't matter that she was nothing to him but a beast, not any more. Her fingers tightened in his arms, holding him close, rolling her sex towards the throbbing outline of his erection.

"Fuck me, please."

"The beast begs to be used?" he teased, easing down, catching the chain that linked her nipples between his teeth, tugging it.

"Yes," she hissed.

"You will have to do so much better than that."

"Master?"

"If you want to be used, you need to beg, fully," he growled against her breasts, his cock pressing at her inner thighs. "Show me how much you have missed me, tell me what you want to feel, how you wish to be controlled."

Condemn herself with her own words, that's what he wanted. It wasn't enough that she had returned to his feet freely, that she had come to him and admitted that she missed being controlled by him, or that she craved to know what that was like again. Now he wanted more of her?

How far did he expect her to lower herself?

All the way, or so it seemed.

He lifted up from her long enough to strip the shirt from his body, tossing it aside, his boots and pants following quickly afterwards. The belt pulled from his pants, folded over in his hands, ready to use on her should he desire to. Then he returned, pressing between her thighs. His cock slid along her inner thigh, teasing her slick cunt lips as she groaned, trying to keep from begging there and then. He enjoyed the slow play, the building need in the body of the woman he now sought to use, why would she risk taking away any of his pleasure?

No, not just his. *Their* pleasure.

She moaned, hips pressing to him, thighs parting wider as she tried to pull him into her warm, moist core. She'd missed this. No matter what man or woman she picked out from those in the temple, it didn't feel the same. The pleasure lacked a level of intensity that she had only ever known under his touch.

"Beg for me, slut." His cock, so close, teased at her sex, yet he still denied to her. "Beg for what you want. You know how to, you remember how to, don't you?"

Yes, she did.

Her nails dug into his arms, piercing the flesh, blood tainting the air as she pressed against him. "Please, Master, fuck me, use me, I beg you. Fill me, let me moan for you." She reached up, nipping softly at his chest, licking along his collarbone. "Let me please you, Master, bend to you, whimper and scream as you slide your cock into my cunt, stretching me as I writhe beneath you."

He groaned, looking down at her, passion lending an unholy glow to his eyes. "Yes, my pet, yes."

"Use me, Master, please."

"Until the end of days." His cock slid into her warm, willing body, thrusting deep within her core, one hand tight in her hair, holding her to him. "Mine. My slut, my pet."

"Yours, Master," she whimpered, lifting to meet each thrust as he rocked deep into her body.

"Willingly."

"Yes!" Her thighs locked about his hips, bound breasts trapped against his chest, the clamps biting into her flesh, urging fresh waves of pain through her body with each deep thrust.

"Fuck back against me, slut, writhe, show me how eager you are," he growled, biting at her shoulder, fresh blood trickling down her arm from the bite. "Rock with me, clench, milk me."

Her cunt walls tightened, rippling about his cock, squeezing with each thrust as she lifted her hips upwards, ankles locking behind his ass. She'd never known a man like him; his thrusts powered her passion, sending her higher with each new jolt of pain and pleasure. Even the scrape of the stone tiles beneath her back added to the joy that threatened to surge out of control.

Sweat beaded over her breasts, tension grew, her body no longer her own, just the way he wanted it to be. The scent of sex filled the air, mingling with blood and the soft, low grunts as her body welcomed his thrusts into her clenching core.

So close, so very close.

"Give it to me, pet. Give me your pleasure, your submission."

She wasn't ready, yet her body tried to obey.

"Release your fears, slut. Scream as you come, scream as the pleasure becomes too much to ignore."

Fear surged into life, one hand sliding between them, closing on the chain between her breasts. Instinctively she knew what he meant to do, and tried to deny him. "Please…"

"You need it."

"No." A soft whimper, her pussy tight about his thick erection.

"Your body says otherwise."

Betrayed by her own desires.

She whimpered, trying to fight against the rising pressure in her core, but each thrust sent her higher. Waves of delight surged through her core, pounding in her veins until all she could hear was the rush resounding in her ears.

"Come for me!"

She screamed, nails biting deep into his arms, back arching, liquid heat wrapping around his cock as she tightened beneath him. Still it wasn't enough for him. With a single yank the chain was pulled from her body, small metal teeth releasing their grip on her throbbing nipples, turning a scream into an animalistic cry of pain and pleasure.

"Mine!" he cried out, sinking his teeth into her neck, tasting her fully as she shuddered beneath him. His cock throbbed against her spasm-ridden walls, swelling as he grunted into her neck, "Always mine!"

Chapter Nine

"Do you think we're finished?" he murmured against her throat.

"Master?" She lay beneath him on the cold stone floor, shuddering from the effects of the orgasm that had surged through her body.

"We've only just begun, my sweet slut." He tugged softly at the cords about the base of her breasts, pulling it slowly free.

Sensation surged back through her breasts, blood forcing its way through the tender mounds until she arched, crying out with the new rush of delight.

"You nearly came from that, didn't you, slut?"

Alayna whimpered, heat burning in her cheeks.

"Good, very good indeed." His hands tightened on her shoulders, forcing her up to her feet and across the room. Before she had the chance to scream, she felt him press her against the low bench, her ass raised high in the air.

She'd barely had the chance to come down from one release when he had forced her from the floor. Her mind reeled, lips parted in a cry of terror and desire. Willow split the air, cracking down on her ass, welts rising instantly under the thin, brutal strokes.

Alayna screamed, struggling against the wood, trying to find a way free of his grip, but chains would have been easier to break free from.

"Mine!" he snarled, laying stroke after stroke across her ass.

Sobs wracked her body, her fingers tight on the edge of the bench, breasts--still tender from the release of the clamps and cord--pressed almost flat against the wood. She barely even had time to realize the switch had been tossed aside before she felt him move fully behind her, his cock pressing against her asshole.

Oil touched the ring of muscle, mingling with her own juices and sweat. She struggled, trying to protest as the thick erection, still slick from her use only a short while before, pressed against her tight dark star.

"My beast, my slut, my whore, aren't you?"

"Yes," she whimpered, hips pressing back against him.

"You want this, to be used as the lowest slave in existence."

No. She didn't want this, not like this, yet her body said otherwise. Hips arched towards him, lifted and welcomed him as he thrust into her ass, tearing a soul-numbing scream from her lips.

"Try to deny it, slut, but you love this." His hands gripped her thighs, cock sliding into her tight, dark hole. "The pain slips away, pleasure rises until you no longer know where one ends and the next begins."

She groaned, head low against the bench, heat building within her sex, a driving force that she could no longer ignore. His cock, slick from taking her cunt, now thrust into the darkest depths of her body.

Alayna groaned, pressing back against him, thighs tensing at each thrust. Her buttocks burned from the switch, cunt rippled as if filled with his cock, passion and pain blending one into the other as she tried to meet each new push into her willing body.

"You're going to come for me, aren't you, pet?" he moaned against her back. "You'll come, scream and give yourself to me."

"I already have," she whimpered, pressing back against him, hips grinding with each delicious thrust into her sensitive body. Shudders ran through her body, pressure building between her thighs as her breath came in short, ragged gulps. Blood rushed through her body, roaring in her ears as she arched beneath him.

Hardened nipples scraped against the wood. Her body writhed under him, thighs tense, slick, heated. She didn't care how it looked, or what she lost by surrendering to him. She needed this, craved this and she had missed his control with every breath she had taken in his absence.

Walls of lies crashed down, destroyed.

His. She belonged to him, body mind and soul.

"I'm yours, Master."

"Scream it for me." One hand released her hip, tangling into her hair, forcing her head back as she lay, trapped against the bench. "Scream it for me and come!"

Sweat stung her eyes as she pressed up from the wood, her taut, well-marked ass thrust back against his body, her scream echoing through the dark chamber as her mind fled into the darkness.

Chapter Ten

Her body ached, but the welts had faded by the time she awoke on the floor. No soft caress or caring arms wrapped about her. Those had never been a part of his ownership. She classed herself fortunate to find a blanket had been tossed over her at some point during her sleep.

"Awake, my slut?"

"Yes, Master," she murmured, rolling over onto her belly as she peered into the dimly lit room. Where was he?

There, a shadow of a figure by the door, already dressed. No one else would have dared to enter the room without his permission, and she could see no other signs of life. "Was I asleep that long?"

"Long enough for the sun to have risen and set again. Up. You have to wash, prepare for presentation."

She frowned, confused for a moment until the memories returned. Such a long sleep? Had it been close to sunrise by the time they had finished? She couldn't recall being that drained. "Your kin?"

"On their way as we speak."

She nodded softly, pushing up from the floor. Her legs felt odd, wobbly, unwilling to work as well as they should. A chill coated her body, turning a stretch into a shiver as goosebumps raised along her skin. "Where do you wish me once I have bathed, Master?"

"My chamber. I am sure you recall where it is."

She nodded softly, hurrying towards the door. His kin. At last she would meet others of his kind and perhaps understand just what it was about them that caused them to be such creatures of cruelty. She had so many questions, but the hope of them being answered was slim at best.

Enslaved By Blood

Barefoot and still naked, she hurried out of the chamber, glancing back once, but she already knew he would not be there. He had other matters to attend to, beyond that of taking care of his property. Especially when he knew the woman was capable of looking after herself.

Hot water closed about her body, welcoming her as she slid into the bath. Cold despite the passion of his touch, she remained chilled to the bone until she had been able to seek the respite of the bath.

The blanket, at least he had given her that. Enough to keep the chill from becoming too much, but still she felt the knives' edge of the cold even as she sat in the bath. Soft towels had been laid out around the bath. Three women stood along one wall, their eyes downcast as they waited to tend her, should she desire it. Despite the collar she now wore about her throat she was still their Priestess, or so it appeared, a fact that relieved her more than she thought it would.

"Did you need anything, Milady?" A soft voice, one she remembered; the maid from the corridor. "You look drained. Almost as if you haven't been fed in a week. I've never seen you looking like this before."

"I feel it, but no. Until my Lord Traven gives me leave to feed, I must refrain from doing so." That part she needed no reminder on. Did she need the blood? Not really, but she needed something in order to help steady her nerves.

"If not blood, then something else? I have seen you take wine on rare occasions. Would that aid you?" The soft-eyed woman knelt at the edge of the bath.

"Why are you so kind to me, even after I turned you away?"

"You are the Priestess."

"And I turned you away." She moved in the bath, twisting so she could see the young woman's face. "I denied you the one thing you wanted."

"You have every right to, Milady. You are the Priestess, and I am but a temple servant. It is never for the servant to say what the mistress should do." A gentle smile graced the woman's lips.

"What's your name?'

"Brianna, Milady."

"A pretty name, and how long have you served in the temple?" Her thighs pressed tightly together in the warmth of the bath. Even after she had served Traven in such a deep, intimate manner, her craving for more sparked quickly back into life. What would it be like to kiss those soft lips?

"Five years now." Twin points of color burned in the woman's cheeks. "I have been here since I became a woman."

"And have you been touched?"

"No, Milady. I have kept to my work, and hoped that one who was worthy would look on me with favor." Brianna shifted on her knees at the edge of the bath, her hair mussed by the soft tendrils of steam that filled the room.

"Rare in the temple," she noted, picking up the soap, building up a lather as she watched the maid closely. "Most have at least known the touch of a man or woman at some point."

"I have kept myself busy, Milady."

"So it would seem." Her gaze lingered on Brianna before Alayna ducked under the water to wash off the soap from her body.

Interesting. One small session and you become the slut in heat. Good, very good, but if you seek to sport with her, save it for another time, my pet. I believe it would be interesting to watch you set this innocent to her tasks. How would it feel to have her tongue squirm into your ass, her fingers buried in your sweet cunt as you grasped her hair, controlled her every move, but always knowing that I could tear you both apart and return you at my whim to the low, helpless slut you truly are?

She shuddered, looking up at the maid with a fresh hunger in her gaze.

Ah, it will have to wait until later. Remember, my kin arrives.

Enslaved By Blood

You have little more than the time to bathe, be oiled and present yourself in my chamber before they arrive.

Not long enough for anything more than offering Brianna a moment of hope for another time. "Dry and oil me." Alayna pushed out of the bath, looking over the maid. There would be another time after the visit, and then they could sport a little. She might even be able to push away the memories of Isabella with the soft, seductive touches offered.

"Yes, Milady." A soft, warm towel wrapped about her body, gentle hands leading her across the room to the padded bench. Strange. Once she had feared this type of preparation, now she welcomed it, knowing it meant she would be found pleasing to her owner.

Gentle touches caressed her body, drying off the remaining water from the bath as she eased down onto the bench. Soft fingers slid the oil over her skin, working it into her body, preparing her sex and ass both. Always ready to be used, that had been one of his rules, one she knew would be fully back in place now he had returned.

She'd fought them preparing her once, shrank back in terror from the intimate touches that turned her into a ready slut for use. Now she relaxed under the experienced caress.

His voice dragged her from the safe, warm place her mind had sunk into. Commanding her attention the way no other could.

Come, my pet. They arrive.

Chapter Eleven

Lamps flickered in his room, bathing the chamber with a soft, welcoming orange glow as she hurried to his feet. She'd barely had time to run a brush through her hair before running from the bathhouse, almost knocking over one of the Devoted along the way.

Traven gestured to a spot at the side of his boots. "Good, they will be here in a moment or two at the most. Kneel and keep your gaze lowered unless commanded otherwise. Do not move without permission and do not speak. Is that clear?"

"Yes, Master." She glanced up long enough to catch a glimpse of his eyes before kneeling fully, her thighs pushed wide, oil glistening on her newly bathed skin.

"They will test you."

She nodded softly, keeping her gaze lowered in case they entered before she had the chance to correct her position.

"Be aware of that, little pet. They will test us both."

She had no doubt of that, just from what she knew of the one that owned her. He tested, with every passing day had tested, especially in the early days of the collar. Small tests, large ones, pushing to see if she would break position, testing her reactions to different sensations, pain, pleasure, control, all rolled into one. That he warned of his kin and any testing they might wish to engage in did not surprise her.

"Do not fail me, pet." His warning came a heartbeat before the double doors opened. She tensed, fighting the urge to look up and see who had entered. Four sets of footfalls, booted ones by the sounds of it, and a fifth pair, barefoot, lighter than the rest, rang through the chamber, the doors closing behind the newcomers.

"It has been a long time, brothers."

Brothers. No women with them?

Alayna barely smoothed her brow clear of the frown before she felt their gaze upon her.

"Too long, but travels tend to keep our kind separated for the most part." A voice like liquid velvet, male, filled with power. It urged her to look up, steal a glance in his direction, but she fought it, her nails digging into her palms, offering a bright point of pain to counteract the tug of that seductive voice.

"You're looking well, Bastian." Her Master spoke, and she tried to draw comfort from his presence. "And Gullian, you seem ill at ease, does my home not suit you?"

"There is something lacking about it." Gullian, at least she presumed that was the one who answered. "I feel you have strayed from our ways, and this temple lacks the level of control that should be an everyday part of their ways."

"Those here are kept under a strict control, have no doubt on that."

"Why should I believe you? Look at the beast at your feet. She has not even attempted to greet or acknowledge our presence. Where is the respect in that?"

"She was commanded not to move until told otherwise."

"Interesting," Bastian mused. "She ignored the pull of my voice in order to obey your command. Impressive. I know of few humans who manage such. Normally they cave at the first caress of control."

"She is not fully human."

Silence settled on the room, one that left her struggling not to squirm as she felt the gaze of at least four men settle on her form.

"What do you mean by not fully human?" Bastian demanded. "You turned one of the temple females? You dared such without seeking sanction from the Blood Council?"

"Why would I need such an action sanctioned? I have the right to take one toy at a time. One turned female to meet my needs and beget, when the time is right, a child on her so that the line, our line, may continue."

"You are young, too young to make such a choice without aid." Bastian's voice lost its smooth, seductive edge. "You should have sent word so we might advise you on which female would be best suited for you."

Her mind reeled, the information crashing down on her almost too quickly for Alayna to sort through it. He needed permission to take a pet, a Chosen? Calm, focus, don't let them see how riled the conversation was making her. She had to keep from disobeying Traven if she did not wish to make matters worse for him.

"According to you, but I rule here, and have done for generations by their measure. I have long since passed the time when I might need the aid of the council for such a simple decision."

"You are still young, and the female might not be suitable for breeding." Gullian protested. "How do you know she will survive it? She seems weak, ill suited for this life. I doubt the creature could withstand even the basic ways of our life."

"How do I know for certain?" Traven's fingers smoothed over Alayna's hair before tightening in a firm grip as he forced her head up. "Because it has been close to two hundred and seventy years by their measurements of time since I turned her."

She tried to bite back the whimper that formed at the back of her throat.

"Look at them, my pet. These are my kin. My brothers." *These are the ones who might try and take you from me if they disapprove of my choice. Look on them and be proud of who you belong to. Look on them, and show no fear.*

Alayna felt her gaze drawn to the four men, each one dressed in the same well-cut dark clothing she had grown used to seeing Traven wear. Handsome, cruel with the violet eyes she had only seen in her Master up until this day. But where he looked on her and left her shivering in need, their attention left her stomach churning, hands clenched tight on her thighs. They looked on her as if she were nothing more than a bug to be squashed beneath their feet, or a meal about to be served up to them.

"She is my Chosen and my property. If you have a problem with that, then speak on it now, as I have no intention of seeing her destroyed."

"That is a matter that must as yet be discussed, Traven. You have pushed too far in claiming the female as your own." Gullian stared at her. "However, I might be persuaded to overlook the matter with the right sweetening of the pot."

Her stomach rolled at the words, and the only thing that managed to keep her from curling up into a ball was the grip in her hair.

"Just what are you talking about?" Traven growled.

"Before I go any further, I wish a taste of your property."

"You will not feed from what is mine."

"Brother, dearest brother, not that type of taste. A kiss. I would sample her mouth before I decide if I need to sample her other skills."

Heavens no.

If Bastian had demanded such, then she could have faced it with a smile, but the longer she looked at Gullian, the more her stomach turned and threatened to empty. He had no right to demand such from her. She didn't belong to him.

Alayna swallowed hard, her teeth sinking into her bottom lip as she struggled to keep silent.

"You push the limits, brother."

"Not at all. You have no right to deny such a thing to me. We are guests in your home. Your slaves and your servants, they are all open to be used, should any of us desire it. And I, for now at least, wish only to taste her lips. Are you going to deny me such a thing? Are you saying you have emotions for the slut, ones beyond ownership?"

His grip tightened, strands of hair breaking under his fingers before he forced himself to relax. "No, not at all."

"Then I make a deal with you. One kiss, one full moment in my arms and if she obeys and manages to please me, then I will sanction your choice."

"A kiss, nothing more?"

"My word on it."

She whimpered, looking quickly around the room, her gaze lingering on the silent, kneeling woman for a moment. Just like she had been warned, the one that knelt there was little more than a shadow of humanity. Her face lacked color, hair rested limp about her shoulders, fear emanating from her with every breath she took.

What had happened to her?

For a moment she reached out towards the other woman, not with her hands, but her mind. Brushing over her, listening, seeking in the same way she knew Traven could do.

A mistake.

Images flooded through her mind. Pain. Humiliation. Death, endless death. The woman didn't even have a name. Had been denied one for more years than she could remember.

Just a beast.

Nothing more than an animal, forced into an immortal life to provide the pleasure Gullian desired.

Cold, alone, fearful, the woman no longer even knew how to speak.

Don't. You must pull back now. You have no permission to pry into the mind of his property. Gullian is dangerous. If there is one here who will try and fight me, to take you from me, it is him. Do not test him. You lack the power to tear his throat out. The mental slap sent her mind running back into hiding, the soft, probing fingers drawn back into their shell.

"Agreed. If she performs well, then my choice will be shown as the right one. If she fails, then I will take her life here and now in front of you all."

She tensed, her gaze drawn towards his face, cold sweat

coating her body. Heavens. He meant it. If she failed, displeased that one who left her feeling sick to her core, she'd die. Here and now, in front of them all.

"Good. For a moment, I thought you were about to show us just how human you have become. I've seen that happened before, dearest brother. Too many years with them and it can taint you, unless you keep a firm grip on the lives around you." Gullian's lips twitched upwards into a mocking smile.

"Enough." Bastian silenced them both. "We will discuss this further, without the property being present."

"After my kiss," Gullian insisted.

"Indeed, go to him, my pet. Crawl to his feet and beg for his kiss." Traven turned his full attention to Alayna's trembling form. "You know what I expect from you."

She tensed, looking up at him, seeing the cold, uncompromising gaze that met her own. If she hesitated or argued with him, it would be dangerous for them both. Slowly she lowered down to her hands and knees, full breasts swaying towards the floor, nipples hard from the cruel grip he had held in her hair.

Her lips brushed softly across the man's boots, ass raised high in the air. Though the welts had healed before she had even awakened, she could still feel them burning across her flesh as if newly placed. She whimpered, licking carefully over the rough leather, trying to ignore the taste of the mud and grit that coated the toe.

A single crack sounded, a crop biting into her ass, pain lancing through her body as she cried out, squirming on her hands and knees, yet still she didn't remove her lips from his boots.

"She has been trained to pain," Traven explained.

"So I see, and she knows not to break position?" Bastian inquired.

"Probe her, see for yourself what she feels towards our brother."

A cold caress worked through her mind, brushing over her thoughts, sorting through emotions, then vanishing as quickly as it had begun. "Interesting. She dislikes Gullian intensely, yet she's obeying you. Would you believe that she fears you will take her from Traven?"

"Interesting, perhaps she is right." Gullian chuckled. The sound lacked warmth. "If she proves of interest I might be tempted to show her the true control of an elder of our kind, instead of the fumbling attempts our young sibling has introduced her to."

She whimpered, lowering her lips closer to the black leather boots, cleaning each grain of dirt from the toes. Obey, serve, show them she had been well trained.

"She knows better than to disobey me." Traven's voice filtered through her thoughts.

"We shall see." Gullian reached down, grabbing the back of the collar. "Stand, slut."

Alayna pushed carefully to her feet, the collar biting into her throat. She wanted to lash out at the man, knock him to the floor and destroy him completely. Cold sweat coated her body, hands clenching into fists at her sides long before Gullian pulled her towards him.

"You will kiss me, slut. Show me what delights you have used to bewitch my brother, and only then will you be given leave to return to your Master."

What if she didn't please this stranger? Would that be enough of a reason to pull her from her Master? From the pain and pleasure he had taught her to enjoy?

No, she would not fail Traven.

She leaned in, nibbling across Gullian's neck, tracing soft, small patterns upwards towards his lips. He groaned, a low sound that only she could hear, his cock hardening beneath the soft cloth of his pants. Whatever he thought of her, she had at least managed that small reaction, one he would be unable to deny once she pointed it out to the other men present.

If she had to go that far.

"She shows some small signs of skill," Bastian murmured somewhere behind her.

"More than she will have the chance to show here. Put her with another woman and the show becomes quite intense." Traven spoke softly.

"Something you will have to show us later." Gullian turned slightly as he spoke, forcing Alayna to shift position against him.

"Perhaps, but if you watch closely, you will soon see why I picked her out of the humans to be my chosen. Her heart walks in the shadows, as much as she might try and deny it. She has a thirst for blood and pain that refuses to be controlled save by the strongest hand. Each time I take her for my pleasure, I know the risk that she might try and turn on me."

"I thought you said she knows better than to disobey you?" Bastian inquired.

"She does, but I never claimed she was tame, did I?"

"Then why do you keep her if she is not fully tamed?" Alayna tried to ignore the concern behind Bastian's words.

"I prefer the challenge, however slight, that she can offer. Who knows, perhaps one day she will be strong enough to claim the life of one of our kind. To challenge us."

She tried to shut out their voices and focus on only the task she had been set as she licked gently across his lips, arching close to Gullian, her breasts caressing across his shirt-covered chest as he arched his neck, pulling his lips away from her touch.

"Perhaps I will take her for my own, Traven." Gullian's hands tightened about her body, nails digging in deep. "She shows far more talent than such as you deserve."

"Don't threaten me, Gullian."

"I will do as I wish. I am the elder here."

His neck. Her gaze fastened on his neck. Blood and power throbbed through his veins. So close to her teeth now, tempting, calling to her. He was open, vulnerable, exposed. All it would take was a single bite. Enough to show them she had every right to walk with Traven as his Chosen and Priestess.

No, she wasn't one of their kind, she didn't have the ability to fight them. Better that she submit and wait to discover her fate. Traven wouldn't let this one take her. No matter the cost, he would keep her close.

"And I will not permit you to take what is mine." Traven's voice dropped into a low whisper.

"Oh, and how are you going to stop me?"

"By any means I can." Traven growled. "She is mine. I turned her. I have trained her. And I will not give her up to you. If you think you can just walk in here and claim her, then you've become senile with your years. Do not seek to anger me in my own home, Gullian."

No, she couldn't risk her master being injured. The others would turn on him, even if he did win!

"He won't fight you, Master," she whispered, nibbling softly at Gullian's throat, licking along the throbbing pulse line, feeling him shudder beneath her touch. His grip tightened on her body, his firm erection pressing against her belly, his hips rolling with each soft kiss.

She licked softly over the vein in his neck, teasing it with the tip of her tongue even as he shivered and clutched her tighter to him.

"And why is that, pet? Ah, don't tell me, he fears me, doesn't he?"

Her breath caught in the back of her throat as she nipped along the tempting line. "No, Milord."

"Then it is because you have chosen to come to me of your own free will." Gullian slid his fingers through her hair, caressing her scalp with his nails. Pain and pleasure surged through her body in equal amounts and for a moment, a brief wonderful moment, she caught a glimpse of the world he could show her.

There was only one way...

"Because fighting the dead is pointless." Alayna replied, sinking her teeth deep into his throat, tearing at the veins beneath. Rich, vital, filled with power, his blood poured into her mouth. "I belong to him, not you!"

Gullian screamed, his hands clawing at her back and hair as he tried to yank her from his body. She snarled, the new source of strength surging through her veins as she sank her teeth back into his throat, biting flesh and veins alike.

Blood spurted across the room as they struggled.

Line of fire erupted from his claws, pain unlike anything she had known burned through her body as he tried to force her away from his throat, but still she held on.

No one had the right to take her from Traven. Not even his kin.

"You...you can't..." He stumbled, losing his balance. "You can't do this."

His heart faltered, missing a beat, a second one, life seeping from his body. It all made sense. The warnings not to bite Traven without permission. The way he had reacted when she had forgotten in the past and even nipped at his neck.

He had lived amongst her kind long enough to know that humans took chances. Gullian, apparently, had forgotten.

"I already have," she murmured, finally releasing her grip from his throat, pushing back from him as he lashed out weakly. Blood poured from the gaping wound, pooling on the stone floor, spreading out across the chamber.

No one moved.

She'd done the unthinkable, and killed one of the Gods.

Alayna stumbled back from the body, her gaze darting around the chamber, moving from man to man--and the kneeling, trembling woman who made no attempt to edge away from the spreading pool of blood.

Would they kill her now?

She glanced around the room, waiting for one of them to move, to strike out at her and end her life. She'd attacked one of them, and they had to be wondering if she would do it again.

She'd gone too far, but it had been worth it.

Traven met her gaze, a cold smile touching his full lips as he snapped his fingers once, pointing to his feet.

Hope surged through her being and without a word she moved to him, falling to her knees, lowering her head to his boots as she covered them with blood-tinged kisses.

"If anyone else has an objection to my decision on who I choose to lift up into the ranks of Chosen and Priestess, I suggest they say something now."

And who would dare to object when I own a woman strong enough to risk attacking one of their own kind?

She smiled, looking up into his deep violet gaze. She was exactly what she was always meant to be, his slave, his Chosen, his eternal Priestess. And now no one would ever dare question his choice again.

Also By Terri Pray...

A Passage From *Deed Wife*

Fresh blisters burned her heels with each step, adding pain to the growing anger her enforced trip north had caused to fester within her. The fury ate away at any joy the flowers might otherwise have offered as she limped her way along the narrow lane.

The very least he could have done was to have met her from the ferry. Even cattle were escorted to a new owner. Instead he seemed to expect Marion to meekly deliver herself into the care of a stranger.

What else would he expect of her?

Not for the first time in her scant years, Marion wished that she had been born a man. At least then the option of leaving the Isles might have been a realistic one. A woman seeking passage alone would be more likely to end up sold to some brothel, or worse.

"What did we do that was so wrong?" Her words caught on the breeze, answered only by bird song.

She knew the answer; it had been drummed into her as long as she could remember. The English had tried to lay claim to a land and a people they had no right to control. They had stolen, used and abused, and that would no longer be permitted. Now all that mattered was not keeping her husband waiting any longer than he had to.

Lights beckoned from the next rise as she took the left hand path at the crossroads, either from a candle, oil lamp or perhaps a mage ball left in the window to light the way. At least there might be a fire, even some hot tea if she was lucky. It was the rest of what might be waiting for Marion that caused her concern. Would he at least wait until a preacher could speak the vows before demanding the rights of a husband from her body?

Marion hoped he would be that patient, or did he want to practice some strange binding ritual as rumors spoke of back home?

Would there be any vows at all?

Not that they were needed, according to the custom of Deed Wife. She had become his from the moment he had sent for her.

There was nowhere to run, and no one would offer her shelter if she even dared to try it. Caught, she could be flogged and then returned to her husband, as was his right. If lucky he would keep her, if not, she might be sold to a brothel. Bound there by spells and chains alike, until she died from the harsh use such women endured.

Her small hand settled on the wooden gate, only then giving her the chance to see the trembling that traveled down her limbs. Fear ruled Marion's heart and threatened to send her running from the gate in search of a shelter that she knew didn't exist. Still her terror gave life to desperate thoughts of swimming the lake, even though the icy water would mean her death and other equally foolish plans that now flashed through her mind.

"I won't let him see my fear." She whispered an oath sworn to the breeze and burned into her own heart.

If she could keep nothing else as her own, it would be her emotions.

The gate closed behind Marion--the soft click locking her fate even as the door to the stone cottage opened.

"Ye took ye own sweet time in getting here, lass." A pair of coal dark eyes scowled from the kilted figure in the shadows of the doorway. "Perhaps a touch of leather against ye back will remind ye nae to be so lazy in coming days. I'll nae tolerate such from ye again, mind ye mark that well."

Her hands clenched into small fists, eyes blazing for a moment before she fought back the anger that could push her even further into trouble. "With respect, Sir, the ferry was delayed. I didn't dally, but did have to ask directions to find my way here. I had no way of finding myself to your door without stopping to ask for help."

His massively built form stepped out from the doorway. He was easily a foot and a half taller than Marion, with dark eyes and unruly, raven shoulder-length hair. He possessed a build that spoke of heavy labor and his hands showed the signs of the hard work that he put in every day. Callum Jacobs embodied everything she had been taught to fear in Clansmen. He was exactly how she recalled, but worse still, her body clenched under her skirts as she lowered her gaze almost shyly under his eyes.

"And I suppose ye think I should be accepting ye petty excuse?" His large arms folded across his chest, his words raising the hairs on the back of her neck. "Expecting to be pampered, are ye? Well, ye will nae find such here. I would have thought that ye father would have better prepared ye before ye journey."

"It's not an excuse..." The words darted from her lips before she could prevent them, the shy gaze vanishing. Her breath caught in her throat as she glimpsed the dark rage flash across his face. "I beg pardon, it has been a long journey and I forget my place. I didn't mean to make excuses, Sir."

A cold sweat formed in beads across her skin and her slender fingers tangled into the edges of her shawl whilst she waited for him to either lash out or grow calm. Her breath quickened as she became aware of his gaze following the neckline of her dress. Not for the first time Marion wishing her father had allowed a new dress to be made before the trip--one less revealing--but the funds had not been there.

Or at least they hadn't for a girl sent northward.

"Mind ye manners with me, lass, I'll not be allowing ye low land ways up here. Now get in there, I'll be wanting to take a good look at what's mine in a while." He nodded and his tone remained as unyielding as his gaze before he turned and walked back into the cottage. "Come along inside, my lass."

It might have been better if he had simply lashed out, at least that was something she was used to coping with. Arguments formed and died on her lips as quick steps carried her down the narrow path into the low-lit cottage. Even with the lamps it took a few moments for her eyes to adjust to the difference in light once the door closed behind them both.

A large fire crackled in the hearth, sparks flying upwards with the draught from the closing door. Three lamps offered light within the main room, from which two doors led off, one on each side of the central room. Well worn but sturdy furniture with a few rugs and blankets added a homely feeling to the cottage that somehow felt out of place to her.

"Didn't bring much with ye, did ye, lass?" His gaze bored through her clothing, leaving her skin itching. "Does ye kin think I will fit ye out? Typical of ye kind."

"No, Sir. My father didn't see the point in sending anything with me, except a few basics. There's a small chest in the village, should you wish to send for it." Her hands clasped tightly together. "I'd have brought it with me, but the Ferry Captain refused to release it to my care without your say so."

"Ye didnae expect him to let a girl like ye touch something that belongs to me now, did ye?" Callum shook his head. "Ye a stupid wench. I can see I have a lot to teach ye. Shouldn't be surprised, it's what I get for taking a low land woman into my house when I could have taken on a decent highland lass who knows how to keep a home. And ye will learn fast or pay the price."

Marion's fingers clenched into her own skirts with her rising frustration. Did he think she was lacking in sense? "I'm not stupid, Sir. I carried the chest with me right up until getting on the ferry. Why would I harm the contents now? Just because I am English?"

He moved faster than she would have given him credit for. Large hands grasped her arms and pulled her forward. The shawl was torn from her shoulders and a cry slipped from lips as panic claimed her heart.

"Let go of me!"

Oh Lord, what did I just do?

Terri Pray

Originally from England, Terri Pray now lives in Iowa with her husband and their two children. She works full time as both an author and the EiC for a small press publishing house. Her work ranges from the mild to the wild, fantasy to erotica, horror through to science fiction.